In the Land
of No Right Angles

ANCHOR BOOKS

A Division of Random House, Inc.

New York

In the Land
of No Right Angles

A Novel

DAPHNE BEAL

An Anchor Books Original, August 2008

Library of Congress Cataloging-in-Publication Data
Beal, Daphne.
  In the land of no right angles : a novel / by Daphne Beal.
    p. cm.
  "An Anchor Books Original."
  ISBN 978-0-307-38806-3
  1. Americans—Nepal—Fiction. 2. Triangles (Interpersonal
relations)—Fiction. 3. Kathmandu (Nepal)—Fiction. 4. Bombay
(India)—Fiction. 5. New York (N.Y.)—Fiction. I. Title.
PS3602.E242915 2008
813'.6—dc22
2008014281

Book design by Mia Risberg

www.anchorbooks.com

Printed in the United States of America
10 9 8 7 6 5 4 3 2 1

For my parents,
Polly and Robert Beal

Black hair
With a red ribbon in it
Your life, our lives
Are one and the same
　—Nepali folk song

I was booked to make a mistake.
I have lived too long in foreign parts.
　—Henry James, *Daisy Miller*

PART I · DAKINIS

Sky Spirits

1990

One

It started out as a little adventure, or an adventure tagged onto an adventure. I was twenty and about to go trekking in the central hill region of Nepal by myself after living in the country for almost eight months when I mentioned it to my friend Will. We were at a party on the rooftop of a small hotel high on a hill at the western edge of Kathmandu, and when I told him where I was going in a few days' time, he lit up and asked if I could do him a favor. "It'll take you an hour out of your way. Two, tops," he said as we looked out at the low-slung, ancient city twinkling before us.

"Sure," I said. Two hours was nothing when you were

talking about a two-and-a-half-week trek. Besides, the errand sounded interesting. He wanted me to find a girl he'd met the year before and give her a message. As it was, the purpose of my solo trek was not only to take pictures, but to say good-bye to the people in a remote, hardscrabble village called Jankat where I'd lived for a month in the winter, and it all seemed a little melancholy. I was pleased to add a more cheerful mission.

With a map to the girl's house and a photograph, I took a bus to Ghorka and asked around town if anyone was headed to Barpak, the first town on my route. A small group of men and women said they were leaving in the morning for their home, and when I mentioned I was friends with some other *bideshi*s—foreigners—who stayed there a few months before, they happily added me to their gang. We headed northwest to the thriving village set in lush green fields where I spent a couple of nights and went to a village elder's funeral high on a hillside. The whole village paraded up a winding path to the burial site as women keened and lamas danced and chanted, spinning in their colorful robes and hats, a kind of Hindu-Buddhist-animist blend of rites. As I was taking pictures, I knew I'd made the right decision, even if it was unconventional, to go trekking on my own, to be only one outsider watching all this. From there, I went northeast with a few people to the northernmost point where I was allowed without a permit. We walked uphill all morning, and I spent the afternoon sliding and jumping down muddy terraces until my knees ached, and then walking along the rushing Buri Gandaki some distance behind everyone else until I arrived at a desolate, tight-lipped little town of stone houses in a craggy gray-and-brown setting of boulders and cliffs, where strings of tattered prayer flags whipped in the wind. When I couldn't find anyone to walk with the next day, I started due south along the river toward Tatopani, the town where the girl lived, knowing from Will's description that I didn't have a long day ahead of me. It was an easy walk compared to the day before, and I met enough people along the way that I didn't mind being alone. I expected to be there by about three, but it was almost four when the rain began to fall, and I still hadn't passed any of the landmarks he'd mentioned.

It was a gentle rain at first—*sim-simi*, like little beans, Nepalis say of this kind of soft, steady rain—and I wasn't fazed by it. It even felt good after the midday heat. But soon enough it was a full-on downpour, a kind of preview of the monsoon to come, and my skirt (an ankle-length, flowered *lungi*, same as all the village women wore), long underwear, double layers of socks, and boots were soaked through. Every step was audible now, not just the footfall, but the *slurp-squish-squelch* that followed. Only the small section of my torso that was squarely under my poncho qualified as damp, and I scanned the trail for signs that I was getting close: a water tap, a clearing of wild pot plants, a sharp bend in the path. But more than an hour after I should have seen them, with no letup in the rain, I came up with nothing. There was no one to ask and no porch overhang to stop under. Was Will messing with me? I wondered. Trying to give me some Buddhist lesson about seeking and not finding? It wouldn't be

totally unlike him, even though I wasn't his student anymore. He seemed to delight in exposing the people around him
to new and unsettling ideas. I felt exasperated at the thought,
but also a little excited. Maybe there was a point even if there
was no point. And then, wasn't this exactly the kind of thing I
wanted, when I decided to come here, to see things from a
completely different perspective, from outside the Western
mind-set? What was that Whitman line that Ginsberg used
and that I loved when I read it? "Unscrew the locks from the
doors / Unscrew the doors themselves from their jambs." Here
I was, a million miles from where I'd started, the landscape
intensely beautiful, a pixelated world of glittering greens,
everything smelling lushly of it. My footsteps splashed along
the muddy path and mingled with the sound of my breath, the
rustle of wet leaves, and the incessant rushing of the river,
invisible beyond the dense growth.

If only I wasn't drenched and hungry. I hadn't eaten anything but a single chapati with peanut butter that I packed that
morning. But I knew that eventually, even if I had to walk in
the dark with a flashlight, I would run into the ramshackle
trekking lodge I had stayed at a few months before. I could
always get a good night's sleep (or as much as a wooden cot
allowed) and look for the girl in the morning. It wasn't my
nature to come this far and give up, and, even for Will, it
would be too bizarre to make up such an elaborate lie. I'd seen
him orchestrate surprising excursions for his students in the
course of the semester program he ran, but nothing like this.
Some of the students loved it, gathering at his apartment

every evening to meet whatever guru or charlatan appeared, but I kept my distance. I hadn't traveled around the world to be in the thrall of an American man twelve years older than me. At the same time, from that distance, I liked him. Having lived in Nepal for the past eight years, he was smart and unconventional. And while I sometimes thought he enjoyed his role as teacher a bit too much, I also saw that he listened to the students and engaged with them in a way that made us all feel lucky. For all his grandstanding, there was something kind about him. He also happened to be a very good photographer, and from the beginning he and I had things to say to each other about people like Diane Arbus and Raghubir Singh, and about things like the quality of light in Kathmandu in the early morning, or how the landscape affected our sense of scale.

Then in January, before the new batch of students arrived, we ate a few meals together. I was staying on for another semester, and I told him that after a kind of hiatus from photography, I was looking for a project to work on in the six months I had left, before my money and visa ran out. "I want to do something that's not just old-school anthropology or cool postcards," I told him. "I feel like I'm finally just beginning to know something about this place so that I can actually take a real picture now." I think he was surprised and maybe even a little impressed that I stayed and wanted something more than the gift-wrapped bauble of a semester of study-abroad, and he took me around town on the back of his motorcycle to meet people, expats and lamas among others, to help me figure out what I might be looking for: life at a monastery or convent, in a leper colony, at an untouchable's home. When I had a stomach bug one day, he brought me ayurvedic medicine, and I got better right away.

I didn't sleep with him, if you're wondering. It didn't come up, or not explicitly. Friends had, including Maggie, my closest friend in Nepal, whom I'd introduced to Will. She was my age and taking a year off from Berkeley to immerse herself in the whole Tibetan Buddhist scene, and I thought they would have things to talk about. Then, while I was in India for six weeks, she tried opium with him, and they slept together, which she regretted afterward. "He just wasn't very nice about it," she told me. "It was like he was so invested in not being 'attached,' in the Buddhist way, that he forgot I was a real person." I was so glad it wasn't me. I wouldn't have known what to do. Right before I left for India in February, after a couple of weeks of spending time together, there was a little frisson between Will and me, but I *knew* I wasn't his type. I saw that when he dated American girls, he liked them hippie-ish and diminutive, and I was, especially at that time, what I would call wholesome-bordering-on-nerdy, too tall by at least six inches, and defiantly redheaded compared to his petite brunettes. I knew I was just a curiosity.

After a party welcoming the spring semester's students, we danced a little. Will asked me to come to Ghorka to give a "lecture" about my experience in the area to the new students, and I told him I was thinking I should go to India if I wanted to get to Dharamsala in time for the Tibetan New

Year. I knew he expected me to go home with him that night, but at the end of the party, I jumped on the back of a friend's scooter.

"What? Why are you going with her?" he asked.

"I'm exhausted," I said, pretending not to hear the irritation in his voice. When I ran into him at school a couple days later, he was friendly enough, as if he'd forgotten all about it. All the same, I fled the country soon after. I was way too inexperienced to get involved with someone like him. He was the Casanova of Kathmandu, and I was just a girl from Des Moines who knew more about sex and romance in theory than in practice. When I got back from India, he had moved on. There was Maggie, and then his Nepali girlfriend. We were just pals now.

Still, as I slogged on, I wondered if this errand of his was a kind of test to see how I responded: impatient, irate, amused, defeated? How much had I let Nepal into my psyche? Not enough to want to be walking at night by myself. Just as I decided to speed up to make it to the lodge I knew about, I saw a little path to my left, looked around, and jogged a few steps through the dripping underbrush, my pack thumping against my back as I went. Then I saw the thatched roof, tall and pointy, thick with straw, and the solid gray stone walls beneath it. I felt like Gretel at the candy cottage. "A well-built house," Will had said. This had to be it!

As I got closer, I saw a porch on the far side of the house and on it, under the eaves, a girl, maybe seventeen, leaning against a post holding a big tin water jug to her hip and watching the rain as if she were reading something in it. Her attitude, wistful and contemplative, was familiar in a way that few things were here. People, by and large, were so rooted in their lives, their minds never seemed to float too far away.

"*Namaste*, little sister!" I called, and she swung around and grinned.

"*Namaste*, big sister!" she shouted, as if she'd been expecting me. "Come quickly!" She set down her jug and helped me off with my pack and onto the dry porch, whisking away my poncho to a covered line at the far end. The whole wall facing the river and porch was open, and Nepalis and Tibetans were gathered in the dim light of the late afternoon, drinking from tin cups. I propped my pack against a near wall, yanked off my boots and socks, and went to sit by the small cooking fire at the front of the room, tended to by a cheerful older woman who had to be the girl's mother.

"*Raksi* or tea?" she asked with a sly grin.

"Tea, please," I said, practically sticking my long, bony, freckled feet in the fire. I wanted all my wits about me. The woman chortled. It was a little test on her part, because a woman, especially a young—read, sexually viable—woman really didn't drink. An older village woman had earned her right, and high-caste women just didn't drink at all. So, she was sussing out, was I in fact a foreigner who didn't know all the rules, or one who knew them and was willing to flout them? I was so cold and sodden I might have had *raksi* if I weren't there for such a specific reason. That, and if the drink hadn't tasted so much like lighter fluid the few times I'd tried it.

Holding the hot metal cup close to my face, trying to drive off the chill, I answered all the usual questions. What country was I from? Where did I come from that day? How long had it taken me? The woman was clearly pleased that I could speak Nepali. I shaved off more than an hour so that I didn't look too pathetic. Did I have a mother, father, sisters, brothers? Why was I traveling alone? Had I eaten? When I told her I hadn't, the woman offered me some cold boiled potatoes with salt, which I gobbled up. I knew it wasn't the best idea, eating food that had been sitting around, but my stomach needed something to chew on besides itself. Then I asked about their family, crops, chickens, the weather, and also, because I wanted to be sure, the name of the place.

"Tatopani," the woman said. It was the right name, though Will made it sound like it would be at least a small town. As far as I could tell, this was the only house. Then I put on my best chipper, happy-go-lucky tourist voice and asked, "What are your names?" It was a strange question for this place. On the one hand it was private, and on the other irrelevant, because even between strangers people called one another daughter, sister, mother, aunt—or brother, father, uncle, son. Occasionally I was called *hajur*, which meant "sir," or *memsaab*, but mostly I was *didi*, which meant "big sister," or very occasionally, *bayini*, which meant "little sister." But the girl's name was Maya, it turned out, which, again, was good. Still, I couldn't be sure she was who I'd been sent to find without getting out the photo Will had given me. The truth was that most women and girls in the region were named Maya—which means "love" in Nepali, "magic" in Hindi, "illusion" in Sanskrit, and is also the name of the Buddha's mother.

"Can I stay here tonight?" I asked the woman, and she glanced over my shoulder so that I turned around. Standing in the doorway between the two rooms was a small, glowering, bowlegged man, presumably her husband. He grunted in assent. Yes, I could stay. After I finished my tea, Maya showed me up a sturdy notched pole to a high loft made of dried, hardened bamboo poles lashed together. She shoved two tin trunks out of the way and watched as I unrolled my damp sleeping bag and spread out some clothes to dry.

"Don't you feel afraid traveling by yourself?" she asked.

"No," I said, and looked up. She seemed genuinely interested. "Sometimes. But I've been walking with groups of people every day until now."

"There are some not-nice people on the path," she said.

"I know, but in my country, women are used to walking alone." I couldn't explain my need to disappear into the place as much as possible, unencumbered by anything more than the inevitable whiteness of my skin and my camera. "Besides, I'm pretty big," I said, and she laughed. It was true, though. At five-ten, I was taller than ninety-nine percent of the people I met.

"Do you know how to fight?" she asked.

"No, not really, but still," I added, "when I'm walking by myself, I can think more clearly."

"I understand," she said, and seemed to, even though everything here was about being with others. She was unusual and very pretty. It had to be the girl Will sent me to find. Just before she disappeared down the pole, I asked her if she would show me the local hot springs. *Tatopani* means "hot water," so there were some nearby, and Will had said they were a good place to wash up. All day I'd been dreaming of a little natural hot tub by the side of the river.

"Sure, when you come down," she said, and disappeared.

As soon as she was gone, I pulled out the photo Will had given me from a sealed plastic bag in my money belt, my portable safe, and peered over the edge of the loft. In the picture, Will grinned, with his dark blond curls wild around his head. He was more than a foot taller than the Nepali girl next to him. She wore a serious expression, a little vertical furrow in her brow, and her silky, long black hair was down around her face. She had on a plaid flannel button-down shirt—not typical village-girl wear. "She looks like a UCLA student, doesn't she?" Will had asked. It was true. She could have been a kind of worldly Mexican-American girl on her way to class or a protest.

The Maya downstairs looked similar, but acted and dressed in every way differently. She bustled in and out of the house, her black braid swinging its red tassel as she got wood for her mother and poured *raksi* for the guests, seemingly totally and contentedly of this place. She wore a fresh *lungi* of ornate orange and purple blooming flowers, a marigold-yellow cotton sash around her waist, and a short black velveteen blouse. A gold nose ring dangled from the center of her nose.

WHEN I CAME DOWNSTAIRS cradling my camera, the house was emptying out. The rain had stopped, and everyone else was preparing to get in a few more hours of walking before night fell. Only the trees and eaves were still dripping as people adjusted the ropes across their foreheads that held the heavy baskets on their backs. A black-eyed mother and son caught my eye. She was barefoot and wearing a kind of shapeless thick felt cloak and hood with a basket, and he was in a dirty ski vest with a backpack and a knitted cap. They seemed to span about a hundred years between them. I asked if I could take their picture, and like so many people in the hills, they looked into the camera unblinkingly, clear-eyed and mysterious (it was the only word for it sometimes). High above the narrow river valley, the sky was bright blue with long, thin white clouds sailing by, colliding and breaking apart over and over, casting a pretty, quicksilver light.

Maya sidestepped a chicken and her bedraggled chicks as she led me down a path to the river. I minced along at a distance, now in flip-flops, trying not to get stung by nettles. A couple hundred feet down, after we passed a boulder the size of a small shed, I called out to her.

"*Bayini*?" She turned. "Will you come here a minute?"

She doubled back nimbly as I got out the photo.

"Do you remember a year ago two foreign men stopped here, and you asked one of them to take you to Kathmandu?" She set down the jugs to examine the picture. "He spoke Nepali and said he had to go north to meditate for a month, so he couldn't take you with him." She held it close to her face, as if some detail would make it all clear. "When he stopped by again a month later, your father told him to go or he would cut him with his kukri."

She suddenly lit up with a grin. "Yes! I remember him! This man here?" she asked, pointing to the picture.

"Yes," I said.

"Yes, yes. He was with another man. I wanted to go with them to Kathmandu," she said, repeating things I'd already told her. I couldn't tell if she really did know Will's face or not.

"Well, he asked me to tell you that there's work as a maid in a foreign woman's house in Kathmandu if you want it—"

"Yes!" she shouted, and threw her arms around me. "I'll come with you! I can't live here anymore! Come down to the river, and we'll make a plan so I can leave with you first thing in the morning." I wondered how many foreigners she'd asked for help in the last year, and if it mattered who came through in the end. I knew foreigners were the only ones it made sense to ask, because they wouldn't have the judgments or hesitation a Nepali would about a girl leaving home alone. Even in an unhappy home, family was everything, and you existed in relation to it as a daughter, wife, mother. There was no such thing as an independent, young single woman. Or if there was, she was the exception and considered suspect or unlucky.

The fact that Maya was even bold enough to have asked Will to help her leave made me curious about her. I'd left everything to come here, but it was different. My parents, though they had no idea why I chose Nepal (Not Paris? Not Florence?), sanctioned the decision and in a modest way supported it, figuring I must have my reasons for going halfway around the world for a year. Maya, if she really did go, would be leaving all she knew, and by doing so would probably be considered unmarriageable and a disgrace.

At the river, there was no hot tub or anything like it, just a rough little nook in the rocky bank, a couple of feet wide. I yelped as I plunged my feet in. The water was icy, and just a thin, scalding stream, the so-called spring, hit me about mid-calf. I quickly scrubbed the mud from my legs and washed up to my elbows, then stretched out on some rocks to dry, practically eye level with the blue-green river churning past. About a hundred feet across, wet cliffs shot up at jagged angles, and the sound of rushing water filled my head. My camera sat idle on a flat rock beside me. There was no way to photograph this—to convey the land's hugeness and the happy feeling of my own insignificance that came from being deep inside it. It was exhilarating to be swallowed whole, and it contrasted starkly to everything I'd known up until now. In Iowa or at school in upstate New York, I'd always stood on top of the land with a kind of misguided self-importance, without even particularly knowing it. Here, I could feel the deep, silent tick of geologic time beating through me. At night, sometimes before I fell asleep, I could see the Asian and Indian continents in a silent, wide-screen version, crashing together to form the curved band of land that became Nepal: the snowcapped mountains in the north bursting skyward, the green and ter-raced foothills rippling through the middle, and finally the smooth, flatland jungles of the south, which, infested with malarial mosquitoes, kept the British and Indians out.

Here, beside the coursing Himalayan runoff, between the

cliffs, Maya and I were just tiny ants dropped in the land, no trailhead or parking lot or superhighway just a few miles away.

Maya squatted beside me. "Okay, so tomorrow morning we'll get up before the sun comes up and leave before my family wakes up. I'll sleep up in the loft with you tonight, and tell my parents I am making sure nobody from down below bothers you."

"You're not telling your parents?" I asked. "Not even your mother?"

"No, there's no point. She drinks too much, and she'll tell my father, and then he'll beat both of us."

"Okay," I said. What could I say? Did I really expect that after her father threatened to cut Will that I would just waltz in, work my girlish charm, and say, "Listen, I know this is completely out of the ordinary, and that you actually need your daughter to help with your fields and *raksi* business, but the thing is, she wants to go, and there's work waiting for her in Kathmandu, so we'll be on our way"?

Actually, I did think that her leaving with a girl close to her age would be less of a big deal in terms of the old-fashioned questions of reputation and chastity. But I saw now that leaving was leaving.

"I'm going back," she said, balancing her two huge aluminum containers of water. They had to be three or four gallons apiece.

"Wait," I said, and got up to take some pictures of her. She made it look so easy. She added, "I'll bring my clothes over bit by bit so you can put them in your pack." Then she disappeared up the path. I dipped my legs into the boiling, icy pot of water one last time. Night was falling fast, changing the thousands of greens all around into a myriad of grays, and I wondered if I should say anything else about Will, who he was, what he was like. All he told me was that she seemed like a remarkable girl, that he had been impressed by her energy and forthrightness, but that he wasn't particularly attracted to her. "It's funny. I forgot about her for a long time, and then, lately, I found myself wondering what happened to her. Then June Erickson called to say she was looking for a maid, and a couple days later you told me you would be walking past her house. It seemed like fate. I think you'll like her." It was part of his Buddhist side, taking care of people. It was hard to live in Nepal as a Westerner and not want to help the people around you. Some did, of course, and simply enjoyed the colonial holdover of hot-and-cold running servants, but not Will. He also had a girlfriend, Chhimi, who was from Jankat, the town where Maya and I would go next. So why, now that I was here and had delivered the message, did I feel nervous about bringing her back to Kathmandu? And what would I tell Will if Maya changed her mind? "She was going to come, but after thinking about it, I convinced her not to." Unfortunately, I cared too much about what he thought of me.

At the house, I started to go inside, but was startled by Maya's father squatting in the shadows of the porch, the orange tip of his cigarette more visible than he was.

"*Raat iyo*, night's arrived," I said in my oblivious, tourist voice again. He stared past me, and I went inside to sit with

Maya and her mother while they chatted in their dialect and prepared dinner, cutting up scrubbed potatoes and sifting pebbles from the rice and lentils. It looked like it would be good food, and I was excited after all the scary meals I'd eaten along the way, swallowing horse pills of rice and *dahl*, hoping I wouldn't get sick.

After a while, I went up to the loft and wrote in my journal until Maya came up the ladder.

"*Sathi?*" Maya said, and I sat up. From the moment I told her about the job in Kathmandu, she always called me *sathi*, "friend," never *didi*, "big sister," again. We were equals from the get-go, unlike anyone else I knew here, and I was touched by it.

"I've brought some things for you to put in your pack. Come look." She unknotted a little bundle on my sleeping bag. Inside was a Nestlé Lactogen can (that nutritionless crap marketed to third-world mothers as better than breast milk). Maya peeled off the plastic lid to reveal wads of tired money and coins. Smoothing out the bills, she organized them by denomination and counted them—about fifty dollars in rupees, a sizable sum for an unmarried village girl in a country where the average yearly income was around a hundred and twenty-five dollars. It was enough for her to start a new life, especially when there was work waiting for her in Kathmandu.

I wondered if she'd stolen it from her parents, or if it was her dowry. Girls barely earned money here, and if they did I thought they handed it over to their parents. "How did you get this?" I asked.

"I made it selling *raksi* and tea," she said. It was baffling because it was a family business, but maybe her mother gave it to her as part of her tacit consent that Maya should go when she could.

"Will you keep this?" she asked, handing it to me, and I was amazed by her trust. "Here, look at this." She held out a little black-and-white head shot of a young Nepali man.

"Who is this?" I asked.

"That's my older brother. He died six months ago." She held the photo up to her forehead briefly, an honorific gesture, with her eyes closed.

I clucked my tongue in sympathy, as I'd heard others do. "What happened?" I asked with a bluntness reserved for foreign languages and for places where people seem to die too often.

"He was at school in Bombay. He was protesting the government, and the police killed him with a *lathi*, a bamboo truncheon. We didn't even know until more than a month after it happened, when they sent a photo by mail. He was so badly beaten we could hardly recognize him." She wiped her eyes roughly with the back of her hand.

"*Sathi*, I'm sorry. That's terrible," I said, and realized that in nearly eight months of my being there, it was the first time I had ever seen a Nepali adult cry, and I took her hand awkwardly. I had gotten so used to hearing that all was karma and "*Ké garné?*" the common Nepali phrase that meant "what to do?"

"He was going to take me away from here to go live with

him. Maybe even this summer. He promised me he would help me. He gave me this." She held up a big bottle of green shampoo, and I wondered if she was going to ask me to take it too—and felt immediately bad. Here she was telling me about her beloved brother's death and I was worried about carrying her shampoo.

"How did he end up in Bombay?" I asked. It was such a long way from this far-flung corner of Nepal. It was a big deal for kids to go to the local elementary school, and a huge deal for them to go to boarding school in Kathmandu or Pokhara.

"My father was a Gurkha, stationed there for the Indian army when I was little. We lived in a compound outside Bombay with other Nepali soldiers' families until I was five. Then we came back here, but my brother went to school in Kathmandu, and they said he could go to university. He was in his second year." She already had a broader, more complicated life than I could have guessed

"I'm sorry," I said again, and rubbed her shoulder.

"*Tik-chha*, it's all right," she said. "I miss him, though. That's why I have to leave here. Because now he's never going to take me away." She showed me a letter from him on graph paper in neatly printed Devanagari that I couldn't read. Then her identity card. All of which, minus the shampoo (to my relief!), she handed to me to keep. We'd only just met, but she'd given me all her money, the only mementos she had of her dead brother, and her most valuable documents. She also handed me a new pair of velvet Chinese slippers, which I tucked with the rest in the top pouch of my backpack.

"It's right here if you need it," I said, in case she wanted to bow out. I felt uncomfortably responsible. She grabbed my hand and pressed the backs of my fingers to her forehead and grinned. "I'm very happy you came here!" she whispered. She was like the weather, this girl. Sad, happy. Happy, sad.

"I'm happy too," I said, and then, just as she was about to scoot down the pole, I said, "*Sathi*, wait. I want to tell you about the man who sent me to find you—"

"Will?" She'd already learned her benefactor's name, which was striking in a place where so little value was placed on names.

"Yes. He likes Nepali girls. A lot." Somehow I could talk more easily about death than sex with her.

"He does?"

"Yes, especially if they're pretty. Do you know what I mean?"

"Does he have a girlfriend?"

"He does. This girl Chhimi lives with him. She comes from the town where we're going tomorrow, across the river and up the hill, called Jankat."

"All right, so there's no problem. I'm going to Kathmandu to work anyway. I'm not looking for a boyfriend."

"Okay," I said. "I just wanted you to know."

"Don't worry, *sathi*!" She laughed and traced the furrow in my brow, the same vertical one she had in the photo. "I understand, and it's all fine."

I was relieved by her easy resolve. Of course she had seen all sorts of men come and go from this *raksi-kanné-tau*, this *raksi* drinking place. She was the innkeeper's daughter, after all.

Dinner was delicious—a mound of steaming white rice and yellow *dahl*, curried potatoes, and greens with garlic, and even some kind of fresh chutney, with no alarming grit or pebbles or rancid-oil taste. I ate and ate, as was expected, and complimented the food, and Maya's mother beamed. She offered me *raksi* again, but I declined. We sang Nepali songs together, and I felt anxious that she didn't know her daughter was about to leave her forever. I wanted desperately to ask her if it was all right, but I knew it would screw up everything. Instead, I asked if I could pay for my food and lodging tonight, since I wanted to leave very early. It was totally uncustomary, but she didn't seem to notice, or if she did, she pretended not to.

Maya went out to a flat spot in the yard to do the dishes, and I followed, but when I tried to take a pot, she swatted my hand. Finally, she let me pour water as she scrubbed them with handfuls of cold ashes.

"Did you tell your mother?" I asked, wanting her to assuage my guilt, even if, at seventeen, she was of marrying age in Nepal.

"No," she said. "I can't or she'll tell my father."

"You're not scared?"

"Don't worry, *sathi*. Everything will be all right," she said, and flicked some oily water at me.

"Okay, if you say so."

"Go to sleep. I'll be there soon."

I pulled my things together in the rafters, and soon enough Maya lay down beside me with a rough blanket thrown over her. I tossed around, exhausted, but my mind raced. I got up and went outside to pee one last time, staring at the strip of moonlit sky where skinny clouds glided by like fleets of canoes. Inside, Maya threw her arm over me protectively, as if I were running away with her, instead of the other way around, and said, "Sleep, *sathi*, sleep."

 Two

It was black in the house when Maya shook me and said, "*Sathi*, we have to get up." I was so tired I felt queasy, and when I shone my flashlight on my watch it wasn't four yet, but it was time to go if we were going to make some distance before the roosters and dogs woke up Maya's mother and the rest of the house. Suddenly a wave of nausea swelled up in me, and I practically slid down the pole trying to get outside in time. I made it to the wall in the yard, where I leaned over and threw up, once, twice, and then trembled there, wondering if I'd gotten it all out or if there was worse trouble ahead.

Maya appeared a few minutes later. "How are you, *sathi*?" she asked.

"I'm okay," I said. "Sick, but okay." It was strange, because the food was so good. The only thing I could think was that maybe I shouldn't have eaten the boiled potatoes when I arrived. Another wave rolled in, and I threw up again. If diarrhea followed, I didn't know how I would walk today. I waited for a roiling in my lower gut, but just felt hollowed out instead.

"We could stay. You should rest," she said tentatively. I looked at her, wearing my backpack. It was still night, and a layer of mist covered the ground up to our waists, but the sky was beginning to lighten. She and I both knew that if we didn't go now it wouldn't happen. Her father would find out, or she would get cold feet.

I just wanted to lie down and sleep, but we had to move. Besides, I thought I'd throw up if I smelled her mother's cooking again. Someone inside sat up and looked at us. "I'll be fine if you can carry my pack," I said.

We started off, my head beginning to ache. About ten minutes up the path, we stopped to fill our water bottles at the tap, and we heard the first rooster crow. We quickly put our things together and moved on, not talking, just walking. I knew that I'd feel easier once we'd covered this portion of the path that I'd walked yesterday, recrossing the spectacularly jerry-rigged footbridge, suspended forty feet up above the frothing Buri Gandaki, and entered the woods to climb uphill. I assumed Maya would, too. Alongside the river, it was easy to envision her father storming up the path, brandishing his knife. I don't think Maya could have guessed how slow I would be, especially now that I was sick. Maybe I had just worn myself out.

I prayed we wouldn't meet any other travelers headed in the opposite direction who could report on us to Maya's parents, and when we did spot a group, I was relieved that the bright colors of their jackets and their gait showed they were foreigners, the first I'd seen since Ghorka. As we got closer, I saw that they were four white men and maybe ten Nepalis, and they all looked dazed and tired. One of the foreigners in front was wearing big reflector bug-eye Vuarnets and asked in English with an unplaceable accent if I knew where they could get breakfast. I told them about the trekkers' lodge beyond Maya's house, not wanting them to stop sooner, and asked where they were coming from.

"Ganesh Himal. We lost a climber and guide in an avalanche," he said, rubbing his stubbled, sunburned neck. That explained their shell shock.

"I'm so sorry," I said. I heard these stories secondhand in Kathmandu pretty regularly, but I'd never met one on the path before. It seemed like a bad omen.

"We cremated them at a *gompa*, a Buddhist monastery, a couple days from here," he said. I wished them a safe trip, and we moved on in our separate directions.

When I told Maya what the man had said, she clucked her tongue. "I knew a climber who died. There's a marker for him on the path before you get to the next town. Did you see it?" she asked. I hadn't. "I was just ten or eleven when he stayed with us. He was a kind man, and he spoke very good Nepali. I was very sorry when he died." So Will and I were not her first foreigners, after all. I felt a pang of jealousy I couldn't explain.

On the makeshift suspension bridge with the water rushing beneath us, we passed a group of Nepalis, and Maya ignored them. It wasn't the custom, but I assumed she wanted to make us more invisible, so I did the same. It was late already, and I was relieved when Maya led us behind a big old half-dead tree on the other side of the bridge to a little path. The volume on the dull throb in my head turned up as we climbed.

"Maya, can we eat something?"

"We'll stop in a little bit, okay?" she said.

As we picked our way through the scrubby uphill forest, I wondered if I had altitude sickness. It wasn't even supposed to affect you under nine thousand feet, and I'd never gone higher than seventy-eight hundred. Still, if it was altitude sickness, ascending any amount was stupid. If it was food, why now, when Maya's mother's was the cleanest food I'd eaten so far, unless it was the food from the night before that? Or was it something else? Whatever it was, at least I had friends in Jankat who could help me if we needed it.

As Maya sailed up the hillside, I lagged. Unlike most uphill paths, it hardly traversed the incline, and I plodded behind Maya, making tiny zigzags within the path itself. In the nearly vertical bit at the end, where the track all but disappeared, we clawed our way up, grasping rocks and saplings in the soft dirt, heading for the lighter sky. Soon after, our hands scraped and fingernails filled with dirt, we emerged from the forest and landed on a hardpacked trail running along the hillside. Maya crowed, and I collapsed on a boulder. We were out of the woods, literally. The morning sun, which had been hidden by the steep hills, was shining, and the sky was a clear, liquid blue. A single, snowy peak shone in the distance, all its tiny facets distinct in the morning light. I felt like I could reach out and swipe a fingerful of snow as if it were frosting on a cake. It was Ganesh Himal (named for the happy elephant god), the same peak where the climbers had died. My headache melted in the face of it, and later I wondered if it was nerves after all.

"Do you think your father will follow us?" I asked.

"I don't know," she said, but she seemed more relaxed, as if, even if he did, she wasn't going back with him now. After some crackers and peanut butter laid out in a picnic on a flat rock, we walked easily along the high, even trail, feeling unburdened after the hard morning. Soon terraces climbed the hillside above and below us, some muddy and fallow, others swaying and swishing with dark green wheat. Around a bend, a whole new pocket of the valley opened up, and after a moment I realized the collection of mottled gray spots I was staring at, maybe a mile away and nestled into the middle of the hillside, was Jankat.

It made my heart ache a little to think of how well I knew the place, and how I was returning to it for what was probably the last time. I pictured its low stone houses, smoky and windowless inside, the roofs made of rough planks held down only by rocks—even nails were a luxury. Sugar, salt, tea, and chilis all came dear from the little money people earned selling their crops in the bazaar a few days away, or doing portering work for traders from the north, who used them to carry goods. My school program was the first trekking work these people had done for foreigners. At three dollars a day per person, Will offered them nearly twice what their countrymen did. But even with the influx of prosperity, evident in new *lungi*s and blocks of laundry soap at the town tap, what had existed for generations was the same. Day after day, the crops were planted, tended, and harvested by hand, stalk by stalk, with dull scythes. The grain was ground in rough stone hand mills. Candles were for special occasions. It was the definition of subsistence living in a way I didn't understand before I stayed there. Jankat was a far cry from the trekkers' towns listed in guidebooks, where tea shops offered Cokes and Fantas, glucose biscuits and stale Cadbury chocolates, and where simple hostels had plastic-coated menus boasting "fried cheeps" and "yak chiz." The problem for Jankat was that it wasn't on the way to anywhere. I knew of it only because of Will, and he knew of it only because he'd met some people from Jankat after he and his friend were robbed by their porters (women they slept with, he later confessed). On the path the next morning, they met a group of people from Jankat, who, after hearing their story, helped them back to Kathmandu. Will liked them so much—and liked the idea of mixing his pie-eyed college students with people who'd had virtually no contact with the outside world—that he hired them to be our porters when we trekked the Annapurna circuit the first month of school.

Now, I knew this place as well as a foreigner could: what it felt like to live without combs or soap or mirrors or cookies, to wear one set of clothes until it was worn out. I knew the rutted, nettle-lined paths between the houses, the people who lived inside them, and the rhythm of their days that began in the dark before the roosters and ended late at night sitting in the pitch dark, talking after the coals burned out.

Suddenly a gaggle of children scampered alongside us, little girls lugging toddlers in nubby slings and boys of seven and eight smoking cigarettes in their jaunty, faded *dhopi* caps that reminded me of overturned boats in faded zigzag patterns. One shy girl with bright black eyes and a big basket of sticks on her back wore a red rhododendron blossom tucked behind her ear that was almost as big as her face.

"*Didi! Didi! Didi!* Big sister! Big sister! Big sister!" they called, darting forward like fish to touch our clothes or packs or hands for an instant. "Where did you come from today? How long are you staying?" Maya, glamorous by local standards, with her sleek, long hair and newish clothes, was as of much interest to them as I was, if not more. They knew me.

Finally, just before we crossed the boards laid across the narrow river that rushed down the hillside at one end of town, we saw Karga. Karga was maybe thirty, and he was the de facto leader of the Jankat people—when it came to my school's program, though not by any means a village elder. It was through him that Will had arranged for the Jankaters to porter that first month of school, and then for three of us to live there during the last month while we did our independent study projects.

"*Oh-ho, iyé pugio!* You've come far enough!" he said with a grin, a kind of standard greeting that always made me smile.

"*Namaste dai*, big brother," I said, relieved to see someone I knew, after nearly a week of strangers. I told him I wasn't feeling too well. He led me straight to his place, where I crawled into the low loft and immediately fell fast asleep. A couple of hours later I woke up feeling revived, and found Maya and Karga sitting on the low wall outside his house, chatting and smoking, laughing easily until his wife, Sunmaya, came back from the fields with their little son, Sarkhi, standing in the basket of wheat on her back. Suddenly, Karga had business to attend to elsewhere.

If Karga was protection, Sunmaya was comfort, and I was glad to see her. She ushered us back inside through the rounded doorway we had to stoop to get through, and quickly relit the small, cold hearth and made us popped soybeans and corn in a cast-iron pot and sweet black tea. Sunmaya, who spoke almost solely in the local dialect the last time I was there, now seemed to speak a little Nepali, and she and Maya immediately got on.

As we talked, thin streams of daylight poured through chinks in the stone wall and filled up with swirling smoke, an effect that always reminded me of some strange piece of modern art, more than anything, and it was the kind of detail I found myself wanting to tell Nick, the man I was sort of seeing before I left. Even though we were barely in contact, just a couple of letters apiece since I'd been here, I seemed to be talking to him constantly in my head, writing him an ongoing letter I would never send.

After we ate, Maya and I went out to visit people I knew, until I had to come back and collapse for a while. The nausea never returned, but the headache came and went with a low-grade fever, and all I had was ibuprofen to combat it. If it wasn't altitude sickness or a stomach bug, what was it? Sickness could come in blasts like this here, and then vanish just as quickly. The second morning, after *dahl baht* (the day-in, day-out meal of rice and lentils, vegetables and chutney), I was feeling a little better, and Maya and I went up the hill to see the mother of Will's girlfriend Chhimi. The fact that she was his girlfriend wasn't official knowledge in Jankat, but Chhimi's mother seemed like a woman who didn't miss much and who didn't care for conventions anyway. She herself was single in a place where that should have meant she was dependent on the kindness of others. Instead she was a tough old doyenne, one of the richest people in the village. She still had the obvious beauty of her youth etched in her wrinkled face, and it was easy to imagine her in another incarnation striding down Fifth Avenue, shopping bags swinging from both hands, with a look that said, "If I am not for myself, who will be for me?"

"*Namaste*," I said as we walked up. Her younger daughter, maybe twelve, who was all shy sweetness, stopped scrubbing a pot to put her hands together. The old woman, sitting with two young men drinking *raksi* on her porch, tilted her head at us. She had a crown of snarled hair and earrings so heavy you could see through the elongated holes in her ears. "How are you, *didi*?" I asked.

"Fine," she said. "Come in. Have some tea." The young men got up to leave. She looked Maya up and down and asked where she was from. Maya answered, looking deferential for the first time since I'd met her, as if talking to a strict schoolmistress.

"Why are you going to Kathmandu?" Chhimi's mother asked.

"To work for a foreign woman." No mention of Will, smart girl. The old woman was definitely sussing out whether Maya was a rival for her daughter. She clearly understood the advantages and challenges of being a pretty girl. Of course, the fact that Chhimi was in Kathmandu on her own was unusual too, but then, her mother refused to live with either of her daughters' fathers, even though the rumor was that both had wanted to. Chhimi's mother asked after her daughter— how she was, when she was coming to visit. In the next few weeks, I told her. I gave her a small stack of photographs of her family, which seemed to please her.

My information gleaned, my usefulness exhausted, we sat in silence over the tea, listening to the coals pop and the sound of people going by on the path, their voices mixing with the breeze. I asked about the old woman's crops and her younger daughter, who stood shyly in the doorway. When our cups were empty, we left.

Sitting on the low wall outside Karga's house, Maya and I kept a lookout for angry posses led by Maya's father arriving at one end of the village or the other. I pretended to read, but I couldn't take my eyes off the trails. Maya turned the beads on her *mala*, saying the Buddhist mantra *om mani peme hung* over and over.

When I asked her why, she said it was for all the bugs she killed while walking on the path the day before, for her karma. I hoped it was for mine, too. On the roof of the house below

Karga's, a man lounged, drinking *raksi* from a skin, and every time some people arrived we'd call to him, "Oh, *dai*, do you know these people?" He always did. Then Karga came back in the middle of the afternoon and said that a group of people arrived who had met Maya's father. He told them he knew where Maya was but that he didn't care. He wasn't coming after her. We were relieved. Though I don't think either of us believed we'd heard the last from him. I knew Maya would have been glad to keep walking, but she also knew that visiting these people was the reason I'd come here, to give them pictures I'd taken and to take some more. Though in truth, I didn't feel up to it the way I had the first time. I just wanted to be there, seeing the people and place, without the camera in front of my face.

The next day, I delivered the last of the pictures and the small presents I'd brought while Maya stayed at Karga's. In the end, I felt silly for making this trip as a gesture of good-bye. Here, you didn't just show up, say good-bye, and leave. You either came and stayed awhile, like two or three weeks, or you just left. After all these months of learning how to be here, I felt clumsily foreign. The only thing that made sense was seeing Sunmaya, who was so quietly contented to have us here. That third night we listened to Karga's transistor radio—the first in the village—while a bunch of kids collected at the doorway. We heard the king had just announced there would be a new constitution after the recent student riots in Kathmandu, where some four hundred people were killed. I was shocked. I knew there had been student protests over the last few months, but I couldn't wrap my head around such violence in this peaceable place. Years later, I saw it was the first intimation of a darker undercurrent running through the culture, something I overlooked at first in my youth and enthusiasm.

IN THE MORNING, a day before we were supposed to go, I woke up and knew I had to leave. I shook Maya awake and told her.

"*Janné bella biyo*, is it time to go?" she asked.

"*Janné bella biyo!* " I said.

After breakfast we said our good-byes quickly and flew along the high, winding hillside path, exhilarated. Maya laughed and sang. Her giddiness was infectious, and I no longer had any doubt about the fact that she had wanted to come to Kathmandu. Our first night back on the trail we stayed in an empty storage shed because no one in the high-caste town where we arrived at dusk wanted us polluting their homes. The next night we landed in a more hospitable place. By the third day the towns had shops and tin roofs. Some buildings even had glass windows in painted frames. It all meant civilization was nigh in the form of Trisuli Bazaar, where the nearest bus stand was.

All this time, Maya cruised along the path with my pack on her back, wearing my blue bandanna over her hair in two braids like a foreigner. In her plaid flannel shirt, with her nose ring permanently gone, she couldn't inhabit her new life fast enough. Except in the unfriendly territory of our first night,

Maya charmed everyone she met. She played a little mouth harp, and people gathered around to hear. She took a flower from her own hair and tucked it behind a girl's ear, tossed a boy's ball, picked up a woman's baby, flirted with a grandfather, and seemed to do it out of a kind of irrepressible affection and delight. People were at ease with her in a way that transcended caste that I'd never seen before. Maybe they thought she was foreign, because no one called after her, "*Eh, Kanchi*," a kind of pejorative often used with pretty hill girls. She was somehow already above it, or outside of it.

But the third night, as we were getting ready to sleep, Maya suddenly started weeping about her brother, her family, her life, and the mother she'd left behind. "I have no future, no life. I should have died instead of him," she said.

"No. Don't say that. It's good you're alive. Everything will be okay. Don't worry," I said, and rubbed her shoulder. "Don't be sad. This is a change, but you have work, and Will and I can help you if you need it."

She sniffed and smiled and said, "You're right, *sathi*, thank you." A few minutes later, she started laughing. Then she grabbed at my crotch, and said, "What's that?" I didn't know what to make of it. I'd been in the fields with the women when they got bawdy, away from their men, cracking dirty jokes. I didn't know if it was the same thing, if she was just horsing around village-girl style, or if she was making a pass at me.

The next day as we were walking, she told me about an "old English man" who lived at her parents' house for three months with his fifteen-year-old Manangi bride, and collected hash each day.

"She was my friend, and each day he would go off and she would help me with my chores, and at night he would come back, his hands black and sticky from the hash, and he would add the lump to a ball of it in a tin." (I thought of the Lactogen can with her money in it.) "She was a very good person, and he was okay, and each night I would sleep with them in the loft."

"Why?" I asked.

"She was my friend," Maya said simply, as if that explained it all. She didn't seem like she was making a big confession about sex. She was just telling me something about her life, though again, I wasn't sure exactly what.

Finally we loped down a long, easy downhill and arrived in Trisuli, where, too late to catch a bus to Kathmandu that day, we meandered through the little bazaar town, enjoying cold sodas and crackers. First thing the next morning, we were on a crowded bus winding around the cliffs' hairpin turns. Now it was Maya's turn to be sick as she vomited all over the floor, but she was otherwise jolly about beginning her new life. I was already thinking about how I could at last hand over the responsibility of Maya to Will and just be her friend, free once and for all.

 *Three*

At Will's place, the landlord's German shepherd, Tiger, hurled his body against the high tin gate, barking ferociously. We waited for the landlady to call him off, and when she shouted that she had him, I popped the latch and entered slowly. The dog sat beside his mistress, panting in their doorway as she held his collar, and they both watched us cross the courtyard of packed earth, past her four-story house of white stucco and green wood shutters to the smaller two-story copy of it where Will lived. When I saw the heavy padlock on Will's door, I wrote him a note saying we were headed to Pete's Bistro for a late lunch and would be at school after that. Maya and I walked quickly past the woman and her dog and secured the gate behind us.

Pete's was a happy little enclave, sun-dappled and unpretentious, in an alley off Durbar Marg, or King's Way, that was frequented only by expats. It wasn't listed in guidebooks, and Nepalis, for the most part then, didn't eat out. With its fresh orange juice, homemade muffins, huevos rancheros, pizza, and even salads, the restaurant offered all sorts of things we students dreamed about while trekking, and at Pete's we knew we could eat them without worrying about the repercussions.

Pete was a Peace Corps guy from the sixties, and he knew how to prepare food so you didn't get sick. I didn't like to think of myself as someone who needed a break from Nepal, but after so much *dahl baht* and so much Nepali, I did. Standing outside the brick wall, I could hear Vivaldi piped into the garden and smell the real, live coffee, when the best you got anywhere else in this tea-drinking country was watery instant stuff. We walked into another world: a big, old crumbling Rana palace surrounded by tables with blue-checked tablecloths under mango and peepal trees. A friendly waiter I recognized led us to a table. Maya hunched in her seat, nervously studying the English menu upside down and chewing a cuticle, a stark contrast to the easy, upright girl striding through the villages.

"Is this like the place I'll work?" she whispered.

"Same kind of house, but just one lady, not all sorts of people coming to eat." Maya moved her silverware around at her place as she thought about this.

The food arrived, spinach and cheese omelets and green salad, a welcome respite from all the cumin, coriander, and fenugreek. The familiarity of it reminded me of my other self, the one that existed before here—a cornfed regular girl who drove her parents' station wagon out into the farm country when she wanted space, babysat her younger brothers, and was a decent cross-country runner. I could almost remember that other existence when I was eating at Pete's, and what it felt like to be me before I started this free-roaming life on the far side of the world. When I first arrived, I signed my postcards, only half-joking, "Dorothy in Oz." I knew on the way from the airport, as the taxi weaved through flocks of women dressed in every shade of red walking to the Bagmati River to bathe for a festival, that I had landed someplace beyond my ken.

Maya held the fork awkwardly, looking baffled.

"Try the spoon," I said, and then she stopped, her eyes focusing on something behind me. Will was striding toward us, looking beatific and slightly leonine with his dark blond curls bouncing and his motorcycle helmet under one arm. Scrubbed, eyes bright, wearing a vest over a button-down shirt and khakis—like the young professor he almost was, with a smidge of seventies style—he beamed a close-lipped smile that reminded me of the kitschy posters of Hindu gods you could buy on the street outside the temples. I knew then that my flickers of suspicion were right. He was too delighted to see us.

"*Namaste*," he said, hands pressed together with lots of direct eye contact for Maya, and he leaned over and kissed me. "You have no idea how happy I am. Thank you." He pulled up a chair and homed in on Maya with a laserlike intensity, asking all the proper Nepali questions about our travels. After a momentary shyness, Maya answered energetically and at length, telling him how afraid we were of her father and how I got sick as we left her house. "What did you have?" he asked me. I told him I had no idea. "Huh," he said, studying my face. He was definitely someone who believed sickness had its roots in your state of mind. "But you're okay now?"

"I feel great."

"Glad to hear it," he said. Maya told him how she threw up on the bus and how I harassed a guy into giving her his seat.

"How is your family?" he asked, and she told him, dry eyed, with no mention of her brother. It wasn't so much what they talked about, but their immediate rapport that was striking. I felt I was on the outside looking in, nose pressed to the glass—How much is that doggie in the window?—and I wondered if I should just leave from here, and let them get on with whatever it was they were doing. "Why don't you both come back to my place?" Will said, as if he were reading my thoughts. I paid, and Maya and I followed him out and caught a taxi while he rode his bike back. Tiger was out, but when he heard Will's voice he skulked away.

"He's never bothered me since I accidentally clocked him in the head with a two-by-four," Will explained.

"Accidentally?" I asked.

"It was. I was swinging it to make him keep his distance, and he came too close."

The landlady watched us again with interest—how many girls had she seen come and go from Will's over the years? We left our shoes inside his cool, dark entryway where he stored his bike and all sorts of gear and padded up the red-carpeted staircase to the living room. It was shuttered against the bright daylight, its walls lined with books and decorated with masks, art, tapestries, and Will's photographs. Down the narrow hallway, past ornate *thangka* paintings and Mughal miniatures, was his bedroom, which one girl in my program described as his tantric love den, with its tiger-skin rug and low Buddhist altar decorated with an ancient human skull, a singing bowl, and a statue of a goddess in a lunge wearing a necklace of bones and holding a knife in one of her outstretched hands. Across from the bedroom, in the dining room, Maya and I settled ourselves on the long cushions around a low table while Will made us tea in the alcove of a kitchen.

"You two will stay here tonight, won't you? The curfew starts in less than an hour, at six. It's been that way ever since the protests," he said.

"Sure," I said, as if I had anywhere else to go. "What about Chhimi? Where is she?"

"She's off in Jankat. She left two days ago, and she'll be back in a couple of weeks."

By going through Trisuli, we'd missed her. The better route was through Ghorka. "Are things okay with her?" I asked, in the most all-encompassing general way I could think of.

"They're okay," Will said, setting down the tea. We were speaking in English now. "To be honest, things have gone a little flat between us. She's changed so much, even in the last few weeks. You should see her. Her clothes, her hair. She has bangs now!" He sounded indignant, and Maya glanced at him before getting up to look around. "She's learning English, and she's got all these city-girl clothes. When I think of the fact that she'd never seen a light switch until a year ago . . . I mean, I'm glad for her in one sense. She's improving herself. But on the other hand, I think we may be outgrowing each other, moving toward just being friends."

"What does she think?" I asked. I was surprised his feelings had cooled so much. Just before I left, he told me that one night Chhimi suggested Will call his friend James to come take pictures of them in sexual poses from a book he had on the carvings on the temples of Orissa. "They came out great," he told me then. "I can't show them to you; they're too private. But she's wild, a very free spirit." Yet in just a few weeks' time, she'd been demoted to prosaic.

"I don't know, but I wouldn't be surprised if she felt the same way," he said. "I feel like I'm going through a serious psychic shift. Two days ago I went to Chatral Rinpoche for an initiation for *dakinis*—you know, the female Buddhist sky spirits who can help you on your way to enlightenment with the right tantric practices? Anyway, I want to do a book on them. Then yesterday, Marcia Wilson called up and said I could come out to meet their maid. I'd been wanting to for months! She's a *devi*."

"What does that mean?" A *devi* was a goddess.

"She's a nineteen-year-old Chetri girl who goes into these trances where she's possessed by a *devi*, and she can take curses off you, tell the future, bless you. There have been so many obstacles to meeting this girl. First the Wilsons were busy with planting. Then my bike broke down on the way out to see her. Other stuff, too. But suddenly, I'm there, and she's gorgeous. She went into her trance after dinner, and tells me my spirit needs opening, that something has been blocked, and she danced with branches from the peepal tree. By the time I went to bed, I felt clearer than I've felt in months about relationships, work, being here, everything. Then, just as I'm about to go to sleep, she appears in my doorway all dressed in white like an apparition." White was the color of the dead here.

"So you slept with her?"

He smiled, half-pleased, half-sheepish. "I didn't know what else she was there for. And then I came home and saw your note about Maya. I started shaking, even though it was eighty degrees out. My teeth started chattering."

"Uh-huh," I said, though I wasn't sure how to respond. I was very aware of the fact that I was both a guest in his house and that I felt extremely protective of Maya. If I questioned his belief in transcendental romance, and he decided I was too boring to have around, I wasn't sure where I'd go or if I'd be able to see Maya. So I just said, "I thought your friend was the one who liked her." Meaning his friend who was safely back at Berkeley.

"I know. I thought so too, but ever since you left, I haven't been able to stop thinking about her. I've been dreaming about her—curious, confusing, pleasurable dreams—every night."

"I think she really is eager to work," I said, hoping to remind him of the original plan.

"That's great. Although June said recently that she didn't want anyone till the middle of May," he said. I wondered if it was true.

"Should I make some food?" Maya asked, walking back into the room, having showered and changed into clothes I'd never seen before. A shower sounded good. I went to do the same.

After seeing only bits of myself for weeks, it was startling to encounter the freckled, angular whole of me in Will's full-length bathroom mirror: tan lines, pinkness, and dirty skin. My red hair was unruly—I raked my fingers through it, hoping I was still lice-free—and my eyes seemed a little wild and almost too wide after not seeing their own reflection. I examined scrapes and bruises, my sharp elbows and skimpy chest. I'd forgotten how different I looked from compact, curvy Maya.

The shower, even tepid, was delicious—to stand under a nozzle rather than crouch beside a bucket or icy tap half-dressed, to simply be naked. I scrubbed off shreds of dirt and washed my hair twice, using Will's imported organic health-food-store shampoo rather than my Indian Herbal Essences—I did feel he owed me something, too, suddenly. Afterward, I put on some passably clean if dingy clothes, and I looked a little more like someone I knew.

Night had fallen, and we were halfway through dinner when the lights went out. "It's been like this every night since the demonstrations," Will said, getting up. I opened the shutters behind me to look out at the dark neighborhood. It was quiet except for some dogs yapping somewhere and people talking in the house across the lane. No Radio Nepal with its nightly newscast and *bing-bing-bing*. No cars or scooters. Just a light wind in the trees, a distant screechy bird, and moonlight spilling over the rooftops. We might have been in a village, except everything was a little taller here.

"What would happen if I went outside right now?" I asked.

"Someone would probably shoot at you. There are tanks

down at the bazaar," Will said, lighting a couple of candles, and I closed the shutters again. It was nice to be inside in the flickering candlelight with friends when the world outside was suddenly so hostile. Will described how just a little over a week before, several thousand students belonging to the communist and democratic parties came together and stormed Durbar Marg, breaking store windows and toppling a statue of the king's grandfather, demanding a true multiparty system and a new constitution. The police charged the crowd, killing an estimated three to four hundred people with *lathi*s—a number that later was found to be much lower. The entire city was under curfew for three days, and still people were in hiding, moving from house to house. "But people seem hopeful that there will be real change, that the country might become a true democracy. Not that I'm sure they're ready for it here."

Maya listened with rapt attention, and again I waited for her to tell Will about her brother, but she didn't. Will got up to get more food, and I squeezed her arm. "Are you okay?"

"I'm fine," she said brightly. I felt like we understood each other in a way that I couldn't say about other Nepali friends, where I always felt a screen of difference between us. Maybe it was that we'd both left home with a little bit of desperation, with the idea that there was a more straightforward happiness waiting someplace else—never mind that I had to go around the world and she had to go less than a couple hundred miles.

"Will you eat something else? A mango?" Will asked, plucking one off the brass plate in the center of the table.

"Yes, let's," Maya said. I'd never eaten one before. They

didn't exist in Des Moines when I was a kid, and they had only recently come into season here. The closest I'd come was the sugary, bright orange box drinks that I depended on for quick energy—"Mango Frooti! Fresh and Juicy!" Will got a knife and board from the kitchen and sliced the fruit into neat wedges, leaving the skin on.

"How do you eat it?" I asked.

"Like this," Maya said, popping an oblong piece into her mouth. Holding it at one end, she pulled it, scraping off the fruit with her teeth so that the juice dribbled down her chin. When I laughed, she dropped a piece in my mouth, surprising me and pleased with her trick. I reciprocated, shoving a wedge in her mouth, and she got Will, and suddenly it was a frenzy of mango eating, until *pop!* a flash went off—Will's camera— and we looked up.

"What—?" I asked, but Maya tickled me, I laughed, and more flashes went off. Even before my eyes readjusted to the dark, I could feel how he looked at us, how we were a pair to him, a sexualized pair, even if I was the less alluring of the two. I felt I should pull away, extricate myself, but I didn't want to, and so I kept laughing. *See, I'm not so different from her*, I felt like saying.

"Eat," Maya said, turning to offer the board to him, and he clicked another picture. "Stop it, eat!" He took a piece and per- formed the surgery much more delicately than either of us as he stripped the pulpy fruit from the shiny skin. Soon the mango was gone, and Maya chewed on the pit.

I left Will and Maya making up a bed for her from the

cushions around the table, and I went to the living room and laid out my sleeping bag on the springy, dusty velvet couch. Lying in the dark, I listened to them in the other room and wondered if this was the right place for me to be after all. They seemed to want me there, to be happy for my company, and yet. They were already a *they*, and I was just me, alone. I thought of Nick, how we had fought the morning I left for Nepal, over sex. We had it, but it wasn't very good—my fault, I supposed. It was my first time, and I had wanted to, because I couldn't bear to bring that old albatross—virginity!—with me to Nepal, but I didn't let go with reckless abandon, either. I was careful and nervous, unwilling to be entangled with someone on the other side of the world as I set off for the year. He blamed himself and was gloomy at the airport. I couldn't wait to leave. As I passed out of his sight, I kept thinking, *I'm free!* Still, I thought of him all the time, or I should say I thought *to* him. I sent him mental postcards describing the people I met and the places I visited. But about Maya and Will, I felt strangely quiet. I didn't know what I would say, or if I would say anything at all.

WHEN I WOKE UP I could hear Maya in the bathroom and found Will whistling something cheerful in the kitchen as he whisked eggs in a bowl. He looked up when I came in.

"She's a wonderful thing," he said, and I knew they'd slept together, that his whole shtick about wanting to give her a new life, to rescue her, was an excuse to get her near him, to have the chance to sleep with her, and find out if she was his latest *dakini*.

I felt vaguely sad, as if the chance for something good were lost, but I just leaned in the doorway and said, "What do you mean?"

Fresh, sunny air poured through the window behind him. "We went to bed in our separate rooms, and ten or fifteen minutes later she just appeared and crawled into bed."

"Just like the *devi*?" I said, putting toast in the toaster.

"Yeah, and I'm sure she's been with Western men before, because she knows how to kiss. Hill girls don't usually know about that."

"Oh," I said, wondering if he would ask me to go, now that I'd procured her.

Will handed me a mug of tea. "Alex, I want to ask you a big favor. Would you mind staying here for a while? It would help a lot in terms of appearances in the neighborhood with my landlords, and also, she seems very attached to you."

I took a sip of tea, pretending to contemplate it, as if there were anyplace else I wanted to be, as if staying in a guesthouse in Thamel for a few dollars a night among boisterous backpackers stopping over between Bangkok and Goa held any appeal, or as if living at my Nepali teacher's house again with her three young children sounded good. For all my reservations about Will, the rest of the city felt irrelevant to me now. That was tourism; this was life. I had less than a month left before my visa ran out for good and I had to go back to the hushed and leafy suburbs of Des Moines for the summer. Staying anyplace else in Kathmandu sounded lonely and boring to me.

"Sure, I'd be happy to," I said, careful to hide the extent of how pleased I was. I knew it was good for Will to think I was doing him a favor—it would keep things balanced.

"That's excellent. Thanks a lot," he said, cracking eggs into a bowl.

Maya emerged, her hair wrapped up in a towel, smelling of flowery soap. "*Sathi!*" she cried, and squeezed me with an exuberance I was getting used to. "How are you?!"

"Good." I was. If she was choosing this, and she wasn't just going to bed with a rich white guy by default, if this was what she was aiming for, great. The last thing I wanted was to inflict the puritanical thinking I'd been raised with. Good for her for going after what she wanted. "How are you? Did you sleep well?"

"Very well."

"Okay, you two, go sit down," Will said, holding a tray heaped with pancakes, honey, yogurt, and a big bowl of fruit salad. That was the other benefit of staying here: Will was an excellent cook and lived well, at least when he wasn't in pilgrim mode. There was also something deeply decent about him, no matter how much of a lothario he was. I could and probably should be cautious around him, but I didn't need to fear or mistrust him. Maggie's experience was her experience, not mine. When I'd decided to stay in Nepal it was to be pushed beyond what I knew and was comfortable with: *Like what the mountain climbers were after, but not on a mountain*, I thought as I chewed on a piece of crumbly brown bread with guava jam. A friend who studied with me in the fall wrote me that after her semester away, back at school in Austin, her experience in Nepal was like a smooth, round marble in her pocket. Aside from the amoeba she'd brought home, "I'm just the same," she wrote. I wanted to come home different from what I'd been—bolder, wiser, happier. And so our little household of three was established.

"What should we do today?" Will asked Maya, and added, "Your boss said she doesn't need someone right away, so you can go to work in a couple of weeks if you want to just look around Kathmandu a little."

"Yes, very much!" she said. "I've only been here once when I was a girl, and then I only saw Pashupati temple."

"You and Alex could go to the bazaar, if that's okay with you, Alex? I actually have a little business to take care of," he said. "I could meet you guys at the Shiva Spot at two for a late lunch."

"Sure," I said, understanding suddenly that part of earning my keep was not only being a confidante to Will, but a baby-sitter or chaperone to Maya. I didn't think I was someone who would do whatever Will asked, but there was nothing else I had planned today, and I liked spending time with Maya. After stopping at school to check for mail—I had a letter from Nick, of all people, after something like four months, but I wanted to save it for later when I was alone—we grabbed an auto rickshaw at the crossroads and rode it across town. It trundled past the palace, where no doubt the king, with his bad eyeglasses and big bank account, was thinking hard about his role to come, and south on Kantipath to Asan Tol. It was good to be back in the bustle and throng of the city, to be pleasantly anonymous again.

In the heart of the fruit and vegetable market, among the tall, shapely mounds of mangoes, parsnips, onions, potatoes, and okra (or ladyfingers, as they're known here), there was a tiny, disheveled old woman with tufty, gray hair roaming around in bare feet, chattering at no one and everyone in her throaty voice. People stared or turned away. But when she said to Maya, "*Bayini*, will you invite me over for supper?" Maya said, "Sure, grandmother. What would you like to eat?"

"Meat, lots of meat. Goat and chicken and *buf*'—water buffalo—and yogurt, and some very spicy chutney," the woman said, and laughed. She wanted a feast. Then she started talking gibberish, and Maya listened and responded as if she understood.

Maya turned to me. "Will you take a picture of us?" She knew I carried my camera everywhere, even though I was taking fewer and fewer pictures by the day, it seemed, and I obliged as Maya threw her arm around the woman. They both grinned, one sweetly, the other madly. Then the woman *namaskaar*ed, bowing deeply to each of us, and wandered off.

Vegetables in hand, we meandered through the narrow, winding alleys, where the buildings leaned toward one another across the cobbled lanes, until we reached the old, ornate palaces of Durbar Square, passing the house where the prepubescent girl considered to be the Kumari goddess was locked inside, protected from the sullying forces of the outside world. Back inside the labyrinth of tiny streets, we peered into the gleaming stores of the metal market at the pots and pans and statues, and finally turned into an alley shimmering with millions of strands of colored beads—mostly the ones called *poté* that married women wore—that I could only ever find by accident, and emerged at New Road, a wide, straight paved street where the shops sold electronics and gold jewelry, and where we could find a taxi at the next intersection. Taped to the electrical poles were small posters with colorful boxes printed on them. When we stopped to look, I realized that they were smeary photos of the dead from the protests, their faces battered and swollen, bloody and lifeless. Maya was solemn as she looked at the pictures, and then there were tears streaming silently down her face.

"*Sathi*, are you okay?" I asked.

"Why does it have to be like this?"

"I don't know," I said, suddenly aware of the people who had stopped around us to stare, much as people had done in the bazaar earlier at the crazy lady. People just didn't cry in public here, and when she let out a long, animal keening noise and bent over with sobs, I shuttled her into a taxi and asked the driver to take us home. She shook, moaning all the way there.

People didn't have these open, emotional displays in Nepal. There was no weeping or shouting, nothing the least bit melodramatic or Mediterranean, but the equanimity here wasn't the same as the Midwestern forbearance that I grew up with either. It was simply as if people's experiences, good and bad, dropped like stones into a deep well. I think it had to do with a strong sense of karma and with the inevitability of things. Here, if your child died, that fact did not orbit your head or become your identity the way it would at home, yet it remained deeply a part of you.

I rubbed Maya's back as she cried, and got us safely into Will's house without being mauled by the dog. I wanted to get Maya away from the snoopy landlady and everyone else. I left her on the couch while I went to get water and a plate of tangerines. She drank a little and put her head on my lap, and I thought about those Brontë and Austen novels where young girls were always doing this in times of trouble or weariness, laying their head on the lap of another, out of the public's eye, by the hearth. It felt good to be the protector when I had felt so out of my depth at times in this last year, which had something to do with Nepal, and everything to do with Nick, whose letter I could just reach in the top of my bag on the floor without waking Maya. In his block-lettered print and black Sharpie pen he wrote:

DEAR ALEX,

I HAVE A FEELING YOU MAY HAVE WRITTEN ME A WHILE BACK, BUT I MOVED AND LOST TRACK OF MY MAIL FOR A FEW WEEKS. SO SORRY IF THIS IS THE CASE. I THINK OF YOU OFTEN WITH YOUR NEW PALS, THE HORIZON ALWAYS IN YOUR EYES, AND I'M GUESSING YOU ARE, BY NOW, COMPLETELY TRANSFORMED BY IT ALL. I HOPE I WILL RECOGNIZE YOU WHEN I SEE YOU NEXT, AND THAT YOU WILL KNOW ME TOO. WRITE IF YOU CAN. OTHERWISE, TAKE PHOTOS AND REMEMBER EVERYTHING.

YOURS,
XO NICK

Yours? Why would he sign it *yours?* He wasn't mine any more than I was his. I knew it was just an expression, but why that expression? It was such a short, thin little letter, I wasn't sure why he bothered to send it, except to remind me that he was still there. It was neither warm nor cool, heavy nor light. It existed in some kind of letter purgatory, and it made me feel annoyed, mildly elated, and sad, all at once. I read it three more times trying to crack its code, then dropped it back into my bag.

I met Nick only a couple of months before I left for Nepal, at a photo workshop in Rockland, Maine, where I was on a work-study scholarship. In the first few weeks, I took some pictures I liked. Then a visiting filmmaker named Nick Kanjian came to stay and to show his indie feature *Hurricane*. I'd actually seen it at the art-house theater at school in the spring and loved it—it was all about the peculiarities and absurdity of a supposedly normal family life. After the Q & A, I went up to talk to him, but when it was my turn, he fixed his wide, light blue eyes on me and said, "Yes?" as if I were already wasting his time.

"Oh, uh, hi," I stammered, because I couldn't imagine what I'd done to offend him. "I just wanted to tell you how much I loved your film."

He tilted his head and smiled, looking less ferocious. "Thanks."

I started babbling about the characters, how I still thought about them, and he said, "Hold on a minute?" turning to talk to an older man before I could answer.

If I hadn't felt a little light-headed I might have bolted. Instead I just collapsed into a nearby seat and stared at the chipping paint on the concrete floor until I heard, "I'm sorry. Now we can actually talk.". Nick sat down beside me, giving me a bashful smile and looking like a different person altogether. He reminded me of some kind of intelligent, skittish animal, the way he nervously patted his head, smoothing down his straight black hair that stuck out in every direction.

We talked about the film some more, and he asked about me. He turned out to know a lot about photography. The whole time we were sitting there, I kept wanting to look at his eyes, but his gaze was so unnerving that I mostly watched his eyebrows rising and furrowing on his pale forehead. They seemed to register whatever emotion he was feeling just a fraction of a second before the rest of his face, and even when his face was at rest, he had a kind of permanently surprised expression because of the way they arched. Besides that, he had a handsome Roman nose, full lips, and skin the color of skim milk.

I went out to dinner that night with Nick and a few of the teachers at a local place called the Clam Basket, and everyone was nice, even though I was the obvious kid of the bunch. Nick stopped by the office the next day to say hello, and the day after that he found me outside the cafeteria and offered me an ice-cream sandwich, no small prize for a sweet tooth like me. When I didn't see him the day after that, I got mad at myself. *He's just being friendly. You're just a kid*, I told myself. He was eleven years older than me, and that difference seemed more like twenty years. Why would he be interested in me? But then he showed up at the office in the late afternoon and asked if I wanted to have a beer with a gang of them later.

In a booth, alone sharing Rolling Rocks while everyone else

played pool, Nick and I talked about where we were from—he was from a small town outside Cleveland where his was one of three Jewish families. "It was perfect until I was about nine or ten, and then it just wasn't any place for a kid who didn't aspire to the varsity football team," he said. Then he told me he'd seen my work that afternoon and that he liked it a lot.

"You did? Which prints? Why? Sorry!" He laughed, and I told him it was just that I admired his film so much, I felt embarrassed. But when he described what he'd noticed and understood, I felt as if he had seen the best part of me, beyond what was in the images.

He came to the darkroom the next day and helped me choose some prints for the group show, asking me about each one. What rattled me was the way he treated me as if I were someone with something interesting to say, a phenomenon I wasn't really used to, not with older, more accomplished men, anyway. Then, on the last Friday night, at the opening of the show, he asked what I was doing the next day. I said I was thinking of taking the ferry out to Matinicus Island, but I wasn't sure if anyone was going to come with me, because it was so far.

"How about me?" he said.

We picked up sandwiches, caught an early boat, and hiked to a little cove another student had told me about. I'd worn my bathing suit under my clothes, and Nick said he'd watch me swim, because he didn't have his. But after I'd swum out a ways, yelping at the coldness of the water, I looked back to see him wading in, fully dressed, Doc Martens, black jeans, T-shirt, and a big grin on his face.

"You're nuts!" I shouted.

He just dunked and came up shaking the water off his head before he swam out to meet me.

"Why didn't you take off your shirt, at least?" I asked.

"I don't know what you're talking about. I always swim in my clothes." He was so different from the big-shouldered, easygoing guys I'd gone to high school with, and even from the artsy boys at college. There was an inner life to him that I couldn't even guess at.

We dozed on the smooth, sun-warmed rocks, and I woke to find him watching me with his clear, light-blue-eyed gaze. Birds twittered and the water lapped at the shore quietly, but I felt as if I had a pinball game playing inside me—*ping, ping, ping*. He leaned over to kiss me, and my whole body rang. With his damp shirt cool against my skin, we kissed some more, and I unbuttoned his top buttons to touch his smooth, pale chest. He had a kind of taut, urban leanness that seemed out of place on these rocks by the sea, and I felt like a Viking beside him, long-limbed, freckled, and sun-streaked. I felt protective of him, but then his hands slid so nimbly and certainly over the shiny, hot fabric of my bathing suit, touching me so that he seemed to be holding all of me at once, and when he slipped his fingers under the bottom edging of my suit, the flashing, wet warmth inside me was so different from the sun's steady heat.

"Is this okay?" he asked.

I looked from the sky to his eyes. "Yeah," I said, touching the warm metal button of his jeans. He pulled a strap of my suit to kiss my shoulder and then I stopped us.

"Someone's sure to come by."

"Do I make you nervous?" he asked.

"Yeah, but I like it." I did too, feeling like I was being pulled out past the edge of myself.

At the rail of the ferry, we stood shoulder-to-shoulder, quiet, our sunburned faces cooled by the breeze, my hair blowing around us. When he got chilled, we sat on the bench, and I draped my legs over his lap and wrapped my arms around him. He put his face into the curve of my neck so that I could feel his eyebrows twitching against my sun-tightened skin. At a lobster shack on the shore, we sat at a picnic table under the bright outdoor lights and cracked open the red shells, sucking out the salty white meat inside, talking quietly, as if we'd known each other a long time.

Almost a month later, after a handful of long, late-night phone calls, I went to visit him in New York just before I left for Kathmandu. I told my parents I was visiting a friend from school. They didn't need to know, and besides, I couldn't explain who he was to me. Even with my backpack, I bounded up the five stories of his East Village walk-up to find him in the doorway, beaming. He pulled me into the narrow entryway, his smooth hair tickling my nose, and right away, first thing, I showed him the work I'd brought, that I'd made myself complete since I'd seen him last.

When he proclaimed the pictures "really good," I could have done a little dance. I'd seen his short film. I'd been thinking about it. I'd done this work for him really, and the photos were a whole jump up from anything I'd done before.

That night we went to a place called the Miracle Grill, where I felt as if I'd landed after orbiting the Earth for years. Was it the tequila, or did he know me better than I knew myself? From there we went to different smoky bars looking for his friends. We never found them, but everywhere we went Patsy Cline was playing, singing "Crazy" and "Walkin' After Midnight" and "I Fall to Pieces" on the jukebox, and it seemed significant somehow. We kissed between bars, holding hands as we went. Somebody whistled from a passing car, and we laughed. At his place, we fed each other watermelon on the couch until we slid onto the floor with a thud.

In the bedroom, jeans were tugged off, and we slipped under the white duvet, all limbs and skin. For what was left of the night we slept restlessly, reaching toward each other, pushing and pulling, but not sex, and then bright daylight filled the room, and a breeze blew the white sheets tacked to the windows up to the ceiling. Pulling off the last of our clothes, we were naked in our fluffy bower, and as we kissed, I could hear children playing on the street below and swore they were calling my name. Then I told him I was a virgin.

"Oh, Alex, I feel blessed," he said.

Ugh, I thought. *Wrong answer.* "It's really not that big a deal."

"It is special, though," he said, and something inside me curled away from him, curdled even, like orange juice poured into milk, as I felt the gap of eleven years between us suddenly open up while he talked about his first time so many years before. When we woke up past noon, I made myself forget the talk and put on an emerald green vintage dress he'd bought from a Scotsman with bad teeth on the sidewalk the night before. The late-summer breeze slipped between the heavy cotton fabric and my skin, shifting all around me so that I felt sweetly naked beneath it. But at brunch I got terrible cramps, and beneath the tabletop I rested my palm low on my stomach and switched from coffee to ice water.

Later I said, "I feel like you're idealizing me, like I'm not who you think I am."

"Who are you, Alex?" he said quietly, and I turned away so he wouldn't see me cry. I spent a little time by myself that afternoon, and the next day I met up with a friend from school for a coffee. "It's weird," I told her. "The more distant I feel from him, the more I want to sleep with him. It's like, what have I got to lose?" A passerby on the sidewalk turned to look at us.

My friend laughed and said, "Well, it doesn't sound like you'll be pining for him."

"I will so *not* be pining for him!" I said, full of false bravado.

That night I told him that I wanted to, and he seemed surprised.

"Are you sure?" he asked.

I shrugged. "Yeah, I mean, why not?"

He seemed hurt but willing, and then we tried to have sex but I couldn't, and we fell into a tense sleep. In the morning I woke up to a light rain outside, and the air smelled of wet pavement and the first dying leaves of fall. I had to be at the airport in five hours. We had sex, but I didn't feel half of what I'd felt even a few nights before. I didn't want to. The whole point of going to Nepal was to be on my own, away from everything here. I couldn't commit in the final hours to a lovesick year of being tethered to anything at home. But even as I pushed him away, I knew I was taking him with me as much as I was taking the emerald green dress, now tightly folded up at the bottom of a duffel I kept at school.

Now, with Maya asleep in my lap, I wondered how much of what she was going through or would go through with Will would be like what I had with Nick. I think she already felt her destiny was tied to his, and I wanted to warn her against it. I wasn't convinced his infatuation would last. And yet this girl, this country girl in the big city, overwrought with her past, with all it hadn't given her, was not so very different from me.

I opened my eyes to Will putting down a tray on the table with three cups of mint tea and a plate of imported chocolate biscuits. He raised his eyebrows at Maya, who seemed to be asleep, and I opened my mouth to speak, then mouthed that I'd tell him later. But Maya opened her eyes and looked at Will, at me, and sat up rubbing her eyes, patting her cheeks, smoothing her hair.

"Are you okay?" Will asked, clicking on a lamp. I went to open a shutter. The flat brightness of midday had begun to soften outside.

"I'm okay," she said, and looked at me. "You tell, *sathi*." I did, in the calmest of terms, because I had a feeling the hysteria of it would reflect badly on both of us. Now that Maya was in this, I wanted him to be able to continue to admire her, and I didn't want to be seen as someone who was encouraging her neurotic side. If I was kicked out of this circle, or if the two of us were cut free from him, how would I help her? I didn't have the connections for jobs that Will had. All I wanted for Maya was a good job, so that she had the option of being self-sufficient. That was my goal. If she was Will's girlfriend too, that was fine. As long as she wasn't stranded when his fit of love or adoration or whatever it was eventually passed. I told the story evenly and ended up with, "So then we came home, just to relax."

"I'm sorry about your brother. That's terrible. How are you now?" he asked Maya. That was the funny thing about Will: He really did *know* that everyone suffered. He'd spent too much time with the lamas and meditating not to.

"I'm fine. I think about him a lot, though, and would like to do *puja* for him."

"We can find a lama to do *puja* here," Will said.

"I know," she said. "That would be good, but I would also like to go to Bombay one day and do *puja* there."

"Maybe one day we can go together," Will said. "I sometimes have business there." Will only ever alluded to his business. The most I knew was that he'd smuggled black-market dollars out of the country in the soles of his shoes and smuggled in from Hong Kong chunks of gold buried deep inside the eucalyptus goo of Tiger Balm containers. Antiquities, hash, diamonds—it could have been any or all of the above. I got the impression that most foreigners who weren't working for an embassy (and some who were) trafficked in something or other just to keep their postcolonial lifestyles afloat. But what business exactly Will had in Bombay, I could only speculate. Even my asking would have made him prickly, I was pretty sure.

"Should we start dinner?" he asked Maya, and turned to me. "Why don't you just relax?" Feeling dismissed, I found the novel I was reading and went to the far end of the living room so they could have their privacy. I was jealous of her, of him, and nonplussed by how much I felt like the third wheel. I was supposed to be the one who understood her and made her feel better. He was the one who was supposed to idealize her and want her for his own tantric transformations.

Alternatively, to him, wasn't I pretty? Wasn't I interesting? Aren't you really interested in me, whom you can talk to about art, books, the state of the world? Soon Maya came to get me and bounded across the room, kissed my forehead, and told me I was a good friend, and I recovered my pride enough to go have dinner.

WE SPENT THE NEXT WEEK in taxis, rickshaws, *tuk-tuk*s, and on bicycles and Will's motorcycle, zooming around town on excursions to Pete's Bistro, Swayambu, Boudha, and Patan. When we were all together, Will would admire Maya, sometimes aloud, sometimes in just the way he looked at her, like he couldn't believe his luck that this creature had landed in his life. He liked the way her long hair trailed almost down to her waist in uneven tendrils, the way she laughed so easily at things Nepalis didn't usually laugh at—like the self-seriousness of Brahmin priests, or a glistening, skinned goat's head attracting flies on a table outside a butcher shop. The way she befriended stray dogs and children, and how she didn't seem to think about the fact that she was low-caste or that there was some proper way for her to act. "Isn't she remarkable? She's so uninhibited," he said more than once, as if it were the highest compliment. I found it strange and titillating to be so intimate with the beginning of a romance that had nothing to do with me. So this was how men saw women. This was what they wanted, or thought they did.

Sometimes Maya and Will would go off alone, and I'd meet up with other friends. Sometimes Maya and I went out together. Will and I never had reason to spend time just the two of us. But every night, because of the curfew, we three were together at our table, as we were at breakfast, and aside from the occasional spasms of jealousy, I was glad to be with them. When I went out for Thai food in Thamel with Maggie and her friend Althea, a highbrow hippie girl taking a year off from Brown, I told them that I could have stood to pay more attention to Maggie's experience with Will when I agreed to bring Maya back, since now they were sleeping together every night.

"I feel bad. I mean, she went to his bed, but I really thought he wanted to help her find work," I said.

"What about her work?" Maggie asked.

"Will says June doesn't need someone till the middle of

next month, so that's when Maya will start, maybe. He gave her the option of going there sooner, but she said she was happy to stay at his place and *gumnu* around town."

"She sounds like she's doing fine," Althea said, though she'd never met her.

"I think she's okay. I'm not sure."

"So try not to worry too much," they both told me.

But that very night at dinner, while we were finishing a kind of improvised stir-fry I'd come up with, since I didn't know how to make *dahl baht* anyway, Maya looked down and started quietly sobbing.

"What is it?" Will asked.

She pushed her plate away and put her head on the table, crying more audibly now. We each put our hands on her from either side. "Tell us."

She gasped. "I'm going to die maybe," she said.

"What do you mean? Are you ill? Are you in pain?" I asked.

"*Hoiyna,* no, it's my *mon,* my soul. I'm not a good person. I should have died rather than my brother. He was a good person. What benefit comes from me being alive? I'm bad. I'm a sinner—"

"You're not," I said. Was this because she was sharing Will's bed? "You're a good person with a good *mon.* Listen to me. Don't say those things. Don't cry." Nepali encouraged this kind of straightforwardness.

Will watched her consider this. "Listen to Alex. The things you say aren't true. You have a good *mon.*" He meant it, but he was also clearly surprised by the violence of her emotions. Will gave her a tissue, and she blew her nose with a little laugh.

"What a lot of *holla*, noise," she said. "Please excuse me."

"You don't have to apologize. We understand," I said. "Life is just difficult sometimes." Was I really issuing these platitudes as if I were my mother, albeit in a language I barely knew existed a year ago? How had I, who had lived so little, who knew only about life in the sticks of Iowa and what it was to be an undergrad, how had I become her counselor or adviser? But she was looking at me so intently that I had to believe what I was saying. "Don't worry. You'll be fine. You're strong," I said.

"It's true. You're right. One minute," she said, and got up to go wash her face. Will looked at me, bewildered.

"What just happened there?" he asked.

"I think she just needed to cry. It seems like she's been through a lot, maybe more than she's letting on."

"Like what?" he asked.

"I don't know exactly. Did she tell you about the old English guy and his Manangi teen bride?"

"No," he said, and I told him. "Weird, although it's not totally surprising. A lot of teahouses function that way, too. The daughters might or might not sleep with you for a little money. It's not overt. It's just kind of understood—if you want it, the option's there. Although she claims she's never had sex before, and we haven't been able to."

"I had no idea about the teahouses." I wasn't sure what to say about their sex life.

"Not all of them, but a lot. Sex is such a paradox here. On the one hand, there are all these strict mores, but then when you scratch the surface, there's an appetite and a creativity that can be very playful." This was classic Will-speak, the intellectualized description of something quite ordinary.

I was relieved when Maya returned. "How are you?" I asked.

"Much better," she said, and pinched my cheek.

THE NEXT MORNING, Will decided it was time to take Maya to the Indian palm reader Mr. Thakur. "I think he might be able to explain something about what's going on with her. You wouldn't believe how spot-on he was with Chhimi. He said her destiny was with foreigners, that she would likely marry one, that she would probably live abroad. He also told me about a year ago that I was constitutionally unsuited to marriage, but that there would come a time in my thirty-third year when I would want to. Then in February, right after I turned thirty-two, I really wanted Chhimi to marry me, but she wouldn't."

I was skeptical. I had been to see Mr. Thakur. For ten bucks, to hear someone talk about my character and future for an hour and a half, I couldn't resist. Maggie came too and, in his fancy-pants, convoluted, Indian English, he had told each of us that we were people with a strong sense of home who liked to travel. Not a great leap of imagination for American girls living in Kathmandu. Though, to his credit, he once told

Will he was either a saint or a criminal genius, or maybe both, because his head and heart lines were merged, which meant he had no guilt—an interesting theory. Who knew? Maybe Mr. Thakur would have some insights into Maya.

Will was fuming when he got home. "You know what he said? He said that while she appeared to be a highly spiritual creature, she was in fact closer to a beast. That she should never have been taken from her village. What a jerk. I have to translate the tape for her tonight. I don't know what I'm going to say."

I laughed at Will's outrage. He hated when people didn't uphold his mystical inclinations. I didn't care, though, because it just confirmed my suspicion that Mr. Thakur, while inventive, was a fake.

 *Four*

A few days later at breakfast, like a squall blown in from nowhere, Maya started hysterically sobbing again. "*Maa morchu hola, maa morchu hola*," she said. "I'll die maybe." She seemed like the crying might make her sick. Will, after trying to console her to no effect, got up and poured some more tea before returning and saying, "Seems like a good day to take Ecstasy."

"Really?" I said, sipping my tea. These past months in Nepal, from the beginning, I had trained myself not to show shock, or in some cases horror, for fear it would either offend someone ("You want me to crap where? Eat what?") or make me look conspicuously out of place or, in this case, too naive. Drugs for Maya, for all of us, hadn't crossed my mind, but maybe the idea was just radical enough to work.

"Sure, I think it's time to show her there are other ways of thinking about things." He said all this in English as she sobbed and rocked next to us. "My sister brought it last year, and we did some then. It's very pure, direct from Escalon in California, where they make it."

Of course it was. He was a hedonist, but also an epicurean, which meant he would have the best designer drugs. One person I met in Kathmandu told me he thought of Will as an experientialist, a word I haven't heard before or since. If he was interested in a drug, it was because he was into anything that could show him the unexplored corners of his mind or another possible road to bliss.

"So we won't freak out and die?" I asked. I had smoked pot a few times, but in general my concern about taking drugs was the same one I had about crossing my eyes too many times when I was little: Push your luck and you'll get stuck that way.

"No, no, I promise. Go call Maggie and Althea and see if they want to come up to Shanti Gompa with us. It's so calm up there. It'll be a great day." He meant it, too. "Maya-*ji*, don't cry. We're going someplace beautiful in the country, where a very holy lama lives with some nuns. You'll feel better, I promise." She stopped crying and said she would like to do that.

I still felt a little leery, but I went to call the other girls, and when Maggie, clearly over her grudge against Will, said, "Great!" I had no way out. Maybe if she'd said, "No way, Will's a jerk," I might have backed out. Instead, she said they'd meet us in front of the Yeti Bakery in an hour. I felt so protective of Maya, not as if she were a daughter or sister, but as if she were an alter ego, not exactly more innocent, but more hapless. I was one of two people she counted on in her new life, and yet the fact that I wasn't Will's equal—in any of our eyes—was problematic, because it meant in order to help her I just had to stay close and lie low.

As we walked down the lane outside Will's house to the main road of the bazaar, Maya held our hands, swinging them back and forth merrily now, saying she would like to start work pretty soon. She hardly seemed like the same person she had been an hour before. The birds were twittering and a mild breeze blew. Because the buildings were so low here, even in the city, the sky always felt nearby as the mountainous, flat-bottomed clouds slid across it.

Will smiled at me over the top of her head, and then said to her, "It's a little like Alex and I are your parents." A thrill and nausea welled up in me, hearing my complicity summed up: She trusted us, her pseudo-surrogate guardians in her increasingly screwed-up life.

"*Ho*," she said, laughing, "I'm very happy we're going to the countryside. My *mon* will feel better."

Mon is one of my favorite Nepali words. It's like *heart* and *soul* and *mind* all wrapped up into one concise little ball of a word, and yet it has a regular, mundane place in the language because of the phrase *mon lagyo*, which means "would like to," but literally translates as "my heart feels." My heart feels that I want to eat, sleep, drink, go, etc. It was true that Maya's *mon* seemed to be in need of some attention and peace, so I was glad she thought a trip to the hilltop nunnery was a good idea. I just hoped the Ecstasy would be helpful too, or at least not damaging.

We found a taxi, and Will haggled hard for the ride way up into the hills to the convent. A few blocks away Maggie and Althea piled in, carrying a big, shiny blue thermos of chamomile tea, a bag of pastries, some Swiss chocolate from Thamel, and the highly unusual treat of strawberries, from some Westerner's garden. Althea, with her ruddy cheeks and curly blond hair, was smiling so broadly she already looked like she was on drugs in her big, floppy flowered hat.

I was nervous but excited. Here was a chance to leave my goody two-shoes behind and be just another twenty-year-old having fun. We careened through the streets, mashing into one another as we headed out of town. Madonna's "Lucky Star" blared on the radio. The buildings thinned out, the air got sweeter, and yellow flowering mustard fields and the neon green stubble of rice paddies appeared on either side of the road, interspersed with little towns of red brick, or white-washed houses with clay-red stripes around their base. We chattered and dozed, and once I opened my eyes to see Will looking back at us from the front seat with something like amusement in his eyes. Were we his harem for the day? Or was he our Pied Piper, leading us into the hills? The car stopped at the Sleeping Vishnu, just before Budhanilkantha, and we got out, stretched, and bought marigolds to throw as offerings to the shiny black stone statue reclining in the stagnant water. Then we headed up into the Queen's Forest, past the army checkpoint, through the woods until the road abruptly stopped where it had caved in last monsoon.

The taxi backed up at a surprisingly high speed, made a tight turn, and rumbled out of sight. From there, Maggie led us up the rutted footpath (she had lived with the nuns for a month in the fall), and Althea bounced along close behind. I envied their two-peas-in-a-pod-ness. Will held Maya's hand, and I came last. We met two nuns sitting on a boulder, passing a handheld prayer wheel back and forth, chatting, and looking very content on a flat rock in the sun, looking out over the green valley.

They told us a lot of nuns were away visiting their villages. (In addition to Tibetans there were Nepali girls from the Thamang and Sherpa castes.) Farther up on the convent grounds, white sheets and maroon robes were flapping in front of a plain, four-story white dormitory, and two older nuns were laying out chilies on a straw mat to dry. We climbed the wide concrete steps past them, until Will said, "This seems like a good place," and we all perched along a low wall as he got out a vial wrapped in foil that I realized I'd seen at the top of his fridge door. Althea opened the thermos and poured a cup of chamomile tea for us to wash down the tiny tablets with.

"What is it?" Maya asked, watching Maggie and Althea.

"*Kushi-banaune-ausadi*," Will said, which means, literally, "happiness-making medicine." "After you eat it, all bad thoughts will go away for a time, and a lot of love will come into your heart."

"*Maya* will come to Maya?" she asked, smiling.

"Exactly."

He really had it all figured out, I thought as I took my tablet. I was a little bit in awe of how he could make the strangest, possibly even harmful things seem right and good.

"I'm only giving her half," he said to me.

"Okay," I said, as if he were actually consulting me and not just telling me. What would have happened if I had said, "This is so wrong. We can't do it." He might have listened if I meant it, but if I just said it out of fear, he would have dismissed it and told me that he knew what he was doing.

The idea that Ecstasy could help Maya was all in line with his Buddhist way of thinking: On the tantric path, moments of bliss add up, giving you little tastes of enlightenment. For Will, as he explained it in one of our late-night talks, sex with your *dakini* while using the right practices—a focused, clear mind picturing the two white deity bodies entwined above your head, followed by injaculation (I didn't understand the mechanics, but I understood it to be a male orgasm with no cum, so that the "milk of human kindness" and the blissful energy were retained in the body)—created a kind of conscious ecstasy that was crucial to your spiritual advancement. In this way of thinking, Ecstasy taken under the right conditions could also allow you to dip into nirvana and give you a preview of what you might attain with practice.

We drank the chamomile tea, picking the soggy, daisylike flowers from our lips. Will led us to meet his friend Hans, who was the translator for the *rinpoche* and lived in a cinder-block house apart from the nuns, with a little yard set off by tall grass and hedges. Hans said hello to all of us in a reserved Swiss Buddhist way and invited Will inside. I got the impression that Will showing up with a group of young girls—as, in fact, we were—was not an unusual enough occurrence to merit any special treatment, not that any of us particularly wanted to go inside on this beautiful day. Maya and I sat on the porch swing lazily kicking it back and forth, waiting for whatever would happen next. Maya hummed a song, and Maggie and Althea went out onto the lawn and sat across from each other, cross-legged and talking intently. After a bit, Maggie loped over to say they were going up the hill to the *gompa*, the temple, and we watched them disappear up a path.

All of a sudden, Maya said, "What's happening? I feel so dizzy. I can't breathe." She gasped in quick, hyperventilating sips. "I'm going to die maybe." It was her refrain of the morning all over again.

"It's okay, it's okay," I said, trying to reassure her, but my own heart rate sped up, and I could hear the muffled panic in my voice as I suggested she put her head between her knees. I was not equipped to deal with this. I didn't know anything about bad trips. The taxi was long gone. How would we get her out of here if she was really in trouble? I knocked on the door and called Will's name, trying to stay calm. After what seemed like an age, he appeared.

"What is it?" he asked in his calmest, most soft-spoken voice through the screen. Hans was behind him, and I didn't want to say too much, to betray our little gang in any way. (Though in retrospect I can't imagine Hans didn't know what was going on, or that we were the first drug-taking visitors to the convent.) Somehow I still felt protective of Will. I knew I ran the risk of being excommunicated from his life with Maya if I wasn't useful or discreet, but it was more than that: I wanted people to think well of him, or at least not to notice the gaps between his intentions and his actions.

"It's Maya, she can't breathe," I said. She was still gasping behind me.

"Excuse me," he said to Hans, and stepped outside. "Where are the others?" I told him, and he said I should go join them as he guided Maya out onto the open lawn, coaching her to take slow breaths. My legs felt noodly as I stumbled up the hill, but there were Maggie and Althea, still cross-legged across from each other, holding each other's hands, grinning and talking under the shade of the peepal tree while the colorful prayer flags flapped around them, sending a prayer out with each dry *tak* of the cloth.

"Something's wrong with Maya," I said, feeling like a

killjoy. They looked up at me calmly through a wide-angle lens of air.

"What's wrong?" Maggie asked, patting the ground next to her. I crouched and lost my balance. My body felt like rubber charged with electricity.

"She can't breathe. She's having some kind of bad reaction. I'm worried." I had other words in my head, like *paralyzed*, *coma*, and *die*, but they were flies trapped inside a jar, buzzing and circling there.

"She just needs to know she's loved. Why don't you bring her up here?" Althea said. *Silly hippie*, I thought in slow motion.

Maggie squeezed my hand. "Sure, the only real thing is love. We just have to tell her that."

I was dubious but desperate. Besides, Maggie had followed the Dead for a year. She knew about bad trips. "So I'll go get her?" I asked.

"Yeah, we'll be right here. Don't worry: She'll be fine," Maggie said.

When I got back, Maya and Will were laughing on the lawn, and she reached up her hand and pulled me down. "*Sathi*, that is a very naughty medicine!" she said, as if she were scolding it.

"Do you feel better now?"

"Yes, much better!" she said, and the frantic feeling I'd had, like spiders crawling up my insides, instantly vanished.

"I think she's fine now. It was just the surprise of it all," Will said to me in English. "How are you doing?"

"Much better, now that she's okay," I said, falling back into the grass, relieved and relaxed. I was Jell-O, I was sunlight, I was spilling around myself. She twisted a handful of my hair and held it on top of my head.

"That's pretty," she said, and I beamed.

"And the other two?" Will asked.

"They're good. They said I should bring her up there."

"Good idea. I'll just go say good-bye to Hans."

Maya and I helped each other up, and we giggled and lurched our way up the hill, all levity now.

"Maggie!" Maya shouted when she saw them, and both girls reached out their arms to welcome us into their little klatch. Just as we began to sit, Maya gasped. "I can't breathe! I can't breathe!" And my whole chest constricted, pulled tight by a wire between us.

"It's okay," Maggie said. "Take a deep breath. You'll be fine."

"Have some tea." Althea held up the cup for her to sip.

I managed to say, "It's okay," but I could barely breathe myself.

"I'm dizzy," she said, and I felt the ground spinning under me.

"Breathe slowly, deeply," Maggie and Althea told her as they rubbed her back and I tried to get air in my lungs.

She started to recover, and my own breathing normalized. It made me feel more than ever that we were actually physically connected in some way. Then she let out a peal of laughter and pinched our cheeks, telling us what good friends we were. A fluffy white shih tzu appeared, dispensing pink-tongued kisses, and we all laughed. Maya loved all the lesser creatures. Will appeared and started taking pictures, and Maggie and Althea moved away from us, back into their own orbit.

Then Maya went into another breathless episode. Immediately I couldn't breathe either, and Will and I tried to bring her back, but suddenly she was crying again, so hard she was unable to speak, and Will said, "That's right, let it out like a river, let it go into the ground." He was talking like a Nepali folk song, and I joined right in: "And let the sun dry up your tears and take them into the sky." The language was made for this kind of talk. But Maya didn't hear any of it. A band of nuns appeared, curious, and one asked Maya why she was crying.

I tried to deflect them, saying she would be okay, afraid they would bust us somehow. But Maya looked up. "It's my brother," she said, and told them the story. They *tsk*ed and said she had to do *puja* for him, that she would feel better if she did, and Maya agreed. Of course the nuns knew best in this situation.

Hans showed up, and he and Will went off to the *gompa* to see the *rinpoche*—the high lama who lived there. After a little while, Will came to tell us it was time for us all to go and make our offerings and ask for blessings. We climbed the stairs of a dark cinder-block stairwell behind the temple until we reached the fourth floor, where across an open rooftop was a little room with a maroon curtain hung in the doorway. Will went in first, followed by Maggie and Althea, who dutifully did their full prostrations for the old Tibetan man—three times over, bringing their prayer-clasped hands to head, heart, and stomach, and then nose to the floor. Maya went next and was shaky, almost falling over as she did, but Will stood up and held her by the arm to steady her. Finally I went in, quietly with my hands in prayer, but I refused to prostrate. I liked Buddhism's pageantry, but the prostrations always seemed too much, corny and a little over the top in the devoutness they suggested. I wasn't a Buddhist, after all. The funny thing was, when I sat down and looked up at the gentle lama in his ski cap with his thick glasses and kind smile—he radiated a kind of beneficence—I realized he didn't care if I prostrated or not. The prostrating wasn't for him: It was for me, or for anyone who wanted to lay aside their ego and bow down not to the lama so much as to the ideas of compassion and wisdom that he represented. Suddenly, I wished I had.

But I missed my chance, so I just sat there with the others in the pale yellow room, looking through the large window at the clouds tumbling by over the brilliant-green patchwork valley. We offered our *kathas*, the white silk scarves Will had provided us with, and the lama placed them around our necks with a few words of blessing. Then he gave us each a red knotted cord and a pinch of bitter herbs, and I accepted them both. I needed all the blessings I could get. I had met other lamas, but with the exception of the Dalai Lama, who had blessed me at the Tibetan New Year in Dharamsala (after two hours in line in the icy rain with a stomach bug, and it was worth it), this man was the first truly holy person I'd ever met. It was like being in the presence of something very good and comforting, like the smell of baking bread or a happy child. The *rinpoche* spoke in Tibetan, but no one translated, and after a few minutes Maya got up and staggered out as if she couldn't take another minute. I stayed, and before we all left, he told us through Will that it was very important that we learn how to meditate and do it regularly, and for the first time since I arrived in Nepal, I knew he was right. People had been pushing meditation since I got off the plane, but when I saw this man and felt the charge of peacefulness that came off of him after a lifetime of meditation, I thought that it might be something for me after all. Maybe Will was right, and it *was* the drug that finally made me see.

We emerged onto the rooftop filled with hope and a humming brightness. We could do anything. Will took a picture of his four blissed-out *dakinis* lined up against the wall with a view of valley and sky behind us. We all held hands, grinning, and Maya clutched the sparkly blue thermos like a talisman. A nun appeared with glasses of a syrupy orange drink called i-squash, and the sugar gave me a sudden and pounding headache. All at once we realized we had to hurry if we wanted to get back before curfew. Otherwise we'd be sleeping on the floor of the temple downstairs. There wasn't time to call a taxi from the convent's one phone, so we headed straight downhill on foot toward the center of town on a path that ran along a winding ridge, like a spine through a forest picked clean of brushwood and carpeted in soft brown dirt and pine needles. Maggie and Althea went first, bounding along, then Will and Maya, striding easily, holding hands, and finally me alone, wondering if they would notice if I disappeared. Toward the end the wind picked up as a mass of dark gray clouds rolled toward us in a silent stampede. We leaped faster until we reached the covered porch of a locked house where we watched hailstones the size of marbles bounce all around us. When it was over, we hurried to Boudha and piled into separate taxis with just fifteen minutes to spare before curfew.

"How do you feel?" Will asked me, and I told him about the headache. "Lean your head this way," he said. I bent across Maya, and he began massaging it, drawing the pain away, and I gave in to the feeling that maybe he did like me after all.

"Too bad we can't go to the Hotel Vajra for a steam bath," Will said. "But then we'd have to split up." Him from us he meant. So we went home and ate a simple dinner of pasta and cheese. Afterward Will said, "Thanks for being so game," and gave me a hug. Maya lifted the back of my hand to her forehead and then kissed my fingers. "Sweet dreams, *sathi*," she said, and they went off to their room and I to mine, where I drifted off to sleep until I was suddenly painfully awake, listening to the wind rattle the shutters. I walked down the hallway to Will's door, which was slightly ajar.

"Will, Maya?" I said softly, but there was no answer, and I crawled back into my sleeping bag and fell into a heavy, knock-your-head-off sleep, too deep to be restful.

"I DON'T THINK that was an entirely unsuccessful experiment," Will said when I came in for breakfast. He handed me a B vitamin telling me it would help regenerate whatever synapses had been messed up by the drug. Maya was in a chipper mood. "I slept so well. I didn't have any dreams," she announced, as if that were the height of rest. Will was definitely pleased with himself. I seemed to be the only one who was groggy, although the fact that Maya was happy and healthy counted for a lot. It was another sunny, breezy, clean slate of a day, and over breakfast Will admitted to me he took only a quarter hit, which made him more responsible in my eyes. "Just being around all of you was a good contact high," he said. "So if it's all right with you, I'm going out to the Wilsons' for the night, to see the *devi*. Do you mind staying with Maya?"

I didn't. I was his obliged houseguest, after all. "Are you going to tell her?"

"You can if you want," he said. He knew I wouldn't, though.

Maya and I spent the day at Pashupati, where the skinny, near-naked *sadhus*—the Hindu ascetics—with their long dreadlocks and white face paint collected *baksheesh* (bribes, that is) from tourists wanting their pictures. Pilgrims bathed in the dirty trickle of the Bagmati, just upstream from the corpses sending off their acrid smoke. Maya patted the bony white cow sitting in the middle of the footbridge with a big red *thika* smeared on her forehead and said, "Hello, *didi*," just before we climbed the hill across the river. Sitting in a little temple, a *sadhu* hissed and spat at us. Maya laughed and said, "He just wants *jiggy-jiggy*," which was slang for sex. It was a nice, uncomplicated day, just two girls out meandering through the city. We picked up some food for dinner and, without Will there, took over the dining room as if it were a college dorm room, pillows all around, with the Cowboy Junkies playing on the boom box.

Maya told me that she thought Will would make a good boyfriend, but that he wasn't any good for marrying, and I felt relieved to hear her say it. "But," she added, "I think I'd like to go to America with him and work for his mother, cleaning her house." I was pretty sure it was her idea, not his.

"What about your work here?"

"Or that. I don't mind. I'd like to travel, though. You know, Will and I still haven't slept together. He's too big," she said, and giggled.

I laughed at her frankness. "I have someone like Will in my life too," I said, and told her about Nick, about the flirtation leading up to the first kiss out on Matinicus Island, then secretly visiting him in New York and the thwarted sex, and finally the way I talked to him in my head all the time but barely wrote him (I had never answered his most recent letter, and wouldn't). I told her I was a little bit afraid of him.

"No, not afraid exactly," I said.

"I understand. He makes you nervous," she said.

"Yes!" I said.

"He does sound like Will," she said. Of course, he wasn't really. Will was more comfortable in his own skin and more of a wanderer. Nick had never been farther than Berlin. But I knew what she meant. It wasn't that Will and Nick were alike.

It was that she and Will were not so different from Nick and me. There was the age difference, or, more than that, the gap in experience (I was the country-born college girl to Nick's New York artist). There was the uncertainty about what came next, and much as I hated to admit it, I knew that I hoped Nick would rescue me from my life as much as Maya hoped Will would rescue her from hers.

"You know, we can do this if we want without them. Have good lives, get good work, be good people," I said.

She laughed. "Of course, *sathi*. Why not?"

It was the first time in eight months of being there that I forgot I was speaking Nepali, and the first time I didn't edit part of myself out of the conversation, so that I'd fit local mores as a chaste, unmarried girl. We were just two girls talking about the men in our lives and what the future might hold.

Maya sat up suddenly. "You know what we should do?"

"What?"

"You, me, and Will—we should 'make friends.'"

"What does that mean?" I asked, having an idea, but not wanting to say. I couldn't believe she was really suggesting it. She had seemed so innocent when I met her.

"We should all three sleep together."

"I don't think so." It was one thing to think it—and the truth was I had, the other night after the Ecstasy when I found myself so keenly alone on the sofa. It was another to do it.

"Yes!" She threw a pillow at me. "You ask him tomorrow."

"I won't," I said, and threw the pillow back. "You can if

you want, but not when I'm around. He doesn't like me the way he likes you."

"Okay, I will," she said, tucking the pillow behind her head and lying back. I was amazed by how bold she was about her desires. I just sat around waiting to be desired, as if that were the same thing. And while I couldn't say so, I was excited at the thought of being drawn into their affair, at least temporarily. Ever since I'd met Maya, all the rules I'd ever known were being unwritten day by day, the ink disappearing from the pages of a book somewhere. Being the sole witness to Maya and Will's nascent, secret affair was both intoxicating and disorienting. At the same time, I knew that to Will, Maya was a numinous creature, crying jags notwithstanding, and I was just someone he enjoyed talking to. The closest he'd come to admiring me was after Maya got up from the dinner table a few nights before, when he had said, "It's like you two are the perfect combination. She's the spirit and body, and you're the mind."

"Really?" I said, laughing. It would have been galling if I hadn't been flattered. The truth was that I wanted to be giddy and in love too, instead of the rational one at the sidelines. Still, it didn't mean I would do something about it.

THE NEXT NIGHT, while making dinner, I was leaving the tiny kitchen as Will went in, and he placed his hands on my shoulders to get by, leaving them there a moment longer than he needed to. I knew then that she'd said something. For all our proximity, he and I barely touched each other, with the exception of the head massage the other day or a kiss in greeting if we hadn't seen each other for a long time. Twice I had held on to his waist when I rode side saddle on the back of his motorcycle, just so I wouldn't fall off, but that was it. It wasn't until we were cleaning up that he said to me, "Maya thinks we should all sleep together."

"Huh," I squawked. "She does?"

"Yeah, funny, right?"

"Funny," I said, busying myself with silverware in the sink. The candlelight flickered on the wall. I was Little Miss Ambivalence, intrigued, but too shy to commit.

I was getting ready to go to my bed when Maya grabbed me by the arm. "Oh, no, you're sleeping in here tonight."

"No. I'm not," I said, and kept walking. It felt too fraught, too strange.

"Yes, you are." She giggled as she pulled me back awkwardly, and my flashlight zigzagged over the walls. Will was already setting up more cushions and sheets to extend his bed on the floor. I waited with my arms crossed, flashlight off, and Maya still gripping me saying, "*Sathi, sathi, sathi.*"

He spread the canopy of mosquito net over the widened mattress, and said simply, "There." And I thought, *Why not?* Increasingly, what happened inside this house felt more real or important than anything outside it.

Maya crawled under, then Will, then me. I lay down beside them in my T-shirt and cotton petticoat, dressed like a proper village girl for bed, and feeling unsure of myself. Suddenly

Will kissed Maya and the two of them tumbled away from me. It was thrilling to be right beside them, entwined, kissing, tussling. Moonlight poured through the open wedge of the balcony door, making the world under the netting a dark and watery private world with its own rhythm and flow, both soothing and laced with danger. Dogs barked somewhere. Will peeled off his shirt, and I could see she resisted when he tried to take off hers—she was still in her petticoat and blouse. There was a distinct pushing away of his hands, a quiet tension that surprised me. I looked away embarrassed and stared at the moving shadows on the bunched netting above me. She had none of the abandon I would have imagined. Then she relented, lying there passively, a far cry from the ribald girl I'd seen elsewhere. His breath quickened and he gave a little moan. I thought of bolting from the bed, but felt transfixed.

"Enough," Maya said, and she rolled away from Will. He faced me—he was the pivot, the hinge—and it was a pleasure, the kissing, the pressure of his strong hands, his warm skin, the muscly length of him. But when I looked over and saw Maya with her face to the wall, I wondered if perhaps she had meant something else, something altogether more innocent— like a kids' slumber party? She looked so upset. Lying on top of Will, I put my hand on her shoulder, and she shook me off.

His hands slid around my waist and under my shirt. My shirt was off, then my skirt, and he moved me on top of him and was working off my underwear when I said, "No."

"Are you sure?" he asked. Even in the dark, his eyes were shining.

"Yeah. It's too much," I told him. He dropped his hands, and I rolled to the side. I sat up to put on my shirt, and he said, "You're a pretty girl, Alex," as if it had just occurred to him.

"Thanks," I said, careful not to let him know I minded that it had taken him so long to decide.

"*KERA, KERA, SUNTALAAAA!* Banana, banana, oraaaaaange!" We woke to the fruit seller's cries in the lane and the sun streaming in. A moment later there was a pounding on the door downstairs.

Maya jumped up, crawling over us. "I'll get it," she said.

"Don't let them in!" Will called after her, and turned to me and grinned. "Talk about East meets West." I was glad he wasn't too disappointed about the sex. A moment later we heard voices on the stairs and sprang up, reaching for our clothes. I just managed to pull a skirt on as Maya and the landlords' teenage son arrived at the bedroom door, and I ducked out and down the hall to the bathroom.

When I came into the kitchen, Will was in a foul mood, banging pots around. He looked up, enraged, his neck a blotchy pink. "He came to tell me they're doing construction next door today. What the hell is that about? Who shows up before eight to tell you that? Are they spying on me?" He knew and accepted that his landlords listened to his calls because they shared a phone line. It was just the Kathmandu way to entertain yourself with gossip—there were only two TV stations, after all—but this was too much.

Meanwhile Maya flipped through a coffee-table book about Mount Kailash, ignoring the hostile racket, but when I leaned over to unlatch the shutters behind her, she gave me a sly half smile and I turned away in order not to laugh.

"Didn't you hear me say not to let anyone in?" Will asked her.

"No," she said, blinking. I didn't know if she was telling the truth or not, and I couldn't tell if he was angrier at her or the landlords. It was a beautiful contradiction, this need to keep up appearances.

"I have to go out today, to see about getting a helicopter for a lama who needs to go to western Nepal," he said as if he couldn't get away from us fast enough.

"Okay," I said, and thought, *I'm not stopping you*. He put down his plate of half-finished food and walked out. From the narrow kitchen window, we watched him roll his motorcycle out the gate and rumble past a group of schoolkids in their navy uniforms, red satin bows like butterflies in the girls' black hair. Maya pushed my shoulder and said in a low voice, "I'm very angry!" and we both laughed until tears ran down our faces. I was glad she was unfazed—that Will's word was not absolute. At the same time, I knew I had stopped standing in the eye of the tornado and gotten sucked into its spin, and I decided it was time for me to get out of town for a little while.

 *Five*

When I came back a few days later from Nagarkot, a village at the edge of the valley where you had a good view of the Himalayas, I found that Will and Maya had gone to Delhi for a quick trip and were due back in a couple of days. I was glad to have the house to myself and was settling into the deliciousness of life as a girl alone in Kathmandu with a big apartment to spread out in—I was hardly ever alone there; no one was—when the phone rang.

"Is it true that Will's away?" Chhimi asked. She was phoning from school around the corner.

"It's true."

"Where did he go?"

"Delhi."

"And who is Maya?"

"Come over," I said, mindful of the eavesdropping landlords.

"Does Will love her? Am I not his girlfriend anymore?"

"Chhimi, come over. He's away until tomorrow."

I liked Chhimi. She was funny and smart and didn't take a lot of crap from Will. Her intimidating mother in Jankat had taught her well. I'd first met her back in September when we all went trekking with the Jankat people. Then she and her friend came back to Kathmandu, ostensibly to work cooking and cleaning at the school, but they lived with Will, and when her friend went back after the first semester, Chhimi stayed. I wondered if Will had planned Chhimi's return this way, that he wanted me to see her first to soften the blow about Maya. When Chhimi came to the door, she did look more citified than ever, even after several weeks in the hills and a long bus ride back. She wore a jean jacket, pink T-shirt, and polka-dotted skirt. As she padded around the house looking for signs of Maya having replaced her, pausing to pick up a magazine here, a pillow there—in fact it was just Will's house as much as ever—I thought of the black-and-white picture Will had shown me from when he first met Chhimi a year ago on the same trip he met Maya. It looked like it might have been taken anytime in the last century. Her expression was somber and shy as she peeked out from a tartan shawl over her head. A gold nose ring hung from the center of her nose, and she stared straight into the camera, unsmiling, unblinking. Now she seemed to be someone else entirely. There was something kinetic about her as she picked up a small bag of Maya's clothes in a corner of the living room and dropped it with a sniff.

"I was supposed to go to Delhi. Will promised me three months ago he would take me to Bangkok or Delhi, and he never did. I can't believe he took her instead of me," she said.

"He went on business," I said, getting up to make us tea, not wanting to defend him so much as wanting some way for it to be all right.

"Is she his girlfriend now?"

I looked at her standing in the kitchen doorway, her arms folded over her chest. Her sense of quiet outrage was so unlike Maya's weepiness or jollity. "You have to talk to him."

That night, after dinner, we were cleaning up in the kitchen when she said, "Did you know I was pregnant in February?"

"No." Although it made sense. I had never had much faith in Will's injaculation plan. "Will said he would marry me if I wanted." Just like Mr. Thakur predicted. "He wanted to have the child, but when I found out I could have it taken out, I wanted to do that. I didn't want people in my village to know that the rumors were true about me and Will. I would never be able to go back there." She clattered the dishes in the sink. "He thought we would have to go to Bangkok or to Delhi, but then he found out about the clinic around the corner, and so I went there." I perched on the windowsill, and she looked at me in the flickering light. "It was all fine, and I don't remember anything, except when I woke up my stomach hurt a lot, and there was a lot of blood. When he got there and found me crying, he said he had been held up at school.

"He promised me then that he would take me abroad, since we didn't go for the operation, and now he's taken her." Chhimi recounted all this in almost a whisper, though we were the only ones in the house, all sealed up for the night.

"I'm so sorry," I said.

"Does he not love me anymore?" she asked.

"You have to talk to him," I said again. If it were Maya, she would have been crying, but Chhimi had a practical resilience

to her. She knew Will slept around. That wasn't what bothered her. It was the idea that she'd been replaced.

WHEN CHHIMI WENT TO SCHOOL the next day to wash her
clothes at the tap in the yard, I went to the airport to intercept
Will and Maya. I was pissed at him for putting me in this position, but I thought the whole reunion might be less painful if
he knew she was back: It would give him a chance to be kinder,
because he would be prepared. Their ten-fifteen flight was
delayed, though, and at two I met Will's friend James—he of
the tantric photographs—picking up a courier package. With
sunburned nose and cheeks, white-blond hair, and aviator
sunglasses, he looked like a pink cartoon pig to me, but I was
glad to see a familiar face, any familiar face, after standing
around all morning. He asked me what I was doing, and when
I told him my errand, he shook his head.

"I don't know how he does it."

"What do you mean?" I asked, wanting to hear him say it.

"Has all you girls wrapped around his finger." I could practically see the glinting edge of jealousy.

"Oh, well, it seemed like a good idea somehow. And I had
the free time."

"Come on, I'll give you a ride back. Will can fend for himself. Besides, you could be here all day." I got on the back of
James's motorcycle. "It's incredible," he said as we pulled up
to Will's house and he turned off his bike. "I can understand
you all sleeping with him. It's the doting on and the worrying
about him that confuses me."

"Not all of us sleep with him." I could be technical if I needed to be.

"Huh," he said, scrutinizing me. "Well, good for you. Call me if you need a diversion."

"Sure, thanks," I said, knowing I wouldn't.

WHEN WILL CALLED FROM SCHOOL, I answered the phone. "I hear Chhimi's back," he said. She was beside me on the velvet couch, flipping through a magazine, with one ear cocked toward the phone.

"That's true."

"Is she right there?"

"Yup."

"Is she angry?"

"Seems like it. You want to talk to her?"

"Sure." I put her on.

"Hi, Will," she said in English, wrapping a piece of her hair around her hand. "Not so good." It was startling to hear her speak English so naturally. I left the room, and in a few minutes she came into the dining room and flopped onto the cushions. We heard the dog barking madly in the yard, and then its whimpering retreat. "Do you want me to let them in?" I asked.

"Sure," she said, and I went downstairs. Will and Maya were dusty and rumpled with travel.

"*Sathi!*" Maya exclaimed, and they both kissed me. They were in good spirits.

"She's upstairs?" Will asked.

I nodded, and he took the stairs two at a time while I picked up Maya's bag. "How was Delhi?"

"What a huge, great, dirty city! There were so many people and so many big houses. I was terrified on the airplane," she said, laughing. "I thought I was going to die!"

Everything makes you think that, I thought to myself, surprised to find myself irritated at her as well. "Come on. Let's go for a walk," I said, turning us around and out the door again so that Will and Chhimi could be alone.

As we left the compound and turned down the lane, Maya said, "I don't think she should be angry. Why can't we both be his girlfriends?"

"I don't know. Do you want to share him?"

"Sure. She and I could be friends. We could do things together when he was busy."

"Really?" I asked. Polygamy wasn't the norm in the area she came from, but it did exist. Maybe half a boyfriend was better than none in her book.

Maya leaned her head way back to look at the sky. "I don't know. Maybe. *Sathi*, you wouldn't believe how many people there were in Delhi!" It was as if every time she looked too closely at her life, she had to turn away. She chattered about the Indian bazaars, the beggars, the millions of cars, and Will's friend who had a store filled with brass and gold religious statues. They saw a Hindi blockbuster called *Chandni*, and she sang a verse from the theme song, waving her hands in a little dance. "It's not like here in Nepal. You can't go anywhere without tripping over people. I missed the mountains, the hills, the sky. But I liked it. Maybe I'll go back one day, look around, go to Bombay."

"I know," I said, and squeezed her hand. I couldn't stay mad at her. She wanted so much to be happy, to find some kind of peace.

When we got back, a Hindi film sound track was on, and Chhimi was in the kitchen scrubbing potatoes, quietly humming along. Maya jumped right in to help, and when Chhimi didn't object, I went to find Will, who was in a room I didn't know existed until then. Its door was behind a tapestry at the end of the hallway with a little padlock hanging off the latch, and he was sitting in the middle of a low bed, beside a duffel exploding with clothes and trekking gear, sorting through papers, surrounded by stacks of mail, photographs, negatives, cardboard boxes. This was why the rest of his house was so immaculate, with each object in its place. It was amazing that I had been here nearly three weeks and never known about this secret repository—its size almost a third of the house—for all the things that didn't fit.

"How did your conversation go?" I asked.

"Better than I could have imagined," he said, looking genuinely pleased. "Maya and I had an excellent trip—we finally slept together—and Chhimi, for all her passion, is admirably pragmatic."

"Did you guys decide anything?"

"No, there's nothing to decide, really. I don't want to issue any ultimatums, or be issued any. I still care about her, so we'll just all have to find our way."

"That was easy," I said. Whatever was happening in the secret room of Will's brain was anybody's guess.

"Things often are when you deal with them straight on."

"So what did you say?" I sat down on the edge of the bed.

"I explained that there was nothing wrong with what I'd done, and that you thought it would be okay if I slept with Maya."

"You're kidding, right?"

"No, you said you didn't think Chhimi would mind." He looked up at me, unabashed.

"Why would I have ever said that?"

"You didn't? I could have sworn you did."

"Never. Never," I said, waiting for his apology.

"Well, either way, she's fine with it. I think she really understands."

My head was spinning. "Will, you've got to tell her I didn't say that. Or I will."

"Of course, go ahead." I was so shocked I didn't know if I was more mad at him or impressed by his audacity.

I went to find her, and when I cleared up what had and hadn't been said, she just looked at me. "I knew you didn't say that," she said, seeming to understand better than I did what was going on.

Dinner was civil, even jovial at times. Maya and Chhimi got along, talking about village life versus city life, and people they both knew. Then, at bedtime, Maya and I slept on sofas in the living room, Chhimi in Will's tantric love den alone, and Will in his secret, messy chamber. I got up to get a glass of water from the kitchen and heard him slide a bolt inside the door, and I realized that even he might have had his fill of the situations he'd created.

I WASN'T SURPRISED the next morning when he said he thought it was a good day for Maya to go meet June. He had to figure something out for both of them before he left in a little over a month. I had less than two weeks until my visa ran out for good, and I was glad Maya was agreeable about starting her job. I still believed that if she had any sort of income she would be in a better place to figure out what she wanted.

Will asked me to go with them to June's, and after a servant let us in, June greeted us in a royal blue *salwar kameez* with her white hair flowing and a drink in hand—it was a little after eleven. Ice, that rarity, was tinkling in her glass.

"There you are," she drawled in her Texas-*memsaab* accent. (Once a Dallas debutante, she had left that world in the early sixties to become the king's uncle's mistress.) She kissed Will and looked Maya up and down. I was apparently invisible.

"*Namaste*," Maya said softly, and glanced downward.

"She's quiet. That's good," June said in English, and then in Nepali, "My girl Gita will show you around and answer any questions. Gita!" The girl who came slip-slapping along the tile floors was the most defeated-looking Nepali girl I had ever seen, her hair yanked back into a painful-looking bun, shoulders hunched inward, and her gaze set on the floor a few feet ahead of her. Subservience was common enough here, but this terrorized affect was something else. Clearly not invited to go with June and Will to the patio for a drink, I followed Gita and Maya to the kitchen.

"Why don't you two look around and talk. I'll stay here," I said, hoping Gita would be more candid if I wasn't present.

From where I sat beside the window in the kitchen I could just observe June and Will's conversation outside.

"What?" June screeched. "She's been with you for three weeks—being ruined, no doubt, by your democratic ideals!" I smiled. She was right, of course.

"No," Will said as he turned his glass nervously, looking down and around. I had never seen him like this before. "She was just so green when she got here. It would have been frustrating to you."

June cackled. "I *like* them green. What a pain in the A-double-S you are, Will." I saw now that what might pass for eccentricity from a distance had to be hell to live with. The fact that she was clearly in her cups before noon, as my dad would say—and a nasty drunk at that—didn't help my impression.

Will continued, "She's a nice girl, strong, full of energy. I think you'll like her."

"I'm sure," she said, uncommitted, as she scrutinized Will.

"I wanted to ask you about her days off?" he asked.

"My girls get every other Sunday, and I don't like them to go too far afield, to get too many funny ideas."

"I was thinking if she had a night too, she'd be welcome to stay with me. I do feel responsible for her now, and my place has become something of a second home to her."

June got up and poured herself a drink, sauntered back, sat, crossed her legs, and asked, "What are you, Will, in love with her?"

He leaned back in his chair, raked a hand through his hair, and said hoarsely, so that I had to strain to hear, "In love with her? No. She is pretty, though, don't you think?"

June laughed her hearty, husky laugh and coughed a smoker's cough. "Well, anyway, she's got two days off a month; otherwise she's here."

Maya and Gita appeared, and I noticed that Maya had already adopted the hunch and the downward gaze.

"So, would you like to work here?" June asked.

"*Ho*," Maya said.

"'*Ho, memsaab*,'" June corrected. "And you think you can be happy and work hard?"

"*Ho*." She looked up. "*Ho, memsaab*."

June nodded. "That's right. Would you like to go back, get your things, and start today?"

She was about to say "*ho, memsaab*" again when Will jumped in. "Actually I think tomorrow would be a better day to start. She can arrive here first thing with all her things organized."

"I shouldn't, but fine," said June. "One more night of indoctrination, Will?"

AFTER MAYA WENT TO JUNE'S, Chhimi went to work for another friend of Will's, another dissolute but somewhat gentler expat, a British Buddhist who needed a live-in nanny for her two kids by her Tibetan ex-husband. They lived in a Rana palace where everything was for sale—furniture, rugs, art, the house itself. Will left for the final excursion of the semester, and I was alone in his house for two nights until I was awakened one morning by a pounding on the door. When I opened it, there was Maya, breathless and otherwise a carbon copy of Gita—same clothes, painful hair, hunched shoulders, everything.

"That woman is a nightmare, a witch. I'm not going back there. She drinks all the time, and she hits us both," she said, slipping off her shoes.

"Come in, come in," I said.

She slammed the door and smiled, and I recognized her again. "Oh, *sathi*, it's good to see you," she said, and pressed the back of my hand to her forehead, a gesture that I always found endearing.

Over breakfast, she told me, "The other girl wants to leave too, but she has nowhere else to go. There's no way I'm going back."

I told her she didn't have to, and then the doorbell rang again. It was Chhimi this time, with a similar story about her boss—not that she was mean, but that she drank too much and there wasn't any food in the house and her room was swarming with mosquitoes. "I can't work there. I'll go back to my village first," she said all in a breath. I told her Maya was upstairs.

"Are all older *bideshi* women nuts?" they wanted to know.

"I'm leaving. I don't care if I see Will again. I don't need this," Chhimi said.

"Me too," Maya said. Maybe they were right, but first I thought a day out of town was in order to recoup.

"Let's go to Pharping and Daxinkali for the night," I said. It was Thursday, a sacrifice day at Daxinkali, when people brought goats and chickens to a shrine for that wrathful, bloodthirsty Hindu goddess Kali and killed them in her honor. I found it difficult not to be distracted from my everyday concerns when I saw animals being sacrificed, and I hoped the same would be true for Maya and Chhimi. Also, Will once told me that the area was "auspicious for women." Not only was there the Hindu shrine, but a true Tibetan *dakini*, or *yogini*—in any case an old, enlightened woman—lived there. For many years she was the "consort" to the *rinpoche* we'd met at Shanti Gompa (nothing so mundane as a wife for these Tibetan teachers). They had four sons, all well-known *rinpoches* in Kathmandu in their own right, and now she lived alone among young lamas in training, advancing her own spiritual practice. I was definitely curious, and I knew that if we just showed up, there was a decent chance we could see her. I wanted to get out of Will's house and find us a dose of something good—some karma or insight, the example of a wise older woman, at the very least some fresh air and pretty scenery. An hour later we were on a bus bumping and rolling along toward the southern edge of the valley.

First we checked out the Kali shrine and watched the animals having their throats neatly slit, one by one, and then a friendly young nun led us along the muddy hillside to a cave where an image of the Buddhist goddess Tara was supposedly

emerging in the stone. I squinted to see it and made a dona-
tion. The nun brought us to another nun, the *yogini*'s assistant,
who, with her shorn hair and bright eyes, could have easily had
her own girl band, and who ushered us into an airy room
where a beatific woman in her late fifties sat cross-legged on
her cushioned platform in a block of sunlight from the window. She smiled broadly, as if she had been expecting us, her
merry black eyes set among friendly creases, surrounded by a
soft halo of black hair. The nun brought us tea and cookies
and took away our offerings of fruit. It turned out the *yogini*
spoke only a few words of Nepali, but she managed to convey
that she would teach us some chants. Chhimi and I were happy
to learn them, but Maya soon got restless, as she had at Shanti
Gompa, and went outside. Inside the room, the breeze blew in
lightly from the valley and mingled with the Tibetan incense,
and I was Ecstasy-*lagyo* just being there.

When we came out, Maya was leaning against the railing
talking to two unsavory young lamas, who had to be the least
likely candidates for enlightenment I'd met in a while. One
was chubby and flat-faced in a yellow down vest over his
maroon robes, and the other scowled in his blue windbreaker
and Ray-Bans.

"They're from Ngyak!" Maya said. "It's just north of my
parents' house in Tatopani, where we have another house. We
speak the same dialect." Still, I couldn't see the appeal. They
were dull-eyed, with hard sets to their jaws. *Skeazy* was the
word that came to mind. She asked me to take a picture of
them, and I obliged as they posed against the backdrop of the

valley, while Chhimi looked on skeptically. I was used to seeing lamas around Boudha in their Converse high-tops, and one of the *yogini's rinpoche* sons was driven around in a sky blue Mercedes. But these two—there wasn't even a spark of something interesting there.

Maya, Chhimi, and I ended up staying the night in the shrine room of a Sherpa lama's house at the bottom of the hill. He seemed happy to have us and not to mind when the lamas from Ngyak stopped by to see if we wanted to watch a movie in town. Maya jumped up to go, and Chhimi and I followed them to the second floor of a shop—a long, narrow room filled with guys watching a pirated kung-fu movie on a small TV.

Maya sat with her lamas on the floor while Chhimi and I were given the only two chairs in the very back.

"What is she doing with them?" Chhimi asked.

"I don't know."

Finally we were so tired and bored we decided to go. Maya walked with us as far as the Sherpa lama's house, but then said she'd just walk her friends back to their room. We waited up for her for a while and finally went to sleep. I woke up at six, when she came in talking at high speed. "You wouldn't believe it! When I walked the lamas back to their room, there was a woman waiting for them there from their village. She was on her way to meet her husband, who is a thief and going to Darjeeling. We had so much in common, and we stayed up all night talking about our *sukha-dukha*," which translates literally as our "happiness-sorrow." "And then we shared a bed on the floor."

Her monologue had the pitch and fervor of a lie, but all I said was, "I was worried about you." She threw her arms around me, smelling of sour sweat, and said, "*Sathi!* You didn't have to worry. Those lamas are very good people and the woman was especially. You'll meet her on the bus. I'm sure you'll like her. She has such a good *mon*."

Chhimi and I nodded, and the old Sherpa lama looked perplexed as he gave us tea. An hour later we climbed up to the top of the bus to sit on the roof in the open air among all the crates and sacks of grain.

"Where is she?" Maya kept asking. "She said she would be here, and she wants to meet you." Finally she went to go look.

"I don't think there is a woman," Chhimi said when Maya was gone.

"I know, but I'm not going to say anything," I said.

When Maya came back and reported that she was worried because she couldn't find her new friend anywhere, I just said she was probably catching a later bus. Maya looked relieved that I wasn't going to press her, and tucked herself between some bags of rice and went to sleep.

BY THE TIME Will returned a few days later, Chhimi and Maya had decided, at least temporarily, that they were a team. They spent some of their savings on tin trunks, which they filled with their things, and were only waiting for Will's return to make their dramatic joint exit.

But when they told him, and he said that was fine if that

was what they wanted to do, they looked at each other. "Just kidding!" Maya said, and they both burst into laughter. Chhimi chided him for finding them such bad jobs, and he promised he would find them better ones. I had to wonder if I had done the right thing by encouraging them to stay. It was as if I just refused to believe that, one, Will couldn't help them improve their lives and, two, that there wasn't some option other than going back to their villages. At the same time, it was hard to imagine what kinds of better jobs there were out there for girls like them.

After dinner in the dark—there were still nightly curfews and citywide blackouts—we brought the candles into the living room, where Will got out a bottle of duty-free Johnnie Walker Black Label and poured a finger for each of us. Everyone was in a good mood, despite the fact that nothing seemed to be working out, and then all at once Maya poured a whole glassful and threw it back.

"What are you doing?" Chhimi looked disgusted.

Maya laughed loudly. "I'm fixing my *mon*."

"I would have pulled out something cheaper if I'd known she was going to do that," Will said to me.

Maya poured another full glass, and Will snatched it from her, holding it over his head, touching the low ceiling, but she tickled him and grabbed it when he lowered his arm, spilling a little on each of them before slugging it back. She wiped her mouth with the back of her hand, shaking with laughter. Then she started weeping about how she would die maybe.

"What is wrong with her?" Chhimi asked.

"I don't know," I said. I didn't know what to do, and suddenly felt tired and detached from it all. When Maya said she was going to throw up, it was Chhimi and Will who hauled her into the bathroom and turned on the cold shower. *I should do something*, I thought, and placed a couple candles on the sink while Chhimi filled a bucket with icy cold water and poured it on Maya, and then another, shouting at her and pinching her on the arm. She seemed furious. Will, who had tried to keep Maya upright, laid her down, closed the shutter on the window, and asked Chhimi not to shout before he walked out. Maya just groaned while the water drained around her, and then pushed herself upright to puke while I held back her hair. After several rounds she began to sob again, and her wailing echoed in the cold, shadowy bathroom as she shivered, and I draped a towel over her.

"Why is she so upset?" Will asked, shining his flashlight on us.

"Can you just get us some dry clothes, please?" I asked, and he turned without a word.

Chhimi, still angry, returned with clean sweats, and helped me strip, dry, and dress Maya, then put her to bed on the nearest couch, her head hanging over the side pointed at a ready bucket. I felt relieved when she fell asleep, and soon fell asleep myself.

The next day Maya slept late, while Will took Chhimi to interview for another job. I stayed around the house, waiting for Maya to wake up. When she did, she had a headache and was subdued, but cheerful.

"What happened, *sathi*?" I asked.

"Sometimes I feel sick in my heart, and I don't know what to do," she said.

"Don't drink *raksi*," I said, trying to be practical.

"I know. I'm sorry," she said, and lifted my hand to her forehead.

IN THE END, I was the first to leave. Having extended my visa to the last possible day, I finally just got on a bus to the eastern border, where I walked across and caught another bus to Darjeeling. Maggie met up with me a few days later, and we toured the tea plantations and stayed in a monastery before we traveled as far as Calcutta together. I went on alone, catching a local train to Bombay (a parched and dusty thirty-seven hours across central India) to catch my flight home. I thought I would never be ready to leave Nepal, but when the day came, I was worn out by not being able to help my friends.

"Be good to them," I said to Will, as the four of us stood in front of his gate, feeling older than I had in months, maybe ever.

"Don't worry," he said. When I looked back from the car, Will and Chhimi were already gone, and only Maya remained in the lane, worrying the beads of her *mala* and repeating some kind of mantra, until my car veered out of sight.

PART 2   SUKHA-DUKHA

Happiness-Sorrow

1994

Six

From the moment I touched down at O'Hare in Chicago, I was sure I would return to Nepal within a year, a year and a half at the latest, after I graduated. It was impossible to imagine I wouldn't. The same way Nick never really left my head, now Nepal didn't either. I revisited the country daily, not just the people, but the language—*rungi-chungi, jilli-milli, olla-molla*—the chanting and cymbal crashing that came from monastery windows, the smell of kerosene and cook smoke (mustard oil sizzling with fenugreek and garlic) and cow shit in the lanes, the glow of butter lamps at a shrine in front of shops festooned with saris and *lungi*s, the direct gaze that came with a *namaste*.

By contrast, I returned to a life so subdued in Des Moines, so absent of stimulus, sensory or otherwise, that I felt as though someone had injected Novocain into my soul. Home was the whir of air conditioners and the smell of baked chicken, boiled noodles, lawns and more lawns. Outside, a perfect grid of streets led me to perfect stacks of sweaters behind spotless plate-glass windows at the mall. Bright pennies glittered on black tiles at the bottom of a shallow indoor fountain. *Twinkle*, *twinkle*, but everything felt airless. I couldn't get enough oxygen in my lungs. Driving out to the farmland with the windows down helped a little. One time I got out and lay down in the middle of an empty country road at night. On the still-warm asphalt, surrounded by the shushing fields, the crickets and cicadas, I stared at the stars and reminded myself that yes, these were the same ones I saw over Jankat. Back at the house, David Letterman gabbled on about something in the blue glow of the living room, interrupted only by the swirling ads for used-car dealerships and high-energy fruit drinks.

My brothers were home that summer, not that I saw much of them. Sammy, who was thirteen, was skateboarding a lot and mowed lawns to keep my parents off his back. Adam was all about getting in shape for football in the fall and worked at a gym so he could have access to all the machines. Every time I bumped into him, usually standing over the blender in the kitchen making a weight-gain shake, he seemed visibly bigger. Or maybe I was shrinking.

On I-80, all the cars were sealed in their discrete and solitary atmospheres of music and chilled air. If I smelled five smells in a day, I felt lucky (cut grass, car exhaust, coffee,

Clorox, toothpaste). I was dazed by the blandness. Two weeks in, my mother knocked on my door. I was reading my diary.

"I think you need to get a job," she said.

"Okay," I said.

An hour later I was driving around downtown, considering my options, when I saw a place called Millet Madness a new health-food restaurant near the university. I smelled cumin when I walked in and asked for an application. My parents were nice enough and glad to have me back, but some days it was hard to believe I'd been away for almost a year—was I like Dorothy after all? Was it all a dream, because everything was just the same?

I phoned Nick soon after I got home, compelled to call, not knowing exactly why. He was surprised to hear from me, but after a few phone calls he asked me what I wanted from him. I said I didn't know. He said I should call when I did. I looked at the green vintage dress in my closet, permanently wrinkled and smelling vaguely of Nepal, but I didn't put it on.

Then one night in early August, the phone rang as I walked in after a movie. "Alex?" Will said. He was calling from his mother's house, outside D.C., and he sounded pleased to reach me. I felt awake for the first time in months and pulled a Tupperware of rice from the fridge, popped it in the microwave, and climbed onto the kitchen counter to eat it with my hand, Nepali-style, while we talked.

Will told me that not long after I left, Chhimi decided to go home to Jankat for the summer, saying she would return in the fall to work and to study English, but she wouldn't live with him. He was taking a leave of absence for the year from the school, and, he said, "Anyway, we both agreed that what we had was over." That sounded like the Will I knew, letting himself off the hook, but then it also seemed like a good plan for Chhimi, as if she were taking care of herself. I was so glad to have any news at all.

"And what about Maya? What's she doing?"

He laughed, as if he still couldn't believe what he'd gotten himself into. "She was vehement about not going back to her parents, said that it was impossible now that she'd run away. I tried to get her a couple of different jobs, but nothing stuck," he said.

"You're not in love with her anymore, I take it?" I asked a little coldly.

"No, I think Mr. Thakur was right in the end. She does appear to be enlightened at first because she has so few inhibitions. But as time went on, I saw—*you* saw—she's very unstable, with all her crying jags and strange stories. It got tiring trying to figure her out." I felt sad that the inevitable had happened, as if it were my loss too, and I was frustrated that his devotion to her had ended so quickly. But he was also my only connection to her, and I didn't want to alienate him.

"So where is she now?"

"I had to find someplace for her. I didn't really trust her to stay in my house alone. So, finally I found a Christian halfway house for single women alone in the big city. Some of them were pregnant, and she wasn't too thrilled with the meek-and-pious thing they were pushing. There was a good amount of doily-crocheting going on, but I promised to come get her when I returned."

"It sounds okay, temporarily," I said, and maybe it was.

"The other thing was she kept disappearing for days at a time," he said. "I heard rumors that she was with . . . do you know him, this guy named Mickey?"

I'd heard of him, but no, I didn't know him.

"He's, I don't know, he's just kind of louche. Always has a lot of girls hanging around his house."

"Unbelievable!" I said. This time my sarcasm was clear.

"No, seriously, he's completely different from me. First of all he's incredibly indiscreet, always going on about his escapades, and second of all, there's nothing else. No Buddhism. No curiosity. No empathy. No inspiration. Just: Live cheap and have sex."

"Okay, okay." I was glad he called, with all his delineations of what was right and wrong. "So maybe she was just hedging her bets."

"Anyway, she talks about you all the time, how you're the only one who understands her and how you're her best friend. I have some pictures that she drew for you and a cassette she made that I'll send you." It was real. We were friends!

In the package that arrived soon after, there were two crayon drawings of hearts and rainbows, with a studiously copied *I love you, my sister*. They looked like the work of a six-year-old, and I couldn't reconcile them with the person I thought of as my friend and equal. But hearing her voice and intonations on the cassette made me feel close to her, her breathlessness as she described her *sukha-dukha*. "I can tell you anything. You are my best friend. Please write to me and come visit soon."

I quickly sent Will a sweater and cassette-letter for him to take her when he went back. I told her I would try to come in a year. "I believe you'll find a good job and a good boyfriend soon, so try not to worry. Your mind and your body are strong, and *sabai raamro hunchha*, everything will turn out fine," I said on the cassette. I didn't mention Will at all, because chances were she would be using his recorder, and he would hear the tape, too.

Then I went back to school in upstate New York, my arty little haven. Once my great escape, it was somehow demure after I'd been so far away. In November, now that I was on the Hudson River Valley line, Nick and I got back together. With him, striding through New York in the caffeinated cold, returning to his place, to tulips in a water glass beside the hissing radiator, I recognized myself again as the person I had started to become in Nepal or, to be precise, in Maine not long before I left. We fought a lot, and we made up. When I was at school we talked late into the night. It was never easy, but I was relieved to feel sharp, to have the sleepiness abate.

That summer I taught photography at a day camp nearby, and Nick and I wrangled our way through another season of ambivalence, until I cheated on him with a hearty, uncomplicated boy of a counselor there. Then, after my teary confession, we broke up, and I thought it was the right thing, even though I couldn't get him out of my head. When graduation came—midyear because of my time away—I found I didn't have the funds or the heart to go all the way back to Nepal, so instead I drove cross-country with my friend in her stepmother's old Honda Civic and set up house in Seattle, where I temped and substitute-taught for a little over a year before moving back to New York. Not for Nick (I told myself), but because a friend of mine knew of an opening as an assistant to a photo editor at the *Times*. Even if I didn't get the job, I would be in the right city for the kind of work I wanted to do. I did get it, though, to my amazement, and then I was a working girl, which came with its own set of privileges and restrictions.

All this time I kept Nepal in my head, and I heard from Will a couple of times a year when he was in the States. He seemed to find me easily enough, and we would talk late into the night about his life as a freelance philanderer—I mean adventurer (he still liked to confide in me)—and of Maya's life. Mine too, but not as much.

For more than a year, she worked as a nanny for an American family in Kathmandu—Will got her the job. But after the couple divorced and returned to the States, she moved in with Mickey. Will told me that she came by regularly and once asked him to write an anonymous letter to Mickey about how he shouldn't hit her and should drink less. Will obliged, thinking it couldn't hurt. Finally she moved out, holding odd jobs, and Will was frank about the fact that he still slept with her. "I even told her that if she wanted to have a baby I would help her, but I couldn't live with her," he said.

According to Will, three years after I left, an eccentric American woman named Candace, a middle-aged New Age artist from Southern California, opened a home in the center of town for young single women on their own called Pukka Sathi—or True Friend—the same thing that Maya called me on her tapes.

Creatively run (that is, without religion), the home's agenda was to help girls learn to support themselves in a society that didn't encourage it. "Maya is a star! You should see her," Will said that summer when he was home. "She's finally learning English. I can't tell you how many classes I've paid for that she's dropped over the years, and now they want to bring her here to study massage at the Aveda Institute in Minneapolis." I was floored, imagining her here, visiting me in New York, coming to holiday meals at my parents' house. Her life was finally beginning to take shape.

The next time I talked to Will, it was in person. We met on a cold spring night at a tasteless macrobiotic place he chose in the West Village. It was only the second time in four years that I'd seen him, and yet his face remained deeply familiar to me. It was older by a little and its wattage slightly dimmed, but there he was: Will. It was as if some part of him was written into who I had become.

When I asked about Maya, he shook his head and said, "Something happened. I still don't know what. Maya has one story. Candace has another. But they kicked her out for lying and being generally untrustworthy, and she's living with Mickey again." He raked his hands through his hair, shorter now that he was moving into his late thirties.

"Does he still hit her?"

"I honestly don't know, and I don't know that I should be too involved anymore. Sometimes I think, even now when she's with Mickey, that she's holding out some hope that she and I will be together. I don't want to encourage that."

"Can you help her from a distance, so she doesn't know?" I asked. I did think he owed her something still, but that too much involvement on his part would be confusing.

"I've tried to do that, arranged trekking guide jobs, even paid people to take a chance on her with different kinds of work. But if I get any closer than that, all hell breaks loose." I didn't know what to say, because Nick and I still had a similar thing. Sometimes we tried to be friends, and he would introduce me to a photography curator at MoMA or a professor at Cooper Union. But any contact with him just seemed to make my head spin with the idea that maybe, maybe we would work out still. It was something I couldn't explain, not even to myself.

That night I dreamed I was in Nepal, and in the morning I knew I would go. Too much time was passing. I was losing the connection. For a long time I had wanted to go back and take pictures there, but I was waiting for the perfect subject. Instead, I realized I just had to go. The next trip, after this one, could be the purposeful trip. This one could be for legwork. I finagled some extra vacation days from a sympathetic boss so I could go for three and a half weeks in August, and when I asked Will if I could stay at his place while he was away during the monsoon, he said yes, if a little grudgingly. He also told me that when he told Maya I was coming, she was very excited. She and I hadn't been in touch, but I hoped that because life moved so much more slowly there, we would pick up our friendship where we had left off.

I was nervous on the last leg of my flight, on the way from Singapore, in a way that I hadn't been before I left. What if it was all a mistake? What if Nepal could be magical only once? I wanted to be wide-eyed again, to have revelations about my life in the face of so much difference, and come home newly enlightened—even if I was on an expedited schedule this time. But I worried that my long absence would render me just another backpacker like every other white kid in Kathmandu. What if Maya was just a girl I'd made up?

Then the plane tipped its wings at the Himalayas poking through the cloud layer below us, and we descended through the thick, grayish white monsoon cover to a curvaceous, dazzling green landscape. Behind me two Nepali teenage boys, who'd gotten on in Dakka, pointed out landmarks among the clay and tin roofs of the city below, the temples and *stupa*s and neighborhoods—Swayambu, Boudha, Pashupati, Patan. I felt pleased that after four years away, I understood their Nepali, I knew the places they were talking about. Hope swelled up like a wave heading toward shore. Descending the tin steps to the tarmac, the air gusting around us, I felt like I should be wearing a chiffon scarf and Jackie O. sunglasses. It was an arrival out of time, and the loose flock of travelers crossed to the main building. The breeze was tinged with engine fumes, lush green hills hovered nearby, and a group of hill women in fuchsia, orange, and yellow crossed at the far end of the runway with big baskets full of rocks on their backs. I felt suddenly dazed by tiredness and the intense sunlight, and as I approached the terminal, I felt a little queasy again until I was distracted by a loud flapping, and looked up. On the observation deck was a Tibetan monk with a beautiful, chiseled face scanning the crowd. His maroon robes luffed around him like sails in the high breeze. A few people down from where he stood was Maya, waving and grinning, her hair whipping around her face. I hurried inside through immigration and down to baggage claim, where the bags limped around on the belt, and then through customs, out to where Maya bobbed on her tiptoes in a white sun hat.

"*Sathi!*" she cried as I reached her. "You're here. I'm so happy!" She wrapped me in a strong embrace. She pulled back and pinched my cheek. "You're so thin! What happened? Are you okay?" It was true, I had been chubby, or *moto*, when I left Nepal, after too many chocolates from Thamel. Although thin wasn't good here: It meant you were working too hard or not eating enough. "I'm good. Very good now that I'm here. Thin is our custom. You know that. Besides, I was never that *moto*!"

"Yes, you were!" she exclaimed, laughing. It was so good to see her, I couldn't believe it. She, too, looked completely different, not like the hill *dakini* she'd been. Her hair was chopped to a sensible shoulder length, and she wore madras pants and a long pale pink blouse over them, the kind a Western woman might wear here if she wanted to be culturally sensitive. I tugged at her white cap. "Nice!" I said.

"Everyone thinks I'm Japanese because of it, even other Nepalis," she said, which didn't surprise me. On the way out of the gleaming marble terminal into the crumbling parking lot, she explained that there was a *bandh*, a word I didn't know from the last time, which meant an all-day strike, as a protest against the government. The shops were closed and there were no taxis, but we found a lone bicycle rickshaw (I never liked them, but Will's new place was too far to walk), and I got in back with my bag while Maya biked alongside us through the empty streets. An ambulance wailed by, and she smirked.

"Funny how many people get sick during a *bandh*," she

said. From Ring Road, we headed through a familiar rotary, a *chowk* (the word bubbled to the surface; they were coming faster now), where the same five-story brick buildings were still covered in huge, sooty, painted ads for Surf soap, Iceberg beer, and Khukri cigarettes. Laundered saris twisted from their rooftops like banners. I knew this! We swerved down narrower streets, deserted except for a few pedestrians, some dogs and cows, and the occasional ambulance, passing familiar tea shops, tailors, pharmacies, and sari shops—all their fronts shuttered in corrugated tin. They reminded me of people hiding their faces behind their hands.

At Dili Bazaar we headed north past Bhatbhateni and the Chinese and Russian embassies, where we turned down a dirt road of new houses made of cinder block, most of them half-finished, with their second floors just rough concrete posts and exposed ironwork, littered with buckets, bricks, and drying laundry. Will's house, though, was completely finished, and one of the best-looking, albeit in a purely functional way. It was only temporary until he moved in September. (There had been an incident with his former landlord's niece that had forced him to leave quickly.) At the end of a rutted and muddy driveway, a scrappy black mutt spun and leaped around the rubbled yard. Will had warned me about him, but said the dog was all noise.

"Ravana! *Chup!*" Maya shouted. They clearly knew each other. (The dog was named after the Hindu demon.) He calmed at the sound of her voice, and I got the keys from the landlord next door. Inside, the first thing I saw was a fax that had fallen from the machine onto the entry hall floor. It read:

DEAR ALEX, WELCOME. MAKE YOURSELF AT HOME, BUT PLEASE DON'T GO THROUGH MY THINGS. LOVE, WILL.

It was classic Will—warm and controlling. When I told Maya what it said, she sniffed and said, "Okay, boss."

More than anything, the place inside reminded me of my elementary school in Des Moines, with the pale yellow cinder-block walls and putty-colored linoleum floors. Will's tapestries and paintings, masks and photos looked like a stage set here, at odds with the mundane setting. The big windows on the ground floor with curlicued iron bars were covered in pretty dark red curtains, but still it all felt stark, too square and boxy for the Nepal I knew. Upstairs, Maya wanted to hang out in Will's room.

"Let's not right now," I said, but when I came back a few minutes later she was sprawled on his bed, the curtains and windows open. A sweet smell of flowers wafted in, maybe jasmine.

"Don't worry. He doesn't really mind, and besides, he won't know," she said. What I heard through this was, he's turned my life so upside down, I'm going to do exactly what I want in his place, especially when he isn't around to stop me.

I sat down beside her. He still had his shrine with the human skull bowl and *dakini* statue in her dynamic lunge with her necklace of bones and a knife to cut through suffering.

"You would not believe how *bodmas*, naughty, he is now!" she said.

"More than before?"

"Yes! It's always: 'A girl, another girl, and another pretty girl!'" she intoned. "The man has a very busy penis."

I laughed and slapped her leg.

"What? It's true. He never gets tired. Once I was mad at him and I stood in his yard and shouted that while he was inside with his Tibetan girlfriend. He was furious!" She laughed.

"Do you still want to be with him?"

"No, I don't want to be with any man right now."

"Have you met anyone you thought was good since I saw you last?" I asked. We had never been able to talk about these things while I was away, because we always communicated through Will.

"There was a boy from Canada last year who was here teaching English. He spoke excellent Nepali, and I wanted him to be my boyfriend, but he said it was better if we were just friends. When he left he gave me these earrings." She touched her ears. I had noticed the hoops—they were polished, city-girl gold—and I wondered if he was gay. Then she said abruptly, "Let's go to my place. I don't want to be at Will's anymore!"

On Will's bike, I bumped along the rocky dirt road beside Maya, and I wondered if an alternate version of me had been bicycling along the roads of Kathmandu with Maya the whole time I'd been gone. We were on the main road heading out of town for less than a mile when we were suddenly surrounded by fields, and she turned down another dirt road. There were two little roadside stores, open despite the *bandh*, and she stopped to get a bag of fresh milk for tea. The steady clicking of a tailor's treadle came from the other. Behind the shops, Maya pushed her bike onto a narrow, muddy footpath, and, single file, we walked between a brick wall on one side and sprouting rice paddies on the other, their water reflecting the gathering clouds above us, studded with green shoots. At the end of the path were two big, bright redbrick houses, like two gashes, they seemed so new. Maya said the second one was where she rented her room.

"See the pink flowers?" she asked.

"Of course." They were bursting pale pink blossoms on plants four feet tall, the only loveliness besides the reflecting water.

"I grew them. I love to garden now. I planted everything here," she said, gesturing to some other bushes in front and hanging plants on the porch in varying shades of glossy green. The other house, otherwise identical, was surrounded by shiny, packed dirt slippery from the rains. "I love to do this kind of work now, with flowers and plants, and my friends in California said they'll bring me to America next year so I can make gardens there."

"Who are they?" I asked casually, surprised to find myself jealous of other Americans promising so much, whether it was genuine or not.

"Just some people I met, a man and woman. They lived here last year," she said. We pulled our bikes up the steps and inside just as the clouds exploded with rain. At the back of the ground floor she unlocked a door behind a curtain and let us into a tidy room painted pale blue. She had a bed, a trunk, a crate of cooking staples, a kerosene burner, and a plastic bucket—it was not uncozy. The concrete walls were decorated with a simple cotton tapestry, framed photos of the Dalai Lama and a Hindu swami I didn't recognize, and a slightly torn Bollywood poster of a man and woman in a torrid embrace, her head thrown back and black hair cascading. When she saw me looking at it, Maya exclaimed, "That's my favorite movie! They both die in the end."

I laughed. I had forgotten how her exuberance encompassed bad things, too. "It sounds so sad," I said.

"It is, but their love was very strong and true," she said as she threw a handful of loose tea and sugar into a saucepan of water on the burner.

I felt a surge of pride to see her on her own, and thought that Will was perhaps being melodramatic when I saw him last. That, or she had rebounded in her resilient way. A crack of lightning made us jump, and Maya set out cookies on a plate while I looked at some photos she handed me. A puff of outhouse stench blew in. "Ugh," Maya said, and wrinkled her nose. "I'm sorry. I had to move here three months ago after I stopped living with Mickey."

"What happened?" I asked, wanting to hear it from her.

"He hit me in the face so hard I had to go to the hospital, and when I got out I went to live with my friend Laxmi, who works in an office." She took the stack of photos and flipped through them until she came to a studio portrait of a high-caste girl wearing big owlish eyeglasses that were meant to make her look distinguished. I wondered how they were friends, but it was just like Maya not to have friendships bound by caste in the usual way. "Mickey came to Laxmi's house and touched my feet, and even kissed them and wanted to wash them. He begged me to come back, saying it would be different. But he's said that before, and I didn't believe him. So I moved here."

"Are you okay now?"

"Yes. I went to my guru in Pokhara, and he told me I have bad karma with men, that I should stay single for a while. He gave me this." She pushed up her sleeve to show a metal amulet in the shape of a cylinder tied to her upper arm on a dirty string. "It's filled with *naag-ko goo*—snake shit—to keep away bad men."

"Does it work?"

"Yeah, it works. He's a very wise man. He said that if I don't have a boyfriend for at least a year I'll have a much better life, and that I'll have much better karma. I also have this to keep bad men away." Smiling, she pulled a kukri out from under her mattress and handed it to me—a wide, curved blade about eight inches long. On the phone, when I called to tell Will I was coming, he told me that she'd become a little bit of a badass, working out and getting strong, determined to take care of herself, which we both took as a good sign after the Mickey troubles.

"You seem good, Maya, happier than before."

"I am. When I turned twenty-one, a little bit of *mon* came to me." There was my favorite word. A little bit of soul came to her. I knew what she meant, because since I'd seen her last a little bit of *mon* had come to me, too. I liked not being so much on the cusp of myself anymore, and I was glad

that both of us had moved away from a certain precarious-
ness. Not that I thought everything was easy for her, and I
imagined she afforded this room with a little help from Mickey
or Will or others, but I did think maybe she was past the hard-
est times.

"Maya-*ji*, listen," I said. "I need your help. I want to take
pictures while I'm here. Not just the way I did last time of anything and anyone. I want to find out about these girls who are
being tricked and taken to India. They—" I couldn't remember
the Nepali word Will had told me. "They have sex for money."

"*Rundi?*"

"Yes, *rundi*." I knew it was ambitious, but the whole time I
was in the U.S. it was the one thing that kept coming up in
articles and photographs I saw, and this surprised me because I
had never heard anyone talk about it when I was here four years
before. But when I asked Will, he said it would be easy to find
out about it in Kathmandu. Girl trafficking was associated with
AIDS, and foreign money was pouring in for any kind of development work to do with AIDS. As a result, social codes and
what people would talk about had changed. "Ask Maya about
it," he said. "She knows all kinds of people around town."

Now she said, "Oh, sure, I know girls who've done that.
Some go to Japan, some to India, some stay right here. Maybe I
can introduce you to them. I don't really know about those
girls who are duped into it, but let's go out and look around.
It'll be fun." I knew I could count on her to be game and
nonjudgmental.

A few nights later, after my jet lag settled down, we went

out to dinner in Thamel, which seemed unchanged to me other than a little busier, and then we biked to the Casino Royale, right in the center of town near Kathmandu's only four-star hotel, the Yak & Yeti. The casino was a huge, garish wedding cake of a white mansion, surrounded by mud, with its name written in pink neon cursive along its top edge. We picked our way across the rough planks laid down to get to the entry. Just before we got there, she told me Nepalis weren't allowed in, but she would pretend she was Tibetan. I'd never heard of that kind of restriction, and she said some of the fancier places in town had the rule now.

"But Tibetans are allowed?"

"They have more money," she said, and told me a story about how a few months before, a gang of young Nepali men had kicked their way inside the casino shouting and punching people, before they were thrown out.

Maya flirted with the ticket seller in her not very believable Tibetan, while I bought us ten-dollar tickets. Considering you could still get a nice room in Thamel for that price, it was a small fortune. From the look on the ticket seller's face, I don't think it mattered what nationality Maya was. A pretty girl was a pretty girl. We went up the grand and shabby red-carpeted staircase, where there was an empty room of blinking slot machines, and then a much larger room filled with people standing around gaming tables under fluorescent lights and chandeliers. Fake wood paneling lined the walls about ten feet up and then gave way to stark white plaster. Maya told me that a lot of Indians came to Nepal now on gambling holidays, and that the men liked Nepali girls in particular, but that all happened inside hotels. The Indians and the Asians were all well dressed in silk saris and suits. The handful of white people—or as Maya now referred to them, in slang I hadn't heard the first time, *kwiréharu*, or "foggy people"—were casual and slouchy in baggy cottons and beads. It didn't take long to spot the young, pretty girls in gold-trimmed silk saris at the elbows of older men, their faces too hill-caste to be sashaying around in the expensive, high-caste garb. Maya pointed out one beside a trim Japanese man in his fifties and said, "I know her. We used to be friends. She went away with him for a few months, and now she's back."

There was no question of us going up to talk to her, though. With both her hands placed neatly on his arm, it was clear she wasn't interested in talking to anyone else. If this was prostitution in Kathmandu, it was definitely the high end of the spectrum. And as women, there was no way in for Maya and me.

We weren't actually going to gamble, so after surveying from the sidelines for a half hour or so, we went downstairs to the disco. It was nearly black inside except for the white snowflakes of light from the spinning mirrored ball, and we danced to a couple of songs with people we could hardly see and then left. As we pedaled away a car full of Tibetan guys called, "Hey, girls, come back! We want to dance with you."

In Thamel, less than ten minutes away, Maya pulled up at a bar called the Green Door, filled with budget travelers and a handful of locals—Nepalis now went out at night. Onstage a Willie Nelson look-alike, complete with bandanna and gray braids, sang Rolling Stones covers through a fuzzy sound system. I got us a Kingfisher to split, and Maya said, "I know those girls. I know where they are, but I don't know how you're going to meet them. Since you're not a man, they're not going to want to talk to you."

"I know," I said. "But let's wait and see." I knew I was embarking on a difficult project, but I also thought maybe she wasn't my way into it. Although it was true she was the reason I was interested. From the first time I saw Mary Ellen Mark's pictures of the Nepali girls in Bombay's oldest red-light district in a book called *Falkland Road*, I'd thought of Maya and Chhimi trying to make better lives for themselves in Kathmandu. In the past, if you wanted out of the family structure, it was usually off to the nunnery or to become a servant. Now there was this. What was the distance between Maya's life and working as a prostitute? Or could her relationship with Will and Mickey and others already be seen as that? I liked to think no, that there was a spacious gray area she could inhabit without being stigmatized.

That night she stayed over at Will's, and in the morning she said, "*Sathi*, is it okay if I see you in a few days? I have some work to do." The way she said it, she let me know that I was not supposed to ask what it was, and I didn't. I was back and we were friends, but her life was her life. I felt disappointed she didn't want to tell me, but I tried to understand: I was just passing through.

I visited other friends around town and some NGOs dealing with trafficked girls and women's issues, where Brahmin women told me, over and over, the same sad tale of young village girls deceived by ruthless Indian men who promised marriage or work and then sold them into sexual slavery.

Then I met an American journalist who had lived in Nepal for many years, writing about what he called "woman-and-child" issues for places like UNICEF. He was a familiar type, graying and lanky, part hippie, but the fact that he was employed doing something legal distinguished him from a lot of other older American expats in town.

"Look," he said, as we sat at a rooftop restaurant in Boudha over *momo*s and beer, "of course, there are girls who are tricked into it, and everyone agrees that this thing with the kids has got to stop, but there are other girls who are just going, migrating, because they're poor as shit and what else are they going to do? There's no work here. So what if you get AIDS, at least you can buy your family a nicer house in the meantime. But no one wants to talk about that because it's not black and white."

Below us the Tibetans walked clockwise around the *stupa*, the huge white mound with its unblinking eyes on top, turning the prayer wheels in the surrounding wall, as they had for more than a thousand years. The strings of fluttering prayer flags were torn and faded, and the mound itself was streaked green with a kind of moss or algae. Everything was the same, but everything looked shabbier than I remembered. The daily rain cleaned the air, but left the city and its inhabitants mud-spattered and soggy.

This self-schooled expert also told me that most prostitution in Kathmandu took place inside hotels or under the cover of apartments. The only visible place was outside the bus station, where he assured me no one was going to talk to me.

Still, I wasn't ready to give up yet. When Maya reappeared, a few days later, in good spirits from her work and bearing a colorful cotton scarf as a gift for me, we biked out to Boudha to check out the *chaang* bars where they served a thick and grainy home brew and where we were also supposed to be able to find prostitutes. The handful of bars along the rutted lane past the *stupa* were mostly empty, until we finally came to one called Sagarmatha House—a modest little restaurant with a few Tibetans and a Nepali couple inside.

"We have to go in!" Maya said, pulling open the door. The Nepali man was young and thin, wearing a white oxford, and the woman was pretty and plump in the telltale gold-threaded sari with matching turquoise eye shadow, looking ill at ease and too fancy for her own comfort. They were obviously of different castes, which was still significant here, and were almost silent as they ate their *momo*s hunched over their bowls, sharing a beer.

I ordered sodas and snacks at the counter, and by the time I turned around Maya was telling them her name was Pema and asking if we could sit with them. The man reluctantly agreed.

I asked if the food was good, and the girl said yes, causing her date to give her a sharp look, and Maya nudged me under the table to let me know that she would do the talking.

When she asked, they said they were just married. The girl said she was from Delhi and Muslim, though she was definitely Nepali and almost certainly not Muslim. Maya told them she was from Dharan, the town in the west where they made "blue movies"—or soft porn—something I'd just recently heard about. Soon enough, despite Maya's warmth, or maybe because of it, the guy was hustling them out of there, and the girl looked back for a moment from the door, as if to say, you're right, but I've got to follow him.

One of the two Tibetan men at the other table asked me in English, "Are you guys cops?"

"Cops?! We look like cops?" I said, and translated for Maya.

"Yeah," he said. "They left because they thought you were police." And I wondered how many white women the Nepali police force employed, especially to do undercover prostitution work. He consulted with his friend in Tibetan, who agreed and then got up to leave. The chatty man moved to sit at our table. "So what are you doing here if you aren't cops?"

"I'm a photographer. I'm looking into a story."

"That girl would never let you take her picture. She was definitely a prostitute, a girl that pretty, out this late. I know something about all that," he said, a hint of boasting in his voice.

"What do you mean?" I asked.

"A few years ago I used to go to them a lot. There are a few places you can look in Kathmandu, though it's mostly underground. If I wanted to sleep with someone, I usually went to the discos, because the European women will do anything for a little hash." I laughed. That neatly put me in my place.

"And now?" I asked.

"Now I don't go. I just finished my second treatment program for heroin. I'm trying to stay straight and just run my
carpet business with my brother."

Nepal had changed and so had I. On my first trip to Nepal
no one came close to revealing such modern problems, at least
not anyone who wasn't a good friend. Granted, he was also
sloshed, which might have had something to do with it. Soon
he was saying, "I can tell you anything. Thank you. You're
like my sisters. I can take you out anytime you want to meet
girls like that, in any club in Thamel."

"Okay," I said. "But not tonight." I took his card, and
we made him promise to walk his bike home. He told us again
we were like his sisters, and to please call if he could do anything
for us. As we left, Maya said, "It's not easy being a woman interested in prostitutes. Everyone suspects you."

 *Seven*

That Friday night, some Americans I knew from the last
time—friendly acquaintances who still lived here—invited us
to something called the Marine Bar. I had never heard of it,
but apparently since the early seventies, three Fridays a
month, the four marines stationed in Kathmandu turned their
house into a dance party and cash bar, open to anybody, local

and foreign, who had ID. A small gang of us met for dinner at a decent place with an outdoor garden on the edge of Thamel, and then rode our bikes north, up Lazimpat past the palace and the Shangri-La Hotel to the embassy district, until we reached a high, white wall, with a handsome black marine out of uniform standing at the front gate. We signed in on his clipboard, and inside the wall was a modern-style, three-story stucco house that at first glance might have been airlifted from California, with its clean lines and big windows. Around back an outdoor staircase led up to a long, narrow balcony lined with "foggy people" and some Nepalese and Tibetans smoking, talking, and drinking Budweiser from cans—another anomaly, given that most beer in Kathmandu came in big brown bottles and tasted like formaldehyde.

This was a kind of update on Pete's Bistro (now inexplicably shoddy in a new location). These people were not the thrifty, backpacking bunch, what a friend back home called the "banana pancakers"—because anywhere across the third world, from Guatemala to Mongolia, you could find them wearing tank tops and Tevas and braided bracelets, sitting in cheap restaurants that were indistinguishable from one another: they all served banana pancakes to foreign kids and played Bob Marley day and night. No, this group was here long-term. They were cleaner than banana pancakers, and even their posture said they were more assured, that they belonged here somehow. They enjoyed the commissary beer and hot dogs, genuinely and ironically, and the big room inside reminded me of a hospitable frat house, half of it darkened and given over to thumping music and whirling disco lights and the other half brightly lit and dominated by a beautiful old wooden bar (probably salvaged from a Rana palace) with nothing on the mirrored shelves behind it except a GI Joe in camouflage and a Barbie in a pink bikini. All the cliques were there, playing Foosball and pinball and milling around: Peace Corps kids clustered around one of their own holding forth in a Malcolm X hat; a few of the hard-living expats in tie-dyes doing their seventies-style free-form dancing; embassy wonks (no ties, but nerdy); teenage diplomat brats in low-cut jeans, platforms, and glittery eye shadow; a posse of Tibetan bad boys working a James Dean look, with motorcycle boots, white T-shirts, and Marlboros, (I recognized them from the streets of Thamel); and then the people I knew, who were all working for one NGO or another or doing research for a thesis. Students at the same time as me, they'd opted to come back to make a semipermanent life here, and I thought of them as Generation K.

Maya knew a few people, and after we had a beer we went off to dance, where I shook off all the Nepali decorum, just like the other Western girls there who bared their bellies and shook their hips. There was nothing like this the last time I was here, no respite from the local etiquette. Even that night with Will and Maya years ago, it was as if my body had been given only temporary dispensation to exist. Too tall by at least six inches, with my freckles and flyaway hair, I would never be considered pretty by local standards, but the loud music erased all that as it got into my bloodstream, and I started to sweat.

Maya, surprisingly, was bashful, and I watched an older hippie-ish couple coax her away from the wall.

"Do you want to dance?" I heard someone say a little too close, and I turned to bump into a brown-eyed expat, shorter than me with a pleasing gap between his two front teeth.

"Sure," I said, as we moved out into a loud, fast remix of "It Takes Two." We danced easily together, and when we paused to talk, he said his name was Ben, that he ran a solar energy company, and that his wife and sister-in-law were sitting over there. The wife had to be eight months pregnant, and we all waved cheerfully.

"Our third," he said about the soon-to-be-born child, adding as he put a hand on my shoulder, "I love meeting people who are passing through."

I nodded, baffled. Soon after, I went outside by myself and crossed the short, springy lawn, the kind I had only ever seen on the grounds of fancy hotels. Passing some embassy kids, I heard a girl drawl in a funny hybrid accent, "I mean, who gives a fuck?" and I found a spot on the putting-green grass and lay back. In the air above me, the woofer beat pulsed out the windows and then dissolved into the night. It was as if I weren't in the heart of a city of half a million or more, the way the stars spangled the black sky.

I missed Will. Of course, it was good to spend time with Maya and with other Nepali and American friends here, but it was different not having his take on the place, which had stayed the same in some respects, but had also changed into something racier and more decaying. Or maybe it was also that I'd changed and saw it differently now. And while it made sense that Maya knew where to locate the city's seedier sides—because she had always known people across the social spectrum—increasingly I wondered what was actually going on with her. The more time we spent together, I wasn't sure if we were "true friends," or if she trusted me anymore.

"Alex?" I heard, and sat up, startled. It was Will. For a moment I thought I was hallucinating.

"What are you doing here? I was literally just thinking about you. I thought you were away till September."

"I was. I am. I'm just passing through on my way to Japan." I got up, and we hugged. "I thought I'd find you out here, hovering at the edge of things."

"Passing through?" I asked as we sat down. "Wait, oh, crap. Have you been to the house yet?"

"I have. It's a mess."

"I know it is. Why didn't you call or fax?" I'd taken advantage of the fact that I had no visitors but Maya, strewing my things around. "I'll clean it up as soon as I get back tonight, and I can move out tomorrow."

"Relax. I'm staying with a friend in Boudha. I just dropped some stuff off," he said.

"Did you see Maya?" I asked. Annie Lennox's version of "Take Me to the River" washed out over us. *Drop me in the water . . .*

"From a distance. She was talking to some embassy guy. We weren't exactly on great terms when I left."

It was the first I'd heard of it from either of them. "Why?"

"Right before I left she came and made a big scene at my friend's house in Boudha about how I had ruined her life and that I should at least take care of her, and how I treated her like a prostitute."

"Do you?"

"No. It was crazy and noisy. Everybody was looking out their windows, and I said I didn't want to see her anymore and slammed the door. I didn't know how to get her to shut up. Of course, I felt bad afterward. I know she doesn't have an easy life, but I was leaving in a couple of days, and I didn't want to rile her up again. She didn't mention it?"

"Nope," I said.

"*Sathi!*" Maya was standing at my feet in the Malcolm X cap, the bill pulled to one side, making her look sweetly delinquent. "Oh-ho, you *bodmas keta*, naughty boy," she said to Will, and sat down next to me. "What's he telling you? Lies?"

"Hi, Maya," he said. "How are you?"

"I'm fine, thank you, and you?" she said in her best Berlitz English, shaking his hand with exaggerated formality.

"Very well. Are you working?"

"A little bit, when I can find it." She picked up my hand and began cracking each of my knuckles. "Who are you sleeping with these days?" I felt as if I were in the middle of a game of chicken between two eighteen-wheelers, and wondered who would swerve first. I didn't want to get run over.

"She's American," he told her. Point for Will.

"Where is she now?"

"In Japan." He reclined on his side, head in hand, unfazed.

"Why are you here, then? Visiting your other girlfriends?"

"Who are my other girlfriends?"

"I don't know. Maybe Alex is."

I swatted her lightly and said, "I don't think so."

"No, I'm just doing some work. What about you? Are you in love?"

She laughed. "*Kosto jiskauné-manché!* What a joker you are! There's no one to fall in love with here. If I had the money, I would just go to another country and never come back." Even though she and Will weren't a couple, they seemed together still. I thought of Nick. For reasons I didn't completely understand, I'd slept with him a few weeks before I left for Nepal. Before that we hadn't spoken for seven months.

"I don't believe you." He lay back and looked at the sky.

"I don't care what you think." She lay down with a noisy sigh, and the three of us were quiet, flattened against the loamy ground under the city sky and sounds of others cavorting. I felt as if I were lying between someone's flat palms, gently but firmly pressed there, listening to the party noise around us. This calm lasted less than five minutes, until Maya jumped to her feet and said she was going home, and I gave her my hand to hoist me up.

"You're sure you don't want me to go stay somewhere else?" I asked Will, brushing bits of grass from me.

"It's fine. I'll come by tomorrow. Give you a chance to tidy up—kidding."

"You're not, and I will."

"Bye, girls." He lifted one hand. "Sleep well."

I waved over my shoulder. Maya and I dashed through the party with a fast good-bye to Ben and friends, grabbed our bikes, and wheeled them out the front gate, where we pedaled pell-mell into the sleeping city as Maya called out "*Ciao!*" to no one in particular. We dodged potholes, puddles, and stray dogs, giddy with our escape from Will, from everyone, sailing down Lazimpat and heading east past the palace, a kind of modern atrocity. Just inside its high walls, the branches of the tall trees were weighted with big, oblong lumps—the famous palace bats that occasionally swooped out over the city. At the far end of a quiet Durbar Marg, a lone red neon sign flashed sleepily, *Wai-Wai*, the favorite ramen noodles brand. We went up through the darkened neighborhoods, and at the turnoff for Will's house we stopped.

"You know what I call Will?" Maya asked.

"No, what?"

"*Sé Makas*, One Hundred Flies."

"Why?"

"Because he's dirty from sleeping with so many girls. He doesn't like the name at all." She chuckled.

"I can understand why."

"*Tuk!*" She spat as if to get a bad taste out of her mouth. "When am I going to meet a good man?"

"Soon, I think."

"*Saphana-ma, hola*, in my dreams maybe," she said.

"*Biphana-ma, hola*, in reality maybe," I said. "I need to find one too, you know."

She laughed and said, "You know what you should call your Nick?" I had told her a little about us.

"What?"

"*Lamkoté*, mosquito, because he won't stop buzzing in your ear."

I laughed. Maya Gurung, genius of nicknames. I knew we

weren't perfect specimens either. I'd been called moody, demanding, and unsentimental, mostly by Nick. Maya was a little nuts, and frankly maybe so was I. We said good night, and she started to ride away, in the opposite direction of her house.

"Hey!" I called into the quiet, chirping Kathmandu night, and she looped back around.

"Where are you going?"

"I have to go to Thamel to take care of some things."

"So late?"

"Yes, don't worry," she said, and biked away. Of course I was worried. What kind of business took place after eleven in Kathmandu? Only one kind of business that I could think of, and yet I felt pretty sure she would tell me if she was a prostitute, or that I would know if that was how she was supporting herself.

I was brushing my teeth when the phone rang. It was after midnight, and I hoped it was Maya. But when I picked up I could hear from the crackling that it was an international call, someone for Will. "Hello, hello?" Then I heard, "Alex, is that you?"

Shit. All in one night? "Nick!" *Nick, Nick, Nick,* my voice echoed down the line, spiraling across the six thousand miles. "Is everything okay? How did you get my number?" I held the phone away from my ear so I wouldn't have to hear my words repeating. I waited through the long pause before his voice came back telling me that he'd called my parents (great—they had never liked him, from the little they knew), that he just wanted to hear my voice, that he was thinking about me and wondering how things were going.

"I'm fine," I said. I set the toothbrush down and leaned against the wall. It was a terrible place for a phone. "How—" His words collided with mine across the wires. "You go."

"No, you."

"I was just going to ask if you'd heard anything about money?" As usual, he was waiting for funding to make a movie.

"No. Not yet. It's frustrating. Are you taking pictures?"

"Some. Actually, no." I couldn't lie to him about work. "I don't know what to take them of." The echo seemed to lessen, or I was getting used to it.

"Why don't you just take them of anything, and see what you have when you get back? If they're all bad, they're all bad. So what? I doubt they will be."

How could I explain that every day I was here, I felt more outside the place, more confused by it? Maya's going off at the end of the night upset me. I was missing something. I was afraid my camera would make me miss more, putting me at a remove I didn't want.

"Alex? Are you there?"

"I'm here. It's just . . . I don't know."

"It's not the same?"

"Yeah. I mean, it's still beautiful and special. But it's such a short trip, and I don't know what I'm doing here." I slid down onto the linoleum floor, cold through my clothes, and closed my eyes. Once again I was saying things to him that I hadn't fully articulated to myself. It was as though he brought me into focus. I became more myself when he looked or listened, and I hated him for it.

"Maybe you're not the same. It's been what? Four years?"

"Yeah."

"And your friends, the Nepali girl, the American guy?" I had told Nick about them, not in detail ever, but he knew they were central to my Nepal.

"He wasn't supposed to be here, but just showed up tonight at a party, and she . . . she's here but remote somehow. We spend all this time together, but I don't really know what's going on with her."

"Alex, it's what? Only a little more than two weeks. Take some pictures. Do what you like to do there. Weren't you going to go hiking or whatever they call it?"

"Trekking, yeah. I have to get that organized."

"So get it organized already." He was teasing me now. He would do this sometimes when I was in a funk. He who always took himself too seriously ribbed me for the same quality.

"Yeah, yeah, yeah."

"And go take some pictures, why don't you? I want to see them."

"Okay." Late-night phone calls were our specialty, much better than the two of us together in real life. "Nick, I should go. It's late, and this is going to be expensive. Thank you."

"Just show me the pictures when you get back. And maybe I can show you the new script." I was a smallmouth bass on a very big hook.

"Sure. Okay, bye," I said.

"Nice to hear your voice, Alex." I hung up. *Love you, love you, love you*, echoed in my head. Did I? No, I didn't, but then what the hell was it? A month before, I ran into him at a mutual friend's birthday party at a bar downtown. I saw him first and when I said hi he offered me the chair next to him in the middle of a long table of people. It was suddenly as if we were always side by side. We hadn't seen each other in seven months, but we could finish each other's sentences. We egged each other on, and people listened to us: We were on fire, the belles of the ball, the Wonder Twins. Was it any wonder, that foggy July night, that I walked back through the empty downtown streets to his place with him and climbed the five flights of stairs I had been climbing for four years? His apartment was the same, but dirtier, with a huge bag of empty beer bottles on the floor. The sheets were gritty and the bathroom sink was clogged. The giddiness of who we were together in front of other people wore off, and the sex was self-conscious and awkward, humming with all the disappointment that came before it. But even now I was afraid that without him I would never become who I was supposed to be. *Whatever*, I thought. *He's right. Just take some pictures.*

THE NEXT MORNING Will showed up early, but I'd gotten up earlier to clean the house and even get a breakfast of poached eggs on toast and a fruit salad together. He let himself in and surprised me in the kitchen. "Hey," he said.

"Hey, yourself. You want to eat outside?"

"I'll get the tea," he said. I watched him walk out ahead of me and thought how strange it was that we had once been so domestic together for more than a month, so long ago, and yet we didn't really know each other. We were polite and cheerful over breakfast. It was nice to see him here. It made Nepal feel more like Nepal. He showed me some recent photos, and they were good, although I saw for certain now that there was something too *National Geographic* in his sensibility for me, as each picture rang out one round note of mystical or gorgeous or sad, etc. We talked about the ongoing instability of the political situation in Nepal, and about his Japanese girlfriend. He met her while he was studying in a master's program at Berkeley before he dropped out. About Maya, he asked, "Is there anything she's told you that you think I should know?"

"Not that comes to mind," I said, and there wasn't. He said he'd stop by before he left and told me to enjoy the house.

That afternoon when I was waiting out the rain indoors, Maya called to say she was busy for a couple of days, but we made a plan to meet the day after next at the Annapurna Coffee Shop and then to go trekking in five days. I'd never been on the Everest trail and neither had she, and we agreed that it was probably a good time to go, since the monsoon season meant it would be less crowded. We couldn't take the bus to the region, because the roads were washed out, so I said I'd buy us helicopter tickets to Lukla, where we'd be that much closer to the mountains when we started. "It'll be beautiful!" she said. "My head always feels better when I leave the city. All that fresh air cleans my blood."

I was glad to hear her so excited, and I thought maybe this was what she and I needed—to get out of the fray of Kathmandu, where we were both distracted, and just walk.

Everything had to happen so quickly this trip—reconnecting with Maya, taking photos, going on a trek—and I felt like someone had hit the fast-forward button and I couldn't stop it. It made me out of sync with this slow-paced place, where, when someone said "now," they could mean within the hour or the day or even the week. The last time I was here the days would endlessly unfold, like a piece of origami, changing shape and color with each turn. Only now did I see how luxurious that time was.

With Maya busy and my girl-trafficking project on hold, I started taking pictures of anything and everything. I walked, I bicycled, I climbed the hills in town. One of the perks of my job at home was that I had more free film than I knew what to do with. Just think of it as sketching, I told myself. It was much more interesting than taking meetings at NGOs, and now that I wasn't rushing here and there trying to meet people, I began to see things, not just see past them. Courtyards through tiny wooden doorways, temples, monkeys, traffic, laundry. I began to feel like I'd actually arrived, that my camera was like a guide leading me places. When it rained, I waited it out in whatever shop or stall or temple I was near, holding the babies, accepting hot tea.

Then, at the appointed day and time, I waited for Maya at the Annapurna Coffee Shop over apple crumble and a fresh lime soda. It was cool and calm inside the luxurious hotel, where everything was made of a warm dark wood. I read all the trashy magazines foreigners left behind, gorging myself on celebrity gossip until I realized more than an hour had passed and maybe she wasn't coming. It wasn't uncommon here for people to break appointments without letting you know. Nobody had cell phones yet. I thought maybe she would stop by later, but when she didn't come over that night or the next morning, I went to her place and found her room padlocked. On a hunch I walked around back and peered in the window. The room was completely empty—the bed, tapestry, plants, trunks, cooking gear, posters were all gone. The only thing left was a dirty straw mat and the photo of her guru on the floor. I felt like I'd been punched. I knew that her life had gotten more convoluted. When we met up for dinner, and I asked her what she'd done that day, her answers were often vague or sometimes overly elaborate. She did tell me that she worked for a man who had an import-export business, and while I understood her to mean she did work around town for him, suddenly I wondered if she was a drug mule. Or if she was in trouble with the law and had to flee.

Maya had told me there was a girl named Nitu who lived upstairs with her mother. She said they used to be friendly until about a month before, when Nitu spread rumors in the neighborhood that Maya slept around. Maya had spat as she told me, cursing her. Still, maybe Nitu knew something.

At the top of the stairs I called her name until a girl about my age came out through a faded flowered curtain tacked up in the doorway. Dressed in a long housedress, the kind they called a *maxi* that always looked like a nightgown to me, she pushed a loose bit of hair back from her face. She was pretty but looked tired.

"Yes?" she said.

"You're Nitu?"

"Who is it?" an old woman's voice called from inside.

I stepped closer. "I'm a friend of Maya's, from downstairs. Can I come in for a minute?" I said, loud enough for the older woman to hear.

"Come inside," the woman said, and coughed violently.

Nitu held back the curtain and offered me a low stool in a room much like Maya's, but in need of fresh paint. Her mother lay on the only cot in the room, with a red-and-black quilt up to her chin. Her thinning, short black-and-gray hair was oiled and pulled back. She looked withered and sick, and studied me intensely until she was racked with coughs again.

"I don't want to disturb you, but I wonder if you know where Maya went?"

The girl held a tin cup of water to her mother's lips, and said, without looking at me, "I don't know anything."

I waited until the older woman was tended to. "Are you sure? It's important. She was supposed to meet me yesterday, and she never showed up." Nitu poured water from a cloudy plastic five-gallon container into a pot and threw in some tea and three big spoonfuls of sugar. The older one gazed at me with rheumy eyes. "I'm worried about her."

The girl carefully put away the tea things in a tin box. "She's gone *bahera*, outside."

"Outside Kathmandu, or Nepal?"

"I don't know. I met her at the water tap two days ago, and she said she was leaving, that she wouldn't be back for a while. She told me she didn't want to stay here because her room was too expensive." Maya had mentioned the high rent to me—it was sixty dollars a month—but only as a passing complaint. I wasn't sure she had told Nitu the truth, or whether Nitu was telling me the truth. Maybe she just didn't want to disappoint me.

"Did she say who she was going with—man, woman, American, Tibetan?" Maya and I were supposed to go trekking in three days.

"No, she might have been going alone." But no one went anywhere alone here.

I didn't know what to make of it, and after drinking my tea, I went back to Will's, hoping she might just be there sitting on the patio, playing with the landlord's feisty little dog. When Will came over to drop off a duffel bag that night, and I told him, he said, "Huh, that's surprising."

"You don't know anything about it?" Suddenly I felt suspicious of him.

"You forget that I'm trying to be less involved here. If I worried every time Maya took off, I'd have a full-time job. Secrecy is one of her few forms of self-protection." He seemed genuine. I asked him where she hung out in Kathmandu regularly, and he gave me a few names of places before he zoomed away on his motorcycle. He said he'd call in a few days before he left for Japan. When he didn't, I didn't think too much of it. With Maya missing, our connection was weaker than ever.

At night I went out looking for Maya at the clubs in Thamel—the Green Door, Third Eye, Inner Piece, among others—always taking her photograph with me. At least one person seemed to recognize her in each place, but nobody knew where she was. I even tracked down Mickey. Halfway to Boudha, off Ring Road and down a muddy lane, he lived in a modest, pretty, old-style brick house behind a high, vine-covered wall. I rang at the gate, and a girl led me inside past the kitchen and up a ladder to where Mickey was stretched out on a low couch sipping from a barrel of *thukpa* and flipping through *Asia Newsweek*. He looked big in proportion to his modest aerie, and his face had a drinker's fullness and flush under a mop of white hair.

"Alex, I've heard of you," he said, shaking my hand from his reclined position, his accent a mixture of posh and laconic. "So Maya flew the coop?" He crossed one leg over the other as he called for the *bayini* to bring us tea. It was funny to see this ham-faced American imitating such a pasha. I waited for him to pull out a hookah pipe.

"I was hoping you might have some idea of where she went. We were hanging out together a lot, and then she just disappeared. Her rented room is empty."

"Sounds like Maya. She wore me out with shenanigans like that. Usually people's inconsistencies don't bother me much, but she really tested me. Don't get me wrong—we had fun, and she is strong! You should see her go when we get out to the countryside, but she was too unpredictable and hotheaded for my blood. I'm just a regular American guy."

Who is falling apart, I thought.

The *bayini* arrived with tea, and he held her hand for a moment and said, "Isn't she pretty?"

"Yes. I'm worried Maya might be in danger."

He laughed, not entirely pleasantly. "In danger? More likely whoever she's with is in danger. You must have seen the kukri she carries around now." I thought about asking him why she needed to protect herself, but didn't. "One thing you probably know about your friend is that she's not always forthcoming about her whereabouts. I suppose she could have gone to see her parents up north."

"In Tatopani? I thought she didn't see them anymore."

"Hardly. She doesn't get along with them—or with her father, anyway—but she's always sending money back there. She might be in Tatopani, but more likely she's at their house farther north in Ngyak. Sometimes she just gets a bug about getting out of the city and she's gone." I thanked Mickey and left him in his little tree house. I wondered if I should turn in the helicopter tickets to Lukla. I supposed I could just get on a bus to Ghorka and start walking. Maybe I could even visit Chhimi, who Will and Maya both told me had married her childhood sweetheart and had a baby, returning to Jankat after a particularly doomed love affair with a student that she ended, to his heartbreak. But I wanted to stay and wait for Maya a little longer.

Before Maya disappeared, I figured her life was complicated, maybe by a boyfriend or by work that she didn't want me knowing about, but I didn't think she was in trouble. She always seemed happy to see me and fairly jovial, if a little tired at times. I thought trekking might give us a chance to talk. The longer she was gone, though, the more I wondered if we were friends. Maybe our lives were too different after all. Sure, there were Nick and Will, but I didn't have to go ask Nick for money to pay my rent. Riding my bike back to Will's, I thought about how I used to imagine my home might be here, at least for a few years, but now I knew it wasn't.

I WAS SOUND ASLEEP a couple nights later in Will's room—it was the nicest in the house—when a loud knocking woke me up, and I jumped out of bed, heart racing.

"*Sathi, sathi!* Wake up. It's me, Maya. Open the window." I opened the curtain and unlatched the balcony door, pulling her inside.

"Come in, come in," I said, hugging her. I felt so relieved I wanted to smack her. She was laughing, and she looked like a teenage runaway, her hair in two messy braids, smelling of stale cigarette smoke, her backpack bulging and half-zipped.

"Oh, *sathi*, I'm so glad to see you," she said as I locked the door and drew the curtain. It was three-thirty.

"Where have you been? What happened to you?" I asked as casually as I could as we sat on the bed. My heart was pounding still, and I braced myself for a lengthy, intricate lie.

"I went to Hong Kong with Will." Of course she did. Of course Will knew. I wondered how I could have thought he wasn't in on it. I felt incensed at both of them.

"But where are your things, your furniture?"

"I left them at my friend's. I couldn't live in that room anymore. It didn't smell good, and it was too expensive and . . ."

she paused, considering her hands in her lap. "I didn't have any money to pay for it."

"I could have given you some."

"I was going to ask you, but I didn't want to give you any *dukha*, and then when Will arrived, I thought I should just ask him. I've asked him before. He owes me that, and he has the money. So I went to his friend's—I had a pretty good idea of who it was—early that morning after the Marine Bar and woke him up while he was still in bed with her. He was mad, but then he said he would give me the money and a lot more if I went to Hong Kong with him."

"Maya-*ji*," I said, then stopped and took a breath. "Why didn't you tell me? I looked all over for you. I didn't know if you were dead or in Ghorka or what."

She cupped my hands between hers and said, "Don't worry, *sathi*. I'm fine. I tried to call you here before I left and no one answered. Maybe the machine was off?" There was no way she was telling me any more, not tonight, anyway.

"Never mind, it doesn't matter." That was a lie and I felt bitter about it, but I didn't have the luxury of getting mad at her.

We went downstairs for tea, and she was sitting quietly at the table turning the beads on her *mala* when she said abruptly, "I'll go. You were asleep."

"No!" I said, whirling around, sharper than I meant. "Where would you go, anyway? It's the middle of the night."

"Please don't be mad at me, *sathi*. My life is very difficult right now. I didn't want to beg from you or from anyone. The truth is I needed money for my father's hospital bill, and Will said if I would go with him and take black market dollars, he could give me all I needed."

"Did he tell the truth?" I handed her a mug of tea, wondering if she was telling me the truth. Everything sounded like a lie, except for the fact that she'd been with Will.

"Yes, and we brought back gold."

"Maya, you could go to prison if you're caught." I'd once visited a British guy in prison here who was there for that very reason. I took him some books and cigarettes, and he said the conditions weren't terrible, but the one thing he'd learned was never lend money to the guards. I didn't think it would be such a great place for a young woman.

"I know, but bad work is the only kind that makes any money. I can't pay rent with the money I make trekking or cleaning once in a while, let alone give any to my parents. I had no money."

If I gave her a wad of cash, would that solve all her problems? Was that what it came down to? "What are you going to do now?"

"I wanted to stay with Will, but he's with this Tibetan woman in Boudha, and he's leaving in three days. He won't give me extra money for the gold, which made me mad. We've been fighting all night. He told me I should just stay here with you, but where will I go when you leave?"

"I'll be here for ten days if you want to stay."

"Okay," she said, and got up. "Can I take a shower now?"

I got her a towel and told her to turn out the lights. When

she crawled into bed beside me, smelling damply of soap and shampoo, she threw a leg and arm over me, and I inched out from under the deadweight. When I woke up later she had one hand in a fist near her face, and I tucked back her damp hair. Her cheek was slightly broken out from her travels, and she looked so much younger than she did awake, when her eyes were clouded and wouldn't always meet mine.

THE NEXT DAY we were walking on Kantipath when Will pulled up on his motorcycle. "Hi, girls," he said.

"Are you kidding me?" I was seething. Maya watched, almost bemused, as the traffic swerved around Will. "Couldn't you have just told me so I didn't have to worry myself sick about her?"

"I told you she was probably fine."

"All you had to say was, 'She's with me.' Is that really so hard?"

"Alex, calm down. Come on, meet me at Ananda. I'll explain. Let me buy you lunch or a coffee or whatever."

While Tracy Chapman played on the stereo and some Australian backpackers drank beer, Will leaned forward confidentially to say, "I would have told you, but it was important that as few people as possible knew. I thought we might be in danger."

"Oh, come on! That I might report you to the police?"

"You laugh, but I'm actually glad I ran into you, because it wouldn't be a bad idea if you and Maya went to Lukla after all, if she were out of the city until customs stops poking around. I don't think they'd hurt her, but they might scare her. I'll even buy your tickets." I loved that he drew me back in by asking me to be her protector again.

"What happens when she gets back?"

"Once they realize I'm out of the country for a couple of months, I think things will cool down," he said. I had no idea if he was bullshitting me, but I wanted to go trekking, and I was pretty sure she did too.

"I already have tickets, but you can contribute. And you can get the check," I said, standing up.

He smiled and said, "You're getting shrewd in your old age."

"You set a good example," I said.

 *Eight*

Our helicopter, manned by Russian pilots and carrying half trekkers and half Sherpas, touched down in Lukla in the late morning. Only as we started walking north along the Dudh Koshi (the Milk River) did I realize fully that leaving the city was the best thing we could have done. The air was sweet after Kathmandu's smog. Walking uphill and down through villages, I found that even with the monsoon cloud cover, the "toilet paper trail"—its nickname because of all the foreigners who littered on it—was very pretty and not nearly as polluted as I'd heard it was. We walked hard, and all the clamoring thoughts of Kathmandu streamed away behind me, like the river rushing nearby, or like clouds across a blue sky, as the Buddhists say.

An hour into the walk, Maya crowed, "My *mon*! It's so much better here! I get so confused in the city."

She took my hand where the path was wide enough to walk together and led us clockwise around the Buddhist stone mounds called *chorten*s. I felt oxygenated and revived.

The only thing I worried about was whether a fifty-something-year-old Polish man named Piotr, whom we'd met on the helicopter, was going to catch up with us and glom on for the rest of the six-day trek. Over lunch in Lukla, he told us in a long and noisy monologue that he was moving back to Poland after fourteen years in Australia—a marriage, divorce, and two kids later—and as he picked up the menu to order his third round of lunch, I pitched us off. When we arrived at the Good Rest Inn in Phakding, just as night fell, I was sure we'd outdistanced him.

Half an hour later, when we were playing with the innkeeper's baby boy while his mother made us dinner, I heard him say, "There you are!" and then saw his tall, bulky silhouette in the doorway. "Why did you walk so far? I thought I'd never reach you. In every town I asked about two girls, and they always told me you had just been there." He was taking off his pack and jacket.

"We just felt like going," I said. It wasn't like getting rid of a guy at a bar, because there was a chance we would be stuck with him for days. His return ticket to Kathmandu had the same date as ours. Through dinner, we listened to him talk about all the places he'd been and people he'd outsmarted and the luck he'd had, as he ate and ate. Maya, who didn't understand the blather, was in a sunny mood and teased him by pulling the bench away when he tried to sit down or hiding his flashlight. Later, in our room with the cold night air blowing in just above our heads, she asked me what he'd talked about, and I told her, "Every story was about how brave and smart he is."

"And how *moto*, fat?" she asked deadpan. He did have the ruddy look of someone who was literally full of himself.

The next day we started out together, but he was so intent on capturing every last twist in the path on his video camera so that he could watch it on the large-screen TV he was importing to Poland that we ended up walking ahead. He caught up with us in the bustling hilltop town of Namche Bazaar (Sir Edmund Hillary's favorite village), and we left him dandling the baby of the house, which made me wonder about his own kids in Australia—my only true pang of empathy for him.

When Maya and I ate our picnic of canned tuna and crackers on a high ridge with the clouds sailing by, she said, "You know that man has a *katara naak*—a dangerous nose—don't you?" It seemed ordinary enough, if a little pink.

"What does that mean?" I asked.

"Like Will, like your Nick. They like the girls and *jiggy-jiggy*, these noses." I laughed—maybe that was what she and I shared more than anything now—and Katara Naak became his name from then on.

For the rest of the day we left arrows marked in the dirt where the trail was confusing, because it seemed like bad karma not to be helpful. There were so few trekkers otherwise, and Maya periodically said, "*Bichara*, the poor thing!" adding, "He's traveling all alone!" But we didn't see him until nightfall at the one dry lodge in Tengboche. In the big common room with a fireplace and carpets, Katara Naak regaled us with stories of his travels in Bali, Indonesia, and Thailand, until I said we wanted to get up early.

"Of course!" he said, and we all lay down on the wide, cushioned benches around the room, the walls of the room ticking and creaking around us.

When the alarm went off at four, I pulled open the curtains above me, and the snowy Himalayas ringed the hilltop meadow like a dream.

"Maya, Maya, get up! Look!"

She leaned up on her elbows and crowed, "*Kathi raamro!* How gorgeous! We pulled on our jackets and shoes—Katara Naak and his video camera were already gone—and ran outside through the wet grass and the last of the ground mist toward a hillock. I kept reaching out my arms; the mountains seemed touchably close. The sky was clear, a drinkable blue, and the sunlight poured through the peaks like an egg cracked open. Maya and I ran to another part of the meadow, where I stretched out my arms again. The monastery walls shone white, its red roof visible at one end of the alpine meadow.

Then, as miraculously as the mountains had appeared, they vanished behind the clouds.

At breakfast, Piotr shook his head and said, "I can't believe you're leaving this beautiful place to risk altitude sickness," as if he knew anything about trekking. "You should stay and enjoy these nice people and the mountains again tomorrow morning."

I got up to pay and felt elated as Maya and I bounded down a grassy slope filled with yellow flowers—piping down the valleys wild—heading north. Finally we were just two girls on the road again, unencumbered by various romances or prospective romances. I told her about Nick, how he had called since I saw her last.

"Don't worry. You'll find someone good," she said. "You're pretty and educated and have money. Your life will be good." She made it all sound so simple. Did it really come down to that? I hoped that in the next few days we could come up with a plan for her. Then she added out of the blue, "You know, one thing I always liked about Will is that he never used *timi* with me"—the informal form of *you*—"always *tapai*"— the polite form, and I felt enraged. Why did she care so much about what he thought and said?

"Maya-*ji*, are you saying you don't like it when I use *timi?*"

"No, *sathi*, you can always call me what you want. It's just that it shows he respects me by using *tapai*, that he doesn't think I'm a little person."

"Do you think I think that?"

"No. It's different with you," was all she said, keeping her eyes on the river coming down the valley. They flicked once in my direction, and I felt certain for the first time that I had disappointed her. That I, too, wasn't exactly who she hoped I would be.

Late in the afternoon we crossed the river at a narrow spot on a wobbly log, and entered the long, low-slung, ramshackle town of Pheriche, covered in fog. Originally a yak herders' seasonal encampment, it was now a bleak strip of trekkers' accommodations lining a single, wide street in a tundralike landscape. Most of the lodges were closed for the monsoon, but at the far end we found a few that were open and settled on the most promising, largely because the boulder in front had been recently painted blue and white, with the name "Om's Home" on it. Maya and I got a windowless room in the plywood building, and went to have tea where we found a couple members of a British expedition, both men in their sixties, on their way to Everest Base Camp as part of a medical expedition studying altitude sickness.

They were exhausted and aching, and Maya, turning on her charm, cheered them up with little songs and her ragtag English. They asked me all about how we knew each other and said they had never met a Nepali girl like her.

"She's so modern!" the older one marveled.

We stayed the next day and night, because it was hard enough breathing without going higher. Maya showed me which pine bushes made the best incense when dried, and we collected several bagfuls. I took a bunch of film that day, some of the two of us using a self-timer as we sat on the roof of an abandoned yak herder's hut in the silvery fog, and many, many of her alone. Through the lens of my Nikon (an F2 that I was pretty satisfied with), I could see things I hadn't when we were face to face. It was like the camera showed me an eerie palimpsest of who she had become over who she had been: gestures flickered behind gestures, expressions glimmered through expressions. When I pulled the camera away, the layering vanished, and the friendship took over.

On the road the next day, she said, "You know, Katara Naak reminds me of a German man who stayed with my family for a couple of weeks when I was a little girl, maybe eleven or twelve. He was going to climb Ganesh Himal, and every day he would talk and joke with my mother, saying that when he came back he was going to take me away and make me his wife. My mother always laughed and said, 'How much will you give me?' I was afraid she was serious. One day I went down to the river to get some water, and he was bathing. He was the first naked man I ever saw, and when he saw how shocked I was, he laughed and laughed. Then, when he left, he walked up the trail a few minutes and suddenly ran back and knelt before me on one knee and kissed my hand. A few weeks later his friends returned and said he died on the mountain."

I asked her if it was the same man she told me about when we first met, who had the marker on the trail north of her house, the one I thought of as her first foreigner.

"Yes! You remember," she said, and got quiet again.

Had she wished him dead so he wouldn't take her away, and then felt guilty when he died? Was this why older foreign men were so irresistible? We even passed a young, smiling British guy on the path that day who tipped his felt hat as he went, and she asked, "Why can't I meet someone like that?" I thought, *Because you don't talk to people like that.*

When we were just a couple hours from Lukla, we met Katara Naak at a teahouse. Again, he told us how foolish we were to leave Tengboche, and I just nodded. Inevitably, we shared a lodge, dinner, and the flight back with him, but in Kathmandu I said we'd take our own taxi.

Maya said, "You know, last night, Katara Naak asked me why you don't like him."

"What did you say?"

"I said, 'Don't think that. She is shy.'"

"But I don't like him."

"*Bichara,*" she said. "He's all alone. He has no wife. His children are far away."

"Yeah, but he has his video camera."

"Sure, I know. Still, I think he's lonely."

"Maya," I said a little impatiently, "it's not your problem that he's lonely."

"Okay. I understand," she said. Not that she agreed.

THAT NIGHT we got gussied up and went out to the Airplane Dance Club—through an unmarked door below street level in Thamel, to a big dark room lit with black lights that made my white shirt glow violet, along with the unfortunate spray-painted graffiti on the wall that said *Raper's Night.* We were almost done with our lukewarm Carlsbergs when I heard a familiar voice say, "Hallo, girls!" It was Katara Naak. I was sure this was Maya's doing, and I could have throttled her, but she just grinned and *namaste*d him. He sat down, rubbing his big hands together on the table as he asked, "So, how do you feel after your trek? You must be very sore?" I just looked at him. I really couldn't believe he still wanted to chat. "Do you want to dance?" he asked.

"I'm really tired," I said.

"Maya?"

I watched them go, and soon after, a Nepali man asked me to dance. I did, but after a little while all I wanted to do was go home. When I told Maya, she did a funny little wiggle and said she'd meet me there. "Okay. Be careful," I said, and she planted a kiss on my forehead.

When I got up to use the bathroom around six she wasn't back. I was worried, but there was nothing I could do, so I got dressed and went to pick up fresh milk from the corner shop. The raggedy fields on either side of the muddy road were damp and sparkly, and the rough-and-tumble landscape made me feel melancholy. Around eight, Maya found me having breakfast and reading an outdated *Kathmandu Post*.

"Hi, *sathi*, I'll be back in one minute," she said, waving as she disappeared into the bathroom to take a shower. She came back toweling her hair. "We danced all night, and then I went to a friend's house nearby to sleep, but she didn't have a phone for me to call you."

I poured her tea and dropped bread in the toaster. "Maya, it really doesn't matter to me if you slept with him." I said. Was it me she didn't trust, or everybody?

She laughed loudly. "Why would I sleep with Katara Naak?! He's too *moto* for me."

"Okay," I said, turning back to an article about Prince Charles's impending visit to Nepal. "Where are you going to live when I leave in a few days?"

She seemed perplexed by the change in subject. "I think I'll stay with my friend Laxmi." I suggested she go check in with her to make sure it was all right, and we could meet for dinner at the Hilltop Restaurant in Patan. It was nine a.m. I had good-byes and errands all day long, and I was already looking forward to the glass of wine I knew they'd have there.

THAT NIGHT, sitting in the big rattan chairs outdoors at the restaurant, looking out at the glitter of the city lights, Maya said, "*Sathi*, I have to tell you something. Please don't be mad, but I do some *na-raamro kaam*, bad work."

"No, I won't be mad." I braced myself for the inevitable, glad she could finally tell me.

"I collect hash and sell it to a German guy, but he's not here during monsoon. That's why I don't have any money."

Hash! What a great idea! I felt relieved to the point of being delighted by the news. Maybe she'd even sold Piotr some. "I think that's fine. I mean it makes sense. How else are you supposed to make money?" I felt proud of her that she was so resourceful. And I felt so hopeful that she could tell me the truth.

"You always understand me, my *sukha-dukha*. You are my best friend," she said for the first time since before she went away with Will, and reached forward to take my hand. As she did, the locket she always wore with her mother's and her brother's pictures in it fell open. Her brother had been replaced.

"Who's that?" I asked. It was a tiny, faraway picture of a man standing on a boulder.

"Oh, it's Mickey. I saw him today on the street. So when I came home I put his picture in. He looked so sad."

"I thought he hit you so hard you had to go to the hospital?"

"Please don't get angry, *sathi*. It doesn't mean anything. I'll take it out in a few days." She pulled her legs up into the chair, leaning away from me.

"Promise me you won't let him hurt you."

"*Kassum*, I swear!" she said, and pressed my hand to her forehead, and I held it there.

At the airport a couple of days later she tried hard to refuse the money I gave her, which wasn't much more than eighty bucks' worth of rupees, but I said, "What am I going to do with rupees in America?" I felt hesitant to give her more, to be just like all the other Westerners in her life. But eighty dollars would maybe cover a month's rent or come in useful, at least until the hash guy came back from Frankfurt.

PART 3   DEMOCRACY

(*No translation*)

1998

Nine

I would love to say that after I left, I was an exemplary friend, a pitch-perfect role model for round-the-world friendships, especially in a time when e-mail was not that common and the person I was friends with and I didn't share a written language between us. But I can't. I wish I could say I regularly wrote letters in care of friends in Kathmandu who could track Maya down and translate for her, and sent cassettes and useful presents, like a Gore-Tex jacket and running shoes, or even just fun ones like sunglasses and a CD Walkman. I wish I could say that in the face of realizing how much more I had than she did, I didn't flinch with the guilt, but was generous and helpful and kind.

What I can say is that I didn't forget about her. I thought about her a lot. For one, I worried, because she was leading a life I didn't completely understand or know how to fix, let alone from far away. And for two, I laughed. I remembered how she called Will *Sé Makas* and made fun of herself on the dance floor at the Airplane Club.

Then there were the photographs I took of her on our trek, which turned out to be the best work I'd ever done. When I came back to New York, knowing I was not part of Generation K in Kathmandu, I rented space in a darkroom right away. The contact sheets from the Everest trek in particular looked good, and as I leaned over the developer in the red light, watching the images appear, I thought, *Who are you?* I wanted to call Nick, but didn't. I showed them to my boss instead. He helped me choose the best ones to submit, and in December, I got a call from a journal I liked saying they wanted to publish them and include them in a group show in New York in the spring. It was the first recognition I'd gotten outside of school. They were the Maya pictures, and when the editor sent me the layout with my short essay, I was amazed to see all her many faces. I sent Maya a small album of prints from my visit, but I couldn't send her the essay being published. I couldn't quite show her that this was how I saw her—this vulnerable, this change-able—or not through the mail, anyway. I would bring them to her in person.

So I felt close to her in one way, but at the same time we were barely in touch. It was strange to think of her so often and to have no idea of what was going on. Part of it was that I refused to call Will—I was still mad. Then, late the following spring, just before the group show opened, he called me, and I was relieved. He said he was in town, that he had a gift and a letter from Maya, and we made a plan to meet for coffee at Caffe Dante in the Village, my choice this time.

After I read the letter he had written for her, I asked, "What does this mean: 'I was sick in my *mon*, but now I'm better'?"

"That's what I wanted to talk to you about." Apparently, she had only just gotten the album I sent, because a couple of months after I left, Maya attempted suicide with an overdose of sleeping pills. I thought of her carefully ripping open each individual foil pouch of the pills to make a pile large enough to do herself harm. A neighbor found her, and after having her stomach pumped, Maya went back to live with her parents.

"Her parents? Why?" I asked, and pushed away the plate of flaky pastry, the custard tasted gluey in my mouth.

"I don't know. She wasn't there more than a month or two before she got sick of it and came back to Kathmandu."

"You've seen her?"

"Once. She's living with friends I've never met, a Sherpa couple. She doesn't want anything to do with me, it seems, which is maybe healthy."

I had planned to show Will the Maya pictures, and I had them in my bag, but then I didn't. It didn't seem right when Maya hadn't seen them yet. I didn't even mention the show.

I didn't hear from him after that for a while. Maya sent a letter with an NYU student she met in Kathmandu. She was living with Mickey and sent a snapshot of the two of them in Thailand—she didn't look well. She said she had e-mail now, and we exchanged a few of those, but I couldn't ever forget that someone else was sitting beside her translating and the immediacy was lost. Meanwhile, my photographs of her were republished in a book and got me into the School of Visual Arts' MFA program.

Then, during my last semester, Will called me up one warm spring day when I happened to be home. I had no reason not to have dinner with him at a Thai place on Second Avenue around the corner from school, so I went.

I recognized him across the restaurant, but he looked different—older, but not just by years. Yes, it was true: He was a little squidgy around the edges, as a friend of mine liked to say, his blond hair darker, his jaw less sharp. But it was something in his eyes, an uncertainty that I wasn't used to. He stood up and kissed me on the cheek. None of that old friction was there, and after we ordered Singhas and curry, he told me Maya was in Bombay working in the red-light district.

Something dropped in me and fell a long way. "Are you sure it's true?" I asked. What if I had focused on her more last time I'd seen her, less on the pictures, less on me?

"You can never be sure. Kathmandu is the same gossip mill it's always been. But I haven't seen her for months, and everyone tells me the same thing."

"Do you think I could find her if I went?" A plan was forming in my head. If it was true that she was in Bombay doing sex work, it could just be a detour, not necessarily her final destination.

"Find her?" He tilted his head at me. "I don't know. Bombay isn't a place I know much about, except that, what, thirteen million people live there? Finding one girl living under the radar? I'd say it's optimistic, but then, you and she do have some sort of karma together. We all do, I suppose." I was surprised to hear him say it because I felt the same way. Will wasn't my friend anymore, and yet I wasn't surprised that he was still in my life.

I immediately started planning a trip. I had a teaching gig lined up at Pratt in the fall and freelance photo research that would wait for me. If I sublet my apartment on Avenue A and Third Street for the summer, I thought I could swing it. Then I got word that a modest grant I had applied for came through, and I bought my tickets the same day, into Kathmandu and out of Bombay, leaving ten days after I graduated.

Will was in Kathmandu, but I didn't even ask about staying with him. Instead I booked a ten-dollar room at the Kathmandu Guest House in Thamel, which turned out to have its own kind of charm—a garden café, big skeleton keys for the doors, and my own pigeonhole at the front desk with a *Kathmandu Post* waiting for me every morning. The other guests were older than the backpacking crowd—thirty-something American couples adopting Nepali kids, artists, and people working there for a few months. I was completely unbeholden to anyone in Nepal for the first time, and suddenly I felt like I could see the city for what it was. I still loved the low rough-and-tumble skyline composed of leaning buildings and temples, whose shapes reminded me of elaborate, winged hairdos. I loved the dinging-bleating-rumbling of the streets, the buzzing of scooters swerving around the rickshaws swerving around the cows. Monkeys visited the flat rooftop outside my window daily, and the street boys in Thamel with their cheeky grins implored, "TigerBalmmadam? TigerBalm? Verygood-verynice-goodpriceforyoumadam!" I liked being jostled and stared at and spoken to, compared to the salmon-swimming-upstream sensation of living in New York. But at the same time, something seemed changed and deeply wrong since I'd first spent time there. Before, when people said, *ké garné*, or "what to do?" it sounded philosophical and good-natured. Now it sounded bitter and helpless. It was understandable, too. Friends with good middle-class jobs struggled to afford the necessities, like modest school fees for their kids, let alone all the stuff being advertised on the hundred stations of satellite TV. (My first visit, the two stations broadcast Pakistani sitcoms, a homegrown *Gong Show*, and the *Mahabarata* series from India.) Granted, a lot of that stuff on TV made my own life easier, but there was something obscene about bombarding people with images of washing machines and luxury cars when most of them didn't have flush toilets and sometimes electricity. Government corruption went unchecked as parliament members passed self-serving laws like the one that exempted them from having to pay taxes on imported cars. Even NGOs were suspect: Money poured into the country. NGO workers drove SUVs and sent their children abroad for school, and nothing at home changed—not the roads, the literacy rates, or the potable water situation. A day didn't go by that people didn't talk about the U.S. visa lottery.

On top of that, the monsoon pounded the city each day,

leaving its streets lakelike and its buildings sodden. Everything around me looked mud speckled and unkempt, and I often did too, depending on what time of day I went out. A few days after I arrived, the garbage workers went on strike, so that trash rotted in slimy piles on the street. City officials predicted an imminent cholera epidemic. At the same time, Internet cafés and cell phones were everywhere. Huge TV screens in every restaurant alternated between World Cup matches and the unfolding Monica Lewinsky scandal. When neither of those was on, there were music videos, the BBC, Hindi films, C-SPAN, cartoons, dim-witted American sitcoms, and a barrage of colors and jingles vying for people's hard-earned rupees. The country had jumped from agrarian to electronic, skipping a hundred years of industrialization on the way, and it gave Kathmandu a kind of postapocalyptic feel.

A few days after I arrived, Will said he'd pick me up to go to a new restaurant in the southern part of the city, in an old Rana palace (of course), where they actually served farmed brook trout (I'd never had fish in Nepal), mixed salad (also rare), and wine. I told him I was still planning on going to Bombay to look for Maya, and that I'd begun making contacts with as many NGO people as I could in Kathmandu to get names of people in Bombay. He suggested asking journalists here for names of journalists there. "You know how it works," he said.

"So what happened the last time you saw her?"

"She showed up at my place in early January, after being out of touch for months, and said she desperately needed two and a half *lakh*, which is more than four thousand dollars. She couldn't tell me why, but she said that her life was in danger if she didn't come up with it."

"In danger?"

"I didn't know if she was lying, or if the danger was real or imagined. I didn't have it anyway, but even if I had, I wasn't sure I wanted to get mixed up in whatever mess she was in.

"Then she asked how much I could give her without knowing what it was for. I said about five hundred dollars, and she argued me up to seven-fifty. She said she'd be by in a couple of days to get it. A week went by, and next thing I knew everyone was saying she had gone to Bombay, and unless you're the prime minister's niece who's a Bollywood star, there's only one reason a Nepali girl goes to Bombay."

"Do you think she went of her own volition?"

"I have no idea, but she seems too savvy to be duped." I had to find her. It didn't matter how long it had been. I wasn't supposed to be sailing forward while she sank. That wasn't our deal. On the way home, two teenage boys with Kalashnikov rifles stopped us at a checkpoint, and I knew I had to get out of there.

I made my rounds to friends' houses for *dahl baht*, to NGOs, and to bars to see what I could find out. A handful of people mentioned Bombay. At one place, a congenial, slightly drunken man named Lobsang told me to meet him at Fire and Ice, a pizza and cappuccino place, the next day. He said Maya was his girlfriend for a while, but he couldn't leave his wife. When she asked him for the same amount of money that she had demanded from Will, he said, "I couldn't give her that much, not all at once anyway, without my wife suspecting where it had gone." He shook two packets of sugar, tore their corners simultaneously, poured them in an espresso, stirred vigorously, and drank it in one swig.

"So where do you think she went?"

"She had a couple of friends who worked on Falkland Road, and she said she hoped to stay with them. I told her not to, that I could get her a job at a friend's store, but I never saw her again."

With this information and a list of contacts, I got on a plane for Bombay a little more than a week after I arrived, fleeing the city and its increasingly fetid smells.

FROM THE MOMENT I touched down in Bombay, I felt I was in the right place. My seatmate, a marble importer who was anxious to see his nine-year-old son, generously offered me a ride in his Suzuki SUV to my guesthouse. I was staying in the out-of-the-way neighborhood of Colaba at the southern end of the city, and I took his beneficence as a good omen. The area, with its grand old pastel houses in colonial style, their facades cracked and streaked in moss beside heavy-boughed trees, reminded me of New Orleans. My room at Winchester's Guest House (only the name wasn't Indian) was simple but clean—four high white walls, a full bed, a ceiling fan, and a little table—with tropical bugs and birds that twittered and clicked outside the window.

The next day, first thing, I walked a few blocks to the

Gateway of India to take a bus tour of the city to get my bear-
ings. But when a private guide stepped forward and said he
would take me to the same sites *and* to the red-light district
(the bus wouldn't), I hired him. After the Gandhi Museum, the
Jain Temple, the Hanging Gardens, and the spot where thousands of men called *dhobi wallah*s did laundry for the rest of
the city, thwacking the hell out of clothes and linens in individual concrete stalls, we drove through the heart of one red-
light area called Kamathipura and onto Falkland Road.

The driver pulled over, and the guide hopped out to get me
a Coke and a cup of tea for him and the driver to split, while I
sat immobilized in the backseat. I opened the door and made
myself put a foot on the curb, but couldn't go any farther. In
the soupy heat, in the face of what I saw, I was unwilling and
unable to move. Nothing prepared me for this, no photos or
articles or testimonies. I had known details for years about this
place, and yet, to my chagrin, I was stunned and terrified by
what I saw—even more so to think Maya was here somewhere.
I thought of myself as someone who had been initiated years
ago to India's extremes, so that I could maintain a kind of equanimity, but I had never before encountered here or anywhere a
whole self-contained subculture based on degradation.

All along the wide street for as far as I could see, women,
girls, and transvestites stood in open doorways of crumbling
four- and five-story buildings with sagging shutters and barred
windows. Wearing grimy, once-bright saris and *salwar kameez*es
and painted-on makeup that melted down their faces in the
wet heat, they looked sad, sleepy, bored, angry, indifferent,
defeated, and occasionally something approximating happy.

The youngest of them couldn't have been more than thirteen or fourteen, and some of the youngest were Nepali. These girls in particular looked dead to me, with their caked-on makeup and spidery lashes. Boys and men sauntered down the sidewalk, arm in arm or holding hands, as they did here, and the girls made kissing noises or clicked their tongues as they passed. But there was not even a trace of the seedy glamour that the old Times Square or any other red-light area I knew about (real or cinematic) possessed. I thought of the journalist in her sixties whom I met at the *Times*, who had lived and worked happily for ten years in Delhi, and who told me when she took a tour of Bombay's red-light areas that she went back to the hotel and threw up. "It's a city without a conscience. The whole thing should be razed," she said.

I sipped the Coke through a tiny straw, my heart racing, and thought, *I am an idiot*. Here I was, an outsider, thinking I could just casually walk in and find my girl, and that the thugs, the *goondah*s, wouldn't mind if I trifled with their business or brought the threat of attention. It was part of the myth I lived with Maya, that only good things would come to both of us if we stood by each other. I didn't even know what I would do if I found her, but I knew she wasn't supposed to disappear into the maw of a billion people and die of AIDS in a dirty slum.

When the guide took my empty bottle back to the tea shop and said we would be leaving, I was relieved and demoralized. I had been in the streets and lanes and eaten in people's humble kitchens before, so why did this make me shake? Here was *teeming* India, the word I swore I'd never use about the place.

Back at Winchester's I took a lukewarm shower in the shared

bathroom down the hall, spying through the open window a pretty, gated, and empty park behind the guesthouse, with its lush lawn, tall palms, and flowering bushes. I ordered tea to my room, put on clean clothes, and went out to Colaba Causeway, the main drag, to find some dinner. By the time I'd eaten a *dosa* and drunk a fresh lemon soda at a veg restaurant, I decided that I had to use my camera if I wanted to find Maya, I couldn't just wander the lanes calling out her name. I had to have a reason to talk to people. Not to mention the fact that I had been given a grant of a thousand bucks to take pictures, so I'd better take them. But I didn't want my camera or my face to get smashed, which seemed like a possibility in a place where I wasn't sure any of the codes of behavior that I knew applied.

In the next week I set out to meet people who might be willing to introduce me to women in the red-light district. They worked at advocacy centers for the women, right in the heart of the red-light areas. And while everyone I met was very polite and informative, they couldn't have been less interested in my hanging around to meet women who came to literacy classes or to pick up their kids from child care, much less taking their pictures. As one woman put it, her even smile intact, "Don't you think they've been exploited enough?" Clearly, my fellow journalists, photo- and otherwise, had not made the best impression, and I got it: These organizations had too much trust to uphold with the women and nothing to gain by my curiosity or what they might have even called my voyeurism.

Sitting in the backseat of a gold-and-black Padmini taxi sedan on my way back to Colaba, I, too, questioned my motives. How much did I want to save Maya, and how much did I want to take pictures? I wanted both: to be a good friend and a good photographer. I wanted to know that what I had started eight years ago, when I was twenty, had not only not gone horribly wrong, but had a larger redeeming purpose of showing this place to the world. Maybe if I could actually find Maya, she would end up being my guide, I thought, as the car sped along the water on Marine Drive. When the gallery show opened she could come to America and speak about her experience. It was fantasy. I knew it even as I clung to it.

Finally, at one journalist's urging, I just went by myself. "You'll see," she said. "They can be very friendly." She gave me the name and address of an ayurvedic doctor on Falkland Road, whom she said might be helpful, and I got on the train at Churchgate and took it to Grant Road in central Bombay, sitting in the ladies' car, where I watched a band of *hijras*—that is, the eunuchs and transvestites—harass people for money.

I walked along a main artery toward Falkland Road, clutching the address of the storefront clinic. The journalist had said, "He's more honest than most of the quacks there, and he knows a lot of Nepali women." But as soon as I turned onto the street itself and saw that long, wide avenue lined by women standing in open doorways, I felt terrified and prickly all over. I ducked into Delhi Durbar, the famous restaurant across from the Alfred Theatre, ordered a Coke (my madeleine), and watched the street from the open-air side of the restaurant under a fleet of ceiling fans. I wanted to figure out how things worked a little, how not to get into trouble immediately. It was a little past midday, and not as many girls were in doorways, and the flow of men on the sidewalk was thinner too. Even the traffic of cars and red double-deckers, rickshaws, and carts was less than the other evening. I ate a little *dahl* and rice and went outside, encouraged by the fact that the restaurant interaction had gone well.

But on the street I was afraid again. I knew the clinic was just a few doors down and that broad daylight had to count for something, but I decided I wouldn't make eye contact and that I'd just slip through the passersby, as if that would render my height and red hair invisible. I peered up at painted wooden signs for the doctor's name while trying to keep an eye out for the ominous puddles of black ooze between the paving stones of the sidewalk. I walked a couple hundred feet without seeing the sign, then back, and again, still not seeing the clinic, at which point a loose gaggle of boys ambled by, and one reached out and grabbed my breast. I gasped, and they laughed as I tried to keep walking as if nothing had happened. A minute later I saw the clinic, which was closed until five. I could jump in a passing taxi and flee, or I could take a deep breath and stay. But if I stayed I had better stop being terrified. I lifted my head and shoulders from their hunch and started walking down the street, slowly now, looking people in the eyes and smiling. If I didn't embrace my obtrusiveness, this would never work.

"*Namaste*," I said, lifting my hands up to a group of Nepali girls in their late teens standing in front of a house. "*Sanché tapaiharu-lai*, how are you?" I asked, and they giggled and elbowed one another. One offered me a stool and another an orange. Where was I from? What was I doing there? These girls, unlike others I'd seen on the street, were well fed and not overly made up. The fact that they could talk to me meant something. But when the madam came out and sent two girls inside with customers, I got up to move on. Next, some *hijra*s invited me to sit with them and talk in their broken English and my broken Hindi. (Hindi and Nepali are sort of like Spanish and Italian in their similarity to one another.)

"Husband?" one asked eagerly.

"No husband," I said, and they nodded sympathetically and insisted I drink a Thum's Up, the local Coke, an expensive treat for them that I didn't want but drank anyway. They clucked over my pitiable chest and skinniness, pressing their fingertips against the freckles on my face and arms, always a source of mystery and slight disapproval here, as if they were an affliction.

One waved her hand at my T-shirt and baggy cotton trousers and said, "Next time, a skirt!" and I agreed. Though, of course, I didn't mind being androgynous here and as much outside the arena of desire as possible. A slightly disheveled *hijra* arrived with her sari falling off her muscular shoulder, looked me up and down, touched my hair with distaste, and frowned. "I fix!" she said, and I dug my brush out of my bag. I winced as she yanked my hair back and clipped my barrette over a browning string of jasmine flowers, their too-sweet smell hovering over me. She walked around to examine her handiwork, chucked me lightly under the chin, and said, "Okay, Indira Gandhi, you can go!"

The other *hijra*s gave me a little push out onto the sidewalk, letting me know that this one was not to be toyed with, and I hustled off into the two-way traffic across the wide street, wondering why she called me Indira Gandhi. Was it because of some unwitting high-and-mighty thing? Was my being here on Falkland Road akin to the imperious way Mrs. G. waltzed into the Sikhs' Golden Temple looking for arms—an act that ultimately got her assassinated? Was I dangerously oblivious?

Across the way, two Indian girls stood on a ledge in front of their house, about four feet off the ground. One called to me, bending down, "Hello! Hello! What is your name? Which country?" I stopped to talk to them, and suddenly they both stood up straight and went dead-eyed on me, swinging their arms in tandem. Next door, a group of children slathered in makeup looked straight past me as I walked a few feet in front of their gaze.

I was out of my depth. It was time to leave, and I walked toward the corner to get a cab. I heard hurried footsteps behind me, and a man pulled up alongside me and asked what I was doing there. I told him I was a journalist. Did I want to go to the movies and dinner he asked? No thank you, I said, and he answered, irritated, "Be careful, or you could get raped and killed doing what you are doing!" I sped up, grabbed a taxi, and poured myself into the backseat of the jouncy sedan, trembling as I bounced along toward Colaba. I was bigger than him, but, still, his words underscored my feeling that I really didn't know what the hell I was doing.

I went back to my room to recover with tea and a shower before venturing out to an air-conditioned Chinese place on

Colaba Causeway, where I ate lots of bland, shiny mushrooms and miniature corn on the cob, and when I paid the twelve-dollar check, I was aware that it was what a girl who did well made in a night.

I was shaken by my recent visit, but I knew I didn't stand a chance of finding Maya if I didn't start spending a lot of time on Falkland Road. So I decided to try one last official avenue and tracked down a doctor who had once been an AIDS star in Bombay, the first to give out free condoms and run education programs in the red-light areas. I knew he had fallen out of favor because he was too self-promoting, but I thought because of that he might be the one who would actually help me. In fact, when I finally found him in his down-at-the-heels office at a remote corner of the Sir JJ Hospital grounds, this was the case. The beleaguered doctor said I could ride in his condom distribution van and that his worker would introduce me to some of the peer educators.

I was amazed when I recognized some of the women and *hijra*s from my last trip just walking down the street. Maybe Falkland Road was more like a village after all, especially when you got into the subset of Nepali sex workers. The social worker introduced me to two Nepali women, one circumspect and polite, the other extremely talkative. When I got out the journal with my photos of Maya in it, the first one glanced and said she didn't know her. The second one, named Seema, looked hard and said, "I don't know, but I will try to find out. She looks like this now?"

"I don't know. It's been four years."

Seema pointed to the house she lived in and told me to come visit her in a few days with the photo. I gave her some copies I'd already made. I felt hopeful at the thought of an ally in the red-light district, although I wondered if maybe she just wanted a friend.

I asked the good doctor if I could accompany his man again, and when he said simply no, I decided to try going by myself once more.

At Seema's house, the *gharwali*—her madam—didn't seem too pleased to see me, and told me Seema was out running errands.

"Are you Nepali?" I asked. She almost certainly was.

"No," she said in Nepali. "I'm from Japan."

"So how come you speak such good Nepali?"

"Just from visiting there as a tourist, like you," she said.

I nodded and moved on, saying I would stop by later. I ended up sitting on the stoop of another small house with only two girls and a madam, and a little boy. They spoke Hindi, so it was hard to have anything more than a pidgin conversation, but there was goodwill. I was calm. I felt I was beginning to understand a bit more of how things ran here.

When I returned to Seema's brothel she told me she was busy and that I should come back another day. I crossed the street, disappointed, when I heard a whistle and turned. A Nepali girl, maybe twenty, sat on a high stool outside her house in a long-sleeved blue blouse, jeans, and little black boots. She had a sly, mischievous look on her face, a kind of "who, me?" expression, and her whole demeanor—clothes, hair, posture— was inexplicably fresh and unrumpled in the dripping heat.

I asked her if she was Nepali, and she said no and grinned. Her name was Manisha, like the Nepali Bollywood movie star—didn't she look like her, she wanted to know? Everybody said so. Yes, I said, and it wasn't a total lie. She had some of the first real charm I'd seen on Falkland Road, a kind of sparkle that transcended her circumstances. We sat outside and she asked me what I was doing. I told her about Maya and wanting to take pictures. I didn't feel I had anything to gain by hiding my purposes with this girl, and she wasn't fazed by any of it either. I asked where she was from in Nepal and she told me. She said her real name was Shanta and showed me the tattoo of it on her inner forearm, partially burned off with cigarettes.

She was part of a house of three, and the other two, Tulsi and Kalpana, both Nepali, were inside playing cards with some other girls. They each peered out to get a look at me without saying anything. All in their twenties, they seemed to run the house themselves, unlike anyone else I'd met on the street, and when I came back a couple of days later, the three of them invited me to sit on the high bed in the front of the narrow house in the heat of the day. They showed me their favorite stars in their gallery of head shots on the wall, ordering me tea and soda I couldn't refuse. They reminded me of Maya, the kind of girls she would have been friends with, and even though they didn't recognize her, I thought they were the right kind of girls to be spending time with.

A couple days later I arrived just before the monsoon started. We sat inside the narrow room on the high bed with the flowered curtain closed across the doorway, and they all said they were there by choice. No one had lured them unwittingly into this life. They all sent money home to support their families and educate their siblings. None had fathers, so they wouldn't have had dowries to marry, which explained why they were here, too. They all talked about moving back when they were "old—maybe twenty-seven or twenty-eight" and buying a house one day.

I realized they were a trio of archetypes: Manisha was the obvious glamour-puss of the three; Tulsi the practical one and even a touch maternal, who took care of the money; and Kalpana was the sweet girl-next-door. With them, I quickly began to see that not everything was the scary chaos that I had first imagined, that there was an order to their days and codes of behavior. When the little girl from a nearby house toddled over, Kalpana scooped her up on the bed and they spoiled her with a packet of cherry Bonkers candy. Each day at dusk a holy man came by with a burning censer, and Tulsi handed him a few rupees for him to swing it into the house, filling it with perfumed gray smoke. A few times a week one of them came home with fresh garlands of marigolds or jasmine wrapped in banana leaf packets to drape over the religious icons.

The way they got ready at dusk reminded me of being in college on a weekend night, the music turned up, everyone trying on one another's clothes, borrowing makeup. Then evening came, and I listened to them bargain with strangers young and old to get a full dollar-fifty for a trip to the second bed behind the first, separated by a curtain. Once, after the first bed swayed with the second one's rocking, Kalpana came out after the man, tugging her long scarf back into its proper place over her shoulders with a look of concentrated distaste before she looked up and beamed us a smile.

On my third visit, Manisha asked about my camera, and I got out a point-and-shoot for them to play around with and the used Leica I'd bought just before grad school for me.

"It's gold?" they asked when they saw the brassing around the edges. When I told them no, they turned their attention to the simpler one. I said I would develop whatever pictures they took.

"And will you make them big?" Manisha asked. They liked the published photographs of Maya, not because of my style, but because they were so much larger than the three-and-a-half-by-fives they had of themselves from studio visits.

As for my Maya plan, I always carried the journal with the photos (the pages were now wilted and gray at the edges) and showed them to tea boys and shopkeepers nearby, but no one knew her, or maybe no one wanted to admit it. Some days, after being on Falkland Road and speaking Nepali for the better part of the day, I was too tired to think about it. I was taking pictures now, and that was important too, I told myself. But I was lonely in this city of thirteen million. Writing e-mails helped a little, and so did reading and watching the occasional chaste fifties movie on the tiny TV on my dresser (movies with twin beds for married couples who wore extensive pajamas). But I needed some distraction besides Falkland Road, besides the seawall walk in front of the Taj Hotel, and *Titanic*, which I'd seen twice at the Regal Cinema up the street.

I'd browsed the bookstalls and the clothing stores on the causeway, wandered through the nearby fishermen's neighborhood, where people shat in muddy fields a mile down from the five-star Taj and used ladders propped against the houses to get to the open-walled room upstairs. Once when I went too far into the alleyways, a man looked down at me and said, "You can go."

There were a few cafés where other foreigners hung out, and I talked with some of them, but everyone was always passing through Bombay as quickly as possible. I'd been invited out to dinner by an Iranian "businessman" staying at the cheap hotel next door (I declined). Still, I was tired of the square girl's life, and of spending so much time alone.

Flipping through my Lonely Planet guidebook for the umpteenth time, I saw that the Upstairs Room down the street was a decent club, and, it noted, a good place to check out high-end prostitution. I could distract myself and do research at the same time. I dashed out to a clothing store called Bright Idea! and bought some cheap, trendy clothes—a pair of men's jeans that were almost long enough, a flowery blouse in psychedelic seventies colors, and a little silver jacket. I wore them out of the store and crossed the street to find a pair of strappy, high-heeled sandals, and ate a *thali* at the bustling veg restaurant around the corner from the hotel before heading back.

When I looked in the mirror, I laughed at my long limbs in the wrong-size clothes—I looked like a marionette, but never mind. After reading a little (I didn't want to be too early), I drew a red bow on my mouth, mascaraed my lashes, twisted my hair into an updo, and powdered my freckly shine. I waved down one of the nearby idling taxis, and the driver's once-over let me know I'd achieved the desired effect. Any kind of sexy would do, even if the whole outfit was slightly off. The bouncer waved me in up the stairs, and inside the dark, mirrored club where lights flashed and spun, I found a stool at the bar and ordered a gin and tonic—it was Bombay, after all.

"Excuse me," I heard, and turned to see a very thin man with a very thin mustache, slicked-back hair, and a long cigarette in a holder dangling from the corner of his mouth. "I just wanted to see your face. You aren't the singer from that *Titanic* movie, are you?"

I nearly choked. "No," I said, wondering if all white girls looked alike, and thought of my seatmate on the plane coming from Kathmandu who had told me good-naturedly, "Now, Kate Winslet has a body Indian men can appreciate, not one of these anorexic types you see in most American films." Never mind that I fit into the latter category, if not by choice.

He held out the red-and-gold pack of Dunhills and I shook my head. "But you are a performer. You sing?" He had the mid-Atlantic intonations of someone who had watched too many American films from the fifties (a genre I was overly familiar with right then).

I sipped my gin for inspiration. "Not at all." I wanted to flee, but then, I was here for this exactly. I couldn't be too picky.

"That's a pity, because I am a talent scout—"

"Would you like to dance?" I asked, and he offered his arm, but I skirted it and led us toward the dance floor. Then I melted into the crowd gyrating to the techno remix of Bollywood stuff, letting it swallow up my dance partner.

I switched from man to man as I made my way around the dance floor, but the only one who looked at all intriguing was one who didn't dance. He was about my age, maybe a little older, sitting by himself at a table crowded with drink glasses, and surrounded by empty chairs draped with jackets and bags. I kept an eye on him and decided that when he started dancing I would go over to him, but he never got up. His friends came back to the table to smoke or finish a drink. They leaned in confidentially to talk, and he always looked pleased to see them, but never sad when they left. I thought about sitting down and introducing myself, but I felt like a fool in my clothes by then, and when I finally got up the nerve, he was gone. My original friend, the "talent scout," approached, and I fled like Cinderella at midnight. In a moment, I was down the stairs and out the door when I heard someone ask, "Do you want this car?" It was the same man I'd been watching all night, his hand resting on the roof of a taxi. His voice was slightly hoarse and his accent absolutely American. I stopped, wondering if he was really talking to me.

"Oh, yeah. Thanks," I said, too surprised to think of anything else. I was about to get in when I saw his cane and stopped. "Sorry, no, you should take it."

He smiled as if I'd said something else entirely. "Or do you want to go have a bite around the corner?"

I slid out from behind the open door, buttoning my silly jacket over my too-small blouse. "Is anything open?" He closed the door, and the taxi screeched as it pulled forward looking for a real customer.

"My friend's father owns Mondegar. We can sit in back while they clean up."

"Sure," I said, glancing at his cane, despite my effort not to.

"It's fine. I can't dance, but walking isn't a problem." It was a handsome mahogany cane, antique, or at least old, and if I hadn't looked down I would have barely been aware of it. It was his right foot in a beautiful, black Italian-looking shoe that appeared almost useless, striking in someone who otherwise had so much physical grace. Maybe because of my silvery jacket, I felt as though there were little showers of sparks coming off of me—if I could take his arm, he might be a kind of lightning rod. But I didn't.

After we'd rounded the first corner, he said, "I'm Karsan."

"I'm Alex. Nice to meet you," I said, trying to mimic his ease. "You're from the States?"

"From there, no." He laughed. "I can't imagine being from there. I'm definitely from here. But I've lived there since I was nine, in Seattle when I was kid, and in L.A. since I was an undergraduate. I write screenplays." Of course he did, but he didn't remind me of anyone else, least of all Nick (now long gone, banished even, but in a cupboard of my memory still). Nick, though able-bodied, was one of the most awkward people I knew, physically and otherwise. I always found it funny that I played the suave one when we were together, all grace compared to his off-putting shyness, which he insisted wasn't snobbery.

As we went up the steps of the café, Karsan gently shooed away a couple kids tugging at our clothes, and they fell back, as if his cane and bad foot gave him a certain authority. At the heavy wooden door Karsan waved through the etched and ornamental glass, and a waiter let us in and showed us toward the back.

"What about you?" he asked as we walked.

"I'm from New York. I'm a photographer."

"You make it sound like a question."

I laughed. "I hope it's not, but I'm still in the early stages, or not where I'd like to be, I guess." It was true. I needed something to show for this trip. The Maya photos were old news now.

"And all that whirling-dervish dancing back there——"

"Oh, God! I'm so embarrassed."

"No, you were fun to watch. You don't seem to worry about looking cool."

"Thanks, I think." As if I weren't sure it was a compliment. Karsan ordered us *pakora*s and *ganga jamuna* shakes, my favorite.

"Let me guess: You've taken on some very ambitious subject here, which you're up to your eyeballs in and not sure you can see through to the end. Street children?"

I shook my head.

"Laughing clubs? Bollywood? *Hijra*s?"

"You're getting warmer."

"Prostitutes?"

"Yeah. Nepali in particular."

He asked why, and I gave him a generic answer about how people were so focused on them as victims that no one really seemed to see the girls—whether trafficked or having migrated by choice in search of work—as people. I didn't feel like telling him about Maya yet.

"You look pained. Are you making any progress?" he asked. The food arrived. I shrugged. "A little. How about you? What are you doing here?"

He told me that he was staying with his grandparents along with his mother, sister, and her toddler son for the summer. His father had died a little over a year ago, and he was working on some Bollywood scripts while he was here. "The whole industry is ridiculous but fun. I can act like a complete idiot if I want, and nobody cares."

"That's hard to imagine," I said. He was so soft-spoken and collected.

He smiled and pushed the *pakoras* toward me. "Eat. You look like you've been on serious rations."

As I ate and we talked, I realized that what I was truly hungry for wasn't romantic attention but company—someone who read books and saw movies and watched C-SPAN. What about the fact that Monica's deposition was now being sold in bookstalls all over Bombay as pornographic reading? (A new taunt I'd encountered was a man simply giving me a knowing look and saying, "Beeell Cleenton, Moanika Looowinsky!" as if that said it all.) I had spent so many hours on Falkland Road with the girls in a kind of easy but circumscribed camaraderie, I'd forgotten what it was like to have real conversations about things outside their world. They had their friends, suitors, crushes, and secrets, while I had e-mail. I tried to paint vivid pictures for faraway friends, but here was someone in the same city of gangsters, film stars, and fundamentalist Hindus; of children who begged for boxes of powdered milk supposedly to feed their infant sibling, but which they then sold back to the store for cash to give to their brown-addicted parents; of air that smelled of fruit, incense, excrement, cooking oil, trash, the ocean, wet pavement, and diesel fumes; of the daily cacophony of Bollywood songs, hawkers' cries, honking horns, devotional music, animals bleating, and broken mufflers. Here was someone who was caught in the same soaking downpours and breathed the same air, so humid it threatened to become water at any moment. There was so much I didn't have to explain, and it wasn't long before I told him about Maya, about looking for her and not knowing what to do next. The waiter told us they were closing up, and Karsan paid despite my protests.

"Don't be so American," he said, handing the waiter the money. He hoisted himself up with a small wince and asked, "So do you think you'll find her?"

"I don't know. With each day that passes, I think so less and less."

"And yet, you know the people and the place better and better each day. Maybe that's what it takes." I was touched by his optimism.

"Maybe." The two children were waiting for us outside, and now Karsan gave them a handful of change. When they turned to me, with their long-lashed, shining black eyes, he told them to go away, and they scampered off. We passed beggars asleep on the tabletops used for wares during the day. A raggedy-haired girl climbed to her feet from a darkened doorway and put out her hand.

"One rupee?" she asked sleepily. I gave her five, and she sat back down on a piece of cardboard where her younger brother was sleeping. The Gateway of India glowed in a halo, of fuzzy fluorescence in the evening mist. A noisy group of Chanel purses, high heels, and tight jeans stumbled past us, and Karsan steered me out of their way. At the flashing blue neon sign for the club, an SUV pulled forward, and Karsan said, "My driver can drop you off at your hotel." Had he actually been waiting for me with the excuse of the cab before? It seemed hard to believe.

It wasn't far, but I accepted his offer and gazed out the shaded window from the chilled car while Neil Young played at a low volume on the stereo. I had goose bumps from the AC and suddenly felt tired. "Here it is," I said as we glided up to the darkened guesthouse.

Karsan asked if he could call me, and I gave him the hotel card from my wallet and said, "Room thirty-one." I didn't ask for his number, waiting to see if he would offer it.

"Alex what?"

"Larson." The driver opened my door.

"How long are you here for, Alex Larson?"

"Another month."

"Good." He put out his hand. "See you soon, I hope."

"Me too," I said in my best placid voice, as I stood where the humid night air clashed with the brisk AC of the car. I didn't look back as I walked up the paved driveway toward the hotel and past the clean lobby of chipped and colorful tiles. All the young boys who worked there sat lined up on the long, springy couch watching an action movie on the TV hung high in one corner, and they barely gave me a glance. I liked the idea of so many people awake and alert while I slept.

 Ten

One day I arrived at Falkland Road later than usual, at dusk, just when everything was getting going, when the heat of the afternoon had lifted and business was starting to pick up. There was anticipation in the air—how much money would be made tonight? I went directly to "my girls'" house, where I sat and stood on the bed, and generally wriggled around trying to get shots of them getting ready, dancing to loud music as they combed newly washed hair, brushed their teeth, and applied lipstick, powder, rouge. A boy I'd never met before with a carefully coiffed pompadour and wearing a spanking white jacket and pants, *Saturday Night Fever*–style, came in. He put his arm around Kalpana and asked me to take a picture, since they were getting married. She stood stiffly beside him, and when he left, said, "He loves me, but I don't love him." When they were ready, Tulsi opened the curtain and took a stool outside, and we all waited in the lavender light of dusk, where everything seemed to float a few inches above the ground—the candy-colored buildings with their glowing doorways and windows, the stream of cars and pedestrians. Even the weary gaze of the hash addict squatting on the stoop next door, her bloodshot eyes lined heavily in kohl, seemed less bleak in the twilight. I was suddenly hungry and dashed across the street to buy crackers before business picked up, at which point leaving the stoop would feel like jumping off the bank into a too-swift river. As I ducked into the doorway of the store I ran smack into someone and reflexively excused myself in Nepali.

"It's okay," came the answer, also in Nepali, and we looked at each other. She was a tough, lean girl, pretty in a hard way behind a face of overpowdered, broken-out skin.

"Maya?" Could this really be her? I'd almost forgotten I was looking for her.

"*Sathi.*" She placed her hand on my cheek gently, a surprising gesture, as if she expected me to be there. The Indian man next to her plucked a thread from his shirtsleeve.

"You're so skinny. *Ké biyo?*" I asked. It was as though all her curves had been stretched into long, sinewy muscles, an effect heightened by her black-and-white tracksuit (completely unlike anyone else's getup here), new white sneakers, and a tank top.

"I got strong from going to the gym before I came here. Now I'm getting weak again. What are you doing here?" she asked, lacing her fingers with mine; hers felt scaly and diminished.

I squeezed her hand. "I'm looking for you."

She said something in Hindi to the guy who was with her and he meandered away, hands in his pockets. "Come back to my house."

I wanted to tell the other girls I was going, that I'd found her, but I didn't want to risk losing sight of her for a moment, so I went with her up the street to a house I'd passed many times near the Alfred Theatre, where I'd even noticed the women were Nepali, but had never been encouraged to stop. The *gharwali*, whom I recognized because of a mole nearly the size of a dime under her left eye, sat on the steps, rooted there in all her bulk, smoking a cigarette and contemplating the street.

"*Namaste*," I said, and she tilted her head in acknowledgment. Maya said something in dialect and led us inside as the *gharwali* looked warily after us. The front area behind the thin flowered curtain was busy. A group of six or so Nepali girls tugged at their clothes, twisted up their hair, dabbed on Fair & Lovely skin lightener, and put on pink lipstick and aqua eyeshadow. The colors had a kind of ringing hue in the stark light.

Maya and I ducked behind a second flimsy curtain on a string, passed a bed, and went behind another piece of cloth to a third bed that was hers, lined up end to end with the others like train cars. The air was close this far back in the narrow, unventilated corridor of a house, and I sipped it carefully through my mouth as Maya lit a candle and stuck it on the shelf above her bed.

"Sit, *sathi*," she said, and I pulled my legs up onto the high wooden bed. She laced her hand with mine again, and I noticed the chipped red polish and how her fingers were peeling. I realized I'd half hoped I wouldn't find her so that I could imagine that things had somehow miraculously turned out for the best—that she had returned to Nepal unharmed, or at least that she was working in an upscale house somewhere for decent money on her own terms.

"How long have you been here?" she asked in a whisper.

"Almost three weeks, and you?"

"About three months, I think. Did Will tell you I was here?"

"He did."

"*Tuk!*" she said, as if spitting, cursing him.

"I think he was worried about you," I said.

"He doesn't worry about anyone but himself. He's a 'Cheap Charlie.' He wouldn't give me any money. And you came here just to find me?"

"I wanted to see you. But I've also been taking pictures." I thought that if she knew I had plans to try to get her out of here, she might disappear.

Maya looked at me with an expression I couldn't read, and then we heard the adenoidal breathing and heavy footsteps of the *gharwali*. She appeared from the next room, blocking the little amount of light, and the two of them had a rapid-fire exchange that I got the gist of, and I stood up. "She thinks you'll get her in trouble with the police," Maya said.

"I don't like the police," I said loudly enough for the *gharwali* to hear as she walked away.

As we said our quick good-bye, Maya whispered in my ear that I should come back in two days at three o'clock.

"She won't be mad?" I asked, and she told me not to worry.

I hailed one of the taxis trolling by and collapsed in the roomy backseat as it picked up speed and sailed out onto a larger avenue, past the blazing lights of the evening bazaars selling clothing, electronics, and produce, and past the towering Gothic train station that I still thought of as Victoria Terminus, even though the Hindu fundamentalists had renamed it Chatrapathi Shivaji Terminus, or CST. Just beyond it we turned onto a grander avenue I never learned the name of, because of the constantly changing street names (you had to navigate by landmarks), cruising past Flora Fountain, the darkened sprawling lawns and tall, slender palms of a fenced-off park, and the ornate, baubled jewel box of the Prince of Wales Museum until we reached Colaba, about a million miles from where I'd just been.

BECAUSE WILL WAS THE ONLY PERSON who would really know what it meant to find Maya, I had to call him, and the next morning I trekked up the street to the little long-distance phone office that was like a sauna inside and ten degrees hotter again inside the Plexiglas booth.

"Alex, how are you? Are you still in Bombay?"

"Yeah, I'm here." I fanned the door to get the air moving. "I met Maya on Falkland Road yesterday."

"Really?" he said in his inscrutable way. I could practically hear him nodding, scratching his cheek, as he asked me about her. I told him everything there was to tell, mostly because I hoped in hearing myself talk I might figure out what to do next. "It's interesting that she had the guts to really do it, to go there and make a life of it."

"I don't know that guts has a lot to do with it," I said. "It's pretty desperate here. I'm worried about her. She doesn't look well. I can't tell yet if she wants to stay here or not."

"I'm just trying to think. Maybe I'll come down. I'm not that busy right now, and I wouldn't mind checking out Bombay."

"No!" I said, and caught myself. I didn't want to show that I cared. "It's just . . . that's not why I called. I can handle it. I was only looking for some perspective." I was dripping now.

"It's no big deal. I'd like to see her, and it seems like we stand a better chance of helping her together than alone. You know, prostitutes often have more straightforward relationships with men than with women." God, he could be infuriating, and I had wondered why our friendship had waned.

"Yeah, no, thanks, I'm aware of that. Please, Will, I'm not sure she wants our help, or that she'll even be there when I go tomorrow, for that matter."

"Don't overthink it too much, Alex. In any case, I don't even know that I can get away."

"Will," I said, and took a deep breath. "Please, I'm asking you not to come."

"I don't think I can, but what's the name and number of your guesthouse, just in case?"

I contemplated lying, but it was bad karma, and I must have known on some level that this was what would happen. *Jé hunchha, hunchha.* "What will be, will be," the Nepalis say. I clearly wasn't finished with Will, and he wasn't finished with me, and neither of us were finished with Maya, or vice versa, whether she liked it or not.

.   .   .

ON MY WAY to see Maya the second time, I got the jitters so badly I went to Delhi Durbar for a Coke and buttered *naan* to settle my stomach. Outside, the street was clogged with the stop-and-start traffic, and I mopped the sweat and pollution from my brow with a handkerchief—a Bombay habit I'd picked up—before feeling steady enough to go.

On the steps of her building, a cracked pale green facade streaked with brown, a girl smoked a *bidi* in front of the red-and-pink flowered curtain that hung in the doorway. I asked her if Maya was inside. She gave a little shrug as a weary stream of smoke came out her nose. I took a step toward the door, and she turned and said something to someone behind the curtain.

Another girl appeared, this one smiling and wearing a royal blue sari made of gauzy fabric. "Come in," she said, holding open the curtain. When I did, I saw that there were two other girls sorting through their strongboxes filled with cosmetics and cheap jewelry on the first bed. "Sit," said the blue-clad one, patting a metal folding chair, as she hopped onto the bed again.

"Is Maya here?" I asked a second time.

"No. She went to buy some things." I looked at my watch. I was ten minutes late.

"Do you know when she's coming back?"

"Maybe in an hour," she said, which I took as very loosely true, given the Nepali concept of time and Maya's previous disappearing acts.

"Did she leave a message for me?"

"You can come back?" she asked, glancing up from trading beads with another girl.

I opened the curtain to leave and thought to ask, "When did she go out?"

"Maybe half an hour ago," the girl said—before I was even supposed to arrive. I didn't know what to make of it all and went down the street to visit Manisha and her friends. When I returned more than an hour later, Maya was standing a couple steps up from the street in a candy pink T-shirt and knee-length black skirt, with her hair up in a big butterfly clip. Her *gharwali* sat right behind her, and Maya smiled at me nervously.

"I got back just after you left!" she said. "You should have waited."

"You said to come at three," I said, wishing I sounded more patient. I had worked so hard to find her, and either she didn't care, or more likely she was ambivalent about my being here.

"I'm a little busy right now," she said, strangely cheerful.

"That's okay. I have to go too," I said, trying to act as if I didn't know I was being put off. I turned to the *gharwali* and asked, "*Didi,* big sister, when can I see my friend again?" She seemed surprised, either by my deference or my audacity.

"The day after tomorrow, at two o'clock."

I thanked her and *namast*ed them both.

I arrived early the next time to find Maya sitting on the stoop, chin in hand in the immobilizing heat. A girl in front of the brothel next door watched us with interest. I could just make out Maya's *gharwali* in the shadows inside, her gaze trained on me, but when I raised my hands to greet her, she ignored me. So I turned to Maya and smiled as if we were meeting on a street corner in Kathmandu, on our way to go get ice cream at Nirula's or go swimming at the Evergreen Hotel, instead of here, hopelessly here.

"*Namaste, sathi*, sit down," she said, sliding a straw mat out from under her for me. Then she clasped my hand between hers.

"How are you?" I asked.

"I'm fine." She continued looking out at the street, distracted despite her grip on me, as if she were expecting someone else. "How's Will?" she asked suddenly.

"I don't know. Fine, I guess, but we aren't really friends anymore." She looked at me.

"Why not? What did he do to you?"

"He didn't do anything to me, but I hardly see him, and we just don't talk much anymore." Never mind that I called him yesterday, and he might be on his way here as we spoke.

"He made my life very difficult," she said.

"How?" I asked.

She lowered her head and said quietly, so only I could hear, "I can't say right now. I'll tell you another time." She lifted her head. "Does he have a girlfriend?"

"Probably. I don't know."

"If he does," she said, "he'll ruin her the way he does everyone, spoil her *mon*." That favorite word of hers, of ours. And *bigrinchha*, "spoil," was the same word used with meat or produce, as if your *mon* were a bruised mango or a hunk of rancid goat meat. "It's like he has a disease of the *mon*. You know, I didn't sweat before I met him, and now a stink comes off me." She fanned her hand, and I laughed, not sure if she was serious. She grinned. "And what about that guy, your boyfriend? What was his name? Nick?" I was surprised she remembered it, with all she'd been through.

"That's finished! Almost three years ago I said good-bye and told him I never wanted to speak to him again. And I didn't."

"Good," she said. "Do you have a new boyfriend?" She nudged me.

"No, not really. There's someone I like, but I don't know what will happen," I said. Loneliness was part of this trip too, coming to terms with the end of a relationship with someone from school. It had seemed healthy and good for a long while, and then, all at once, it wasn't anymore. "What about you?" I knew that a lot of women on Falkland Road had boyfriends or a husband, and still worked.

She laughed. "How can I have a boyfriend here? They just eat girls' money. There is one Nepali man who is like a brother to me, but he's away. He's in the navy."

"What's his name?" I asked.

"Prem. He wants to marry me, but he has a wife back in Kathmandu who is crazy. He says she'll kill both of us if we get married." I thought of Lobsang's similar dilemma, and wondered if there were any single Nepali men who might be interested in Maya.

The *gharwali* came out and sat in the doorway, regarding us through her cigarette smoke, and we were quiet. "Do you do this work in your country?" she asked me, nodding her chin up and down at my body. I thought of how her mole and her ugliness gave her a kind of clout.

"No. I take photographs."

"At an office?"

"Yes." It was the easiest way to say it. It wouldn't make sense to her otherwise. As far as I could tell there was office work, manual labor, and this work. Period. She scrutinized me to see if I was lying. "So how do you know her?" Again, she just tipped her chin at Maya.

"We met many years ago in Kathmandu," I said.

"You didn't do this work in Kathmandu together?" the *gharwali* asked again. It was impossible for many people on Falkland Road to understand why I was here if not to work.

"No, we didn't," I said, and hoped I wasn't contradicting whatever Maya had told her. A toddler behind us began to wail in the tense heat, and I could feel trickles of sweat running down my sides under my clothes.

"So why aren't you taking pictures right now?" she asked.

"I can do that," I reached into my bag as everybody around us watched. I removed the case and cover of the Leica, but when I lifted it to take a picture of her, she raised her arm in front of her face.

"No, not me. Him," she said of the funny-looking little boy who had emerged and stopped crying at the sight of me. He had a patchy, nearly bald head, and wore a graying tank top and little lime green underwear. I started to take his picture, but his mother stepped out, holding an infant, and scooped him up with her free arm.

"Wait, his clothes are no good right now. Let me clean him up," she said, and disappeared inside. Maya cracked my knuckles one by one between her rough fingers as we waited for her to return. The *gharwali* smoked, and we all ignored the gathering crowd on the sidewalk. When the mother stepped outside again, she was in a fresh sari, and the boy's face had been washed. He wore a starched, colorful, clean shirt two sizes too big and tucked into matching belted shorts—a gift from a customer? His father? The swaddled baby had newly applied kohl under her dark eyes. Maya cooed and told the boy how handsome he was, and he turned his face into his mother's dress. The *gharwali* disappeared inside. When I'd taken nearly two rolls of pictures of the little family, the *gharwali* shifted her weight out the door. She was swathed in a canary yellow and red sari, and wearing makeup—her face powder was thick and pinkish white against her light brown skin, and her large mole was darkened.

"I'm ready to have my picture taken."

"Here?" I was surprised.

"Yes, and then inside. And then bring them to me when they're done." I would have to get these developed here after all. There had to be one good lab somewhere in this huge city.

She stood first with the family, then on her own. She leaned in the doorway and sat on the steps. A man she knew posed with her for a while, but when two boys began horsing around, insisting that their pictures be taken, the *gharwali* took us inside and arranged herself on the first bed, beside a gallery of Bollywood head shots. She called some of the girls (though not Maya, who remained outside on the stoop, perhaps to stand guard) to sit with her, until she lost her temper at them for not working. I quickly snapped a few more while she yelled. She gave me a hard look for that, but at the same time I could see she had grudgingly accepted me. I was not a threat, and I would bring her photos.

When she leaned outside and hollered for a Thum's Up from a passing tea boy for me, I knew for sure I had made progress. She wanted me to sit beside her then and tell her about myself, why I spoke Nepali, and why I was here. Maya watched from just inside the doorway.

"Are you going to try to take her away?" the *gharwali* asked.

"Why would I take her away?"

"To be a *thulo manche*, a big person. Don't white people like to do that?" She raised her eyebrows at me.

I laughed. "How could I, anyway? I'm just one person," I said.

"You can hire some people."

"I'm not going to hire anybody," I said, sucking up the last of my soda. Of course, I did want to whisk Maya away like a fairy godsister, off to a perfect life that made up for all the shit she'd lived through so far.

"She causes me a lot of problems, your friend," the *gharwali* said, and Maya walked outside.

"Really? Like what?"

"She doesn't like to work, and she's always complaining, getting the other girls upset. It's a wonder I don't just throw her out." The *gharwali* took the empty bottle from me and stood up. She called out to Maya, who appeared in an instant.

"You two can go out tomorrow afternoon," the *gharwali* said. "But you have to be back before five o'clock."

MAYA AND I sat on opposite sides of the cab, not speaking for the length of Falkland Road.

"What's going on?" I asked as she studied the lineup of *hijra* houses at the end of the street.

"I want to go home, and my *gharwali* knows that."

"She won't let you?"

Maya sighed. "No. I owe her a lot of money."

The car jounced down one of the big avenues, past endless stores with dusty displays and sun-faded posters of everything—toilets, sandalwood, auto parts, skin lotions. "How much?" The expanse of dirty sea opened up before us— someone's old slop water stretching out to a gray horizon.

"Forty thousand rupees." About a thousand bucks. Not the same debt she'd had in Kathmandu.

"Why do you owe her so much?" It was an amount that could take her a few years or more to pay back.

"I came with a *dalal*—a trafficker—which was stupid, because I could have come alone. Then I borrowed money from my *gharwali* to send to my parents because my father was sick again." Whether this was true or not, I didn't really care anymore. However she wanted to make sense of her life was up to her. I did wish I were in a helicopter at the moment, or more specifically hanging from a rope ladder attached to a helicopter, James Bond–style, and that I could just airlift her out of this. I didn't even care if my rescue fantasies made me consummately American.

"Is money the only problem? I can help you with that." I was learning finally, after all these years, that sometimes it was just about the money.

"No, because another girl came with me. She's in another house, down the street, and we promised each other that we would go together. She owes her *gharwali* a lot of money too."

"Will you tell me when I can help you?"

"Sure, yeah." She turned her head to look out the window.

At the beach, to my surprise, Maya insisted on paying the driver, and we crossed the busy street to the expanse of dirty sand and walked down to the lapping waves, prettier up close. The stretch of curved sand looking out over the Arabian Sea that was Chowpatty Beach was an unexpected soft spot in the hard city, like the depression of flesh at the base of a collarbone just below the neck. The beach wasn't pristine, but there was something hopeful about this open space, the fact that anyone could come for a breath of relatively fresh air—in contrast to the fenced-off parks I kept noticing. We took off our sandals and walked into the water, where we held our cuffs up just over our knees, out of reach of the small breaking waves.

Keeping her eyes on the muzzy horizon, Maya said, "The truth is, I came with a guy, because he said we could buy clothes in India and take them back to Kathmandu to make money. I knew about trafficking, but I thought I could trust him, and I needed the money after a boulder dropped on our house in Tatopani."

"What?" I wondered if she was joking.

"My parents were asleep with two other guests in the house. At around one in the morning a boulder dropped off the cliff and smashed half the house, but no one was hurt. Now they live in Ngyak and don't sell *raksi* anymore. My father has bad problems with his lungs and has to go to the hospital a lot. Then the man I was supposed to be buying clothes with sold me to the *gharwali*, and I felt so stupid. I refused to work, and she just laughed and kept me locked in a small, dark room, shouting at me through the door until I said I would. I told her I would kill myself, and she said, 'Go ahead if you want to.'"

It was unlike Maya to be so duped, and I wondered if this was just the version of the story that put less blame on her. It didn't really matter. "I know there's not much work at home. It's hard to be a girl and earn money there," I said.

"My father always told me that I didn't bring them enough money, not like the other children who left our village. I told him if he wanted me to earn money, he should have given me an education, because what can I do?" she asked as she loosened her hair, long again, from its elastic so that it fell like a curtain in front of her face and whipped around loosely in the breeze. I saw tears trailing through the powder on her cheeks. It occurred to me then that she might be in trouble beyond what she would tell me. I put my hand on her shoulder and she sniffed. She was so restrained compared to what she'd once been. "Come on. Let's go sit down," I said, and we went back to the beach and tucked in together under a cheap purple umbrella that I carried everywhere because of the monsoon. "*Sathi*, we can figure it out. Please don't cry."

"I still haven't found out what happened to my brother's body. That was the real reason I wanted to come, and I wanted to find a priest who could do *puja* for him. Then I would have some peace, even if I wasn't happy. I would know that at least I was a good sister. Still, I don't know if he was buried or burned or put in the garbage."

Her brother had been dead nine years, a low-caste Nepali student in one of India's biggest cities. The chances of the police being able to tell us anything were pretty much nil. "Maya-*ji*, don't you think your brother would want you to go home instead of doing this work? Can't you do *puja* there?"

Tears were still flowing silently down her cheeks. "If I go home now, after doing this work and not finding out what happened to him, how can I face my parents?"

A group of young boys ran hollering past us, splashing into the sea, shouting and laughing. "Do you want to go to Nepal?"

"I do! But I need to bring money with me. Also, I don't know what I'll do if I go back. Here I can get money from a lot of different people, and I don't have to worry about having one boyfriend. Also, no one can say anything about me here, because we are all the same. We're all sinning together."

"Could you do this work in Kathmandu?" At least she would be in her own country, and I had heard that there was a lot of prostitution in Kathmandu now, mostly run by agencies where you could choose a girl from a book of photos and she would meet you at an arranged time and apartment. It wasn't ideal, but it had to beat this.

"I can't. I know too many people, and they will tell my parents." I wondered what her parents thought she was doing now. It was four o'clock, and we got up to head back. A cluster of policemen at the edge of the beach gave us long looks as we passed.

When we saw the *gharwali* with her arms folded over her chest on the brothel steps, Maya said in a whisper, "Come again another day, *sathi*," so I went down the way to see Manisha and the girls.

A little past nine, I began to feel woozy beyond the usual tiredness and decided it was time to get out of there. When the taxi deposited me on the corner, I stopped to get a Sprite, thinking it might settle my stomach, but an hour later it geysered up out of me with impressive force. At times I felt I was watching someone else being sick all night long, sitting on the toilet and puking into a bucket at the same time. Too weak to go out the next day, I swung between teariness (at the thought of my own death and at Maya's predicament) and resignation that for now my body was not my own.

On the third day I was beginning to wonder if a doctor

might be a good thing, just to confirm I wasn't dying. Then my phone rang, and the man downstairs—an older queeny type named Mr. Subramanyam who had given me disapproving looks each time I saw him, ever since I tried to get my room rate lowered the third day I was here—told me there was a Mr. Will to see me. I couldn't believe it. Didn't he have better things to do? I said I would call back in ten minutes when I was ready for him to come up. "Yes, madam," Mr. S. said in his way. I was never sure if he was mocking me.

In a little fury, I made the bed and opened the window and turned the fan on high to blow out the sick air. Then I changed and washed my face, by which time I felt like I was going to throw up or faint or both. But I called to say he could come up. I could get mad later.

When I opened the door, Will looked like health embodied, tan and golden. There was something dazzling about him again that was not the case the last time I saw him in Kathmandu. I sat down on the bed.

"I feel awful," I said.

"You're all skin and bones, Larson. What happened to you?" he asked, pulling up a chair as I lay back.

"I thought this bug was on its way out, but I feel terrible." He checked my forehead and asked my symptoms, and I told him the gory details. Black tea arrived, and he held the cup near my lips, making me sip.

"That's all I can do," I said. I was worn out.

"It'll pass. It happens to all of us. Why don't you rest?" he said, and pulled a sheet over me.

"Maybe just for a little while. I think I'm almost better," I said, vaguely aware of him turning down the fan. A wave of gratefulness washed over me as I slipped beneath the surface of sleep, raised only by the cold compresses and sips of water Will insisted on. Every time I woke up I expected him to be gone, but he was there reading a book, writing, or once, with his back to me, meditating. Somewhere in the murky sea of sickbed thoughts, I thought, *There is something good here*.

When it was dark outside, he said he would be in the room across the hall if I needed anything, and wrote down his room number, repeating, "Thirty-two, thirty-two," as he walked out.

All the next day and evening I was sicker still, and Will woke me up at intervals insisting I drink a muddy, bitter herb water. It was nice to be taken care of, and a huge surprise that it was Will doing it. He had been kind and occasionally generous in the past, but I'd only heard about this kind of caretaking with him. It was as if he sensed that I was about to give up on him entirely. Of course, I had known he might come when I called him, but if and when he did show up, I thought I'd be in charge. I'd found her. I knew this city better than he did, but here he was shepherding me out of my wretchedness.

By the time I woke up early the next morning, whatever had been swimming like a mean little beast all over my body had quieted. I looked in the mirror above the dresser: My skin was broken out and my eyes were dull, but at least there was a trace of color in my cheeks, and I didn't feel like I was going to fall over just from standing up. I called for toast and tea and began to organize my bag, suddenly feeling a little frantic that I might have lost Maya. I hadn't been to Falkland Road for nearly a week, and it was the only thing I wanted to do. When Will found out where I was going, he asked to come with me.

"Maybe you could come tomorrow?" I didn't feel totally clearheaded, and I wanted to check with Maya before I brought him. I was afraid the sight of him might drive her off.

"I'd really like to go today," he said. I was indebted to him, and I had only myself to blame.

In the springy backseat of the bulbous taxi sedan, he asked, "Do you think there will be trouble?"

"I don't know," I said, and then, when we were in the heart of central Bombay but before we reached Falkland Road, I asked the driver to pull over.

"What's wrong? Are you sick?" Will asked.

"No. I just want to know. What are you going to do?" The bony black shoulder of an ox appeared outside his window. Someone honked behind us.

"Madam?" the driver said, and I peeled off twenty rupees.

"I hadn't really thought about it. I thought I'd see what the scene is like. I thought we agreed: Maya's in trouble; it seems like together we could help her." It was his sweet-talk tone.

Even if what he said made sense, I felt on edge, and I could hear the panic creeping into my voice as I said, "We didn't agree. You know I'm grateful to you for taking care of me, but I told you not to come. She may freak out when she sees you. She doesn't really consider you one of her allies."

"You know how dramatic she is," he said.

"Besides which, she implied that you had something to do with her being here."

"And you believe her—as if she hasn't lied to us since the beginning? Alex, did it ever occur to you that I might actually care about what happens to her? I simply thought it might take two people to bring her back to a place where she could even recognize herself."

I felt embarrassed, though not entirely convinced, as I stared at the back of the driver's head and his short, oiled black hair. Will was right. No one had appointed me the rescuer. "Okay, you're right. I'm sorry."

He put his hand over mine. "Don't worry about it. It's nerve-racking, I know. However glib I may seem about it, I don't want her stuck in some hellhole. I feel responsible, not wholly, but enough. I thought I might as well try."

"*Chalo*, let's go," I said to the driver. He glanced back at me in the mirror, and I looked away.

MAYA WAS leaning against the cracked wall outside her brothel, scratching her ankle and looking listless in jeans and a white ruffled blouse. She didn't see us get out of the cab, but when she did, she pulled herself upright.

"*Namaste*, Maya-*ji*," Will said from the sidewalk. "How are you?"

"*Tuk!*" She spat in his direction. "Don't come any closer."

"Why?" he said, taking off his sunglasses. Maya's *gharwali* stood beside her now, and I saw her searching the assembled crowd around me, probably looking for the *goondah*s who protected the brothel. Maya whispered something to the *gharwali*, and then said to me simply, "You can go."

I turned around and left. I had betrayed her by telling Will about her, and I felt sick as I walked down the way to see the other girls. I found them inside their house with the curtain drawn, sitting on the first bed chatting. It was so much easier for me to accept their situation as inevitable and bearable, compared to Maya's. I hadn't played any role in their demise, and I didn't know them before, what they might have been.

OUTSIDE THE HOTEL, I found Will's darkened window without looking for it. I listened at his door, but no one seemed to be there. I was tired but too agitated to sleep, so I changed, put on lipstick, and went to the Upstairs Room. Karsan had never called, which was disappointing, but what could I do? I looked around for somebody I knew in the smoky, mirrored crowd, but there was no one. Then I saw Maya on the dance floor. I hardly recognized her in her low-waisted blue jeans and baby blue T-shirt that said in gold cursive, *American Girl*. She wore almost no makeup—at Will's bidding, I was sure—and danced with a kind of abandon, lost inside the music. Gone was the bashful girl at the Marine Bar a few years ago. I stood behind a mirrored pillar as I watched them: Will with his face flushed and dreamy, slow-moving in his mellow, outdated style despite the fast beat. Then he stepped back to watch her dance on her own with an almost paternal look on his face.

Maybe he did have a more straightforward relationship with her than I did.

After a beer at the bar, I got up to go back to the hotel.

"Alex?" I heard on my way out, and turned to see Karsan finishing a drink five seats down. I gave him a low-key wave, and he got up to meet me. The truth was, there was no one I would have rather seen at that moment, but I was wary. "Are you leaving?"

"Yeah, I'm worn out," I said, but I didn't move. His handsomeness had something princely to it, more effete than my usual taste, and I noticed again his feline smile and the way his black hair curled against the caramel-colored skin of his neck.

"Can I give you a ride?" We were standing at the top of the dirty white marble steps leading down to the exit. It was almost ten days since I'd first met him.

"No thanks, I could use the air," I said. As we walked down the stairs, I listened to the soft rubber-tipped thud of his cane and his feet on the steps behind me. Outside, he gestured to a motorcycle that a street boy of about thirteen was guarding.

"I've got my bike. Are you sure?" he asked. "I'm sorry I didn't call. I've been caught up in family stuff."

"Don't worry about it," I said. The boy rolled the bike over, a Royal Enfield. Even to my untrained eyes it was pretty.

"You sure you don't want to go for a spin?"

"Where?" It did sound better than my guesthouse room.

"Wherever. Around. The city's nice at night."

I shrugged and waited for him to swing his bad leg over before I got on. We took off helmetless, which was a stupid idea, but safety was the least of my worries, and the great rush of wind was a tonic. Along the water the air tasted sweet without the usual traffic. Karsan's silky locks tickled my nose, and his neck smelled warmly of almonds and sweat as I curved my body around his jean-jacketed back and squinted at the night. We followed Marine Drive all the way around, down the length of the Queen's Necklace, the string of white lights along the water, as it narrowed into a little street and then ended at the ruins of an old fort surrounded with blooming shrubbery. He took my hand as I got off the bike, and I felt like a kid in the face of such easy elegance. We climbed a stone wall just higher than my head and kissed. His hand on my bare hip felt electrically light as he moved it to my back and over the ridges of my spine. Wordlessly he let go of me and eased himself down the wall to where his cane waited. I was about to jump down, but he stood before me.

"Are you holding me captive?"

"I want to look at you."

I smiled, pleased to be admired. Since Will arrived, I had felt his tenderness and impatience, but never his regard. I would always be too *something* for Will.

"Will you take off your shirt?"

"Let me down first," I said, thinking of creepy-crawly things and passersby, though we seemed to be alone. He moved out of the way and I jumped, landing in a crouch, pebbles in my palms. He stepped in front of me and gave me his hand.

"Now will you?"

"Here," I said, as I unbuttoned the top half of my blouse and reached around to undo my bra and slip it off through a sleeve. He pushed the collar away and kissed my neck. Stones and patches of damp moss pressed through the thin cotton of my shirt as his hands found their way around me and down my sides, and then before I knew what was happening he made my knees go weak. I laughed. "Oh, well, okay, then." He rested his forehead on my shoulder, breathing softly, and we turned so that he could lean against the wall as I pulled at the worn edge of his T-shirt and then at his belt. He looked up at me and smiled, as if surprised to find us both here together, in the same corner of the universe.

"I should take you home and let you sleep. You've been sick."

I told him I felt better than I had in a while. "But yeah, it's probably a good idea." All I wanted was to tangle myself up with him under the fan's thumping spin, to lose track of where I ended and he began.

Afloat in the current of air, we barely said a word until we pulled up to the guesthouse on the other side of the city maybe twenty minutes later. "I should go," he said, keeping the engine on and one hand on the accelerator.

"Of course," I said. What was I thinking? This was India. This was Karsan. I wasn't entirely sure he existed, except for the night watchman's curious stare. We kissed each other hastily on the cheek, very continental and chaste, before Karsan took off down the empty street. When I turned to go inside, I saw the lights on in Will's room and shadows moving behind the frosted glass.

. . .

"*SATHI! SATHI!*" Maya shouted through my door the next morning, pounding with her fist. "Get up!" I opened the door, and she toppled me with a bear hug, smelling of green-apple shampoo and wearing another new outfit. "Did you sleep well?" she asked. Her ebullience sloshed all over everything, reminding me of an earlier version of herself.

"I did, and you?" I asked, pinching her cheek.

"Right after you left yesterday"—as if she hadn't ordered me away—"Will gave money to the *gharwali* so that I could leave for a few nights. At first she wouldn't let me. She said he was going to take me away. He promised he wouldn't, but she didn't believe him. Finally I gave her my gold earrings and bracelet to show I would come back, and she let us go. He took me shopping and we had Chinese food, then we went to a movie and a disco. It was great!"

"So you're not angry anymore?" The question of whether she actually would go back to the brothel could wait.

"No!" She picked up my hand and kissed the back of it. "I was only afraid there would be problems with the *goondah*s, so I didn't want you to be there."

"I thought you were mad at Will?"

She lowered her voice. "He's done some bad things to me, but even still, he's an old friend now."

"And you have pretty new clothes," I said. I wasn't going to spoil her good mood.

"I know!" She lifted her legs in the air to admire her pink-

and-orange-striped pants. I called the front desk for breakfast and told her to wait for me while I washed up.

When I came back from the bathroom, Will and Maya were sitting at my little table having breakfast. Sunlight poured through the barred window, making a striped parallelogram of shadow on the wall behind Will's head.

"How are you?" he asked, handing me tea.

"Fine," I said. "I stayed with the other girls I know on Falkland Road, took some pictures, had dinner late at Leopold's."

"I thought I saw you at the Upstairs Room."

I sipped my tea. "Oh, yeah, I didn't want to interrupt. You had a good time?" I could play this game of Conversation Lite.

"We met up with my business partner," he said, switching to English, cutting Maya out of the conversation.

"What kind of business?"

"Buying and selling stuff," he said, and when I raised my eyebrows, he added, "I can't say what."

"And you need help taking it back?" Was Maya going to be his mule, with gems sewn into the hems of her new clothes? Diamonds on the soles of her flip-flops? Kathmandu, now, more than ever, was a nexus for all sorts of trafficking—not just girls, but guns, drugs, antiquities, rhinoceros horns (nature's Viagra, apparently). "Please don't," I said, and he held my gaze as if he were actually considering my request. His benevolence was real, but self-interest was never far behind.

"What are we doing today? Where can we go?" Maya asked cheerily.

"What about Elephanta? Do you want to go in a boat?" I asked her.

"Great!"

"Okay, so I need a half hour," I said, ushering them to the door.

Reunited, the three of us strode into the sunny day, birds singing in the manicured tropical park behind the hotel. I felt content simply at not being left out. We sailed through the heat, past street kids and hawkers, unbothered, and Maya walked between us, holding our hands, like so many years ago in Kathmandu on the way to Shanti Gompa. Of course, she was no longer a kid and neither was I, and the three of us were no longer a trio. Now we were one and one and one, but we could pretend for a little while. As if "We-ee belong together!" like the lyrics of a song I used to listen to in college. At the Gateway of India, we boarded a small and not very sea-worthy boat just about to pull away from the floating dock, the kind I could imagine reading about in the *Times*: *A passenger ferry sank with more than fifty people drowned, two of them Americans.* I was thankful the water was flat and churned slug-gishly around us as the boat trundled off. A stink of a breeze blew over us, and Maya took my hand.

"It's like a time warp," Will said in English over Maya's head, as he stretched his arms back over the railing.

"Totally. I can't quite believe it," I said.

"Water?" Maya asked, handing me the bottle.

We rode the rest of the way in silence, listening to the loud hum of the fumy engine and the splashing of the water against the thin hull. The expanse of gray water under smogged blue sky was interrupted only by oil rigs, tankers, and refineries. Finally the green island came into view, and we docked at Elephanta's long pier.

"How pretty!" Maya said, in what I'd come to think of as her "I can still have fun" tone as we walked past the colorful fishing boats. She repeated her exclamation as we climbed the steep flight of steps to the caves, past vendors peddling fans, cheap flutes and drums, necklaces, and scarves. When she and Will paused to admire some jewelry, I kept going, wondering if the most helpful thing would be for me to defect from this pseudo-trio, so they could proceed unimpeded to do whatever they needed to. Wasn't two always more streamlined than three?

Will and Maya found me inside the main cave at the top standing in front of a two-story-high, full-breasted goddess and a stalwart, buff god.

"*Sathi*, look," Maya said, giggling as we stood before the giant black phallic *lingam*, some three feet high, hovering beside us on its platform. I smiled. It was an old trope between us, the corny sexual jokes. An Indian tourist asked to have his picture taken with me, and I agreed.

At a snack stand outside, we drank Cokes and watched the monkeys menace tourists for their food from nearby branches. An overeager young tour guide wanted to take us on the path behind the caves, but we assured him we could find our way and set off on our own. Will led us along the narrow path that cut through the underbrush as it wound around the back of ⁣ grassy hillside. Leaving the range of other touri⁣ surrounded by a tropical quiet of softly chirp⁣ buzzing insects, and soon arrived at a former nav⁣

big, round concrete hold built into the hillside, with a view of the rest of the island. We sat down. Wedging the handle of my open umbrella in a crack, I lay back as I listened to Maya and Will point out the small village, the harbor, and boats on the horizon, until I dozed off. I woke up with a start to find them gone.

"Maya? Will?" I called anxiously, but there was only a thick, sun-drenched silence in response—the air was like a sponge. I broke out in a sweat, my mouth feeling suddenly dry as I called their names again. My voice sounded thin and muffled. The sun hadn't moved very far in the sky, but they seemed to be utterly gone. I walked around the bunker to find the path, when I heard something inside. Afraid of snakes, I only leaned in the doorway and balanced on my tiptoes so I could see past the curve of wall. The close air smelled of plants and mildew, and then I saw shadows moving rhythmically against the wall, tall like humans.

I caught my breath. It wasn't so surprising, really. So why did my heart thunk so loudly in my chest as I ran away back toward the main temple area and the restaurant there? They must have known I would wake up and find them. It's not a big deal, I repeated to myself, but my eyes stung and I gasped for air as I jogged back. I don't want to see this anymore. I don't want to bear witness. If she is going to suffer, let her do it without me watching. I was headed to the dock, when I saw the tourist restaurant perched on the side of the hill and ducked in to order some food I didn't want. It arrived almost immediately, and when I looked away for a second, a monkey swooped down and stole all of the chapatis from the plastic basket. I burst into tears.

"Hello, don't cry. They do that to everyone. Take this," another foreigner said. He handed me an eight-foot pole. "Just wave it at them when they get near." I looked up at the monkey eating my lunch high in the tree and thumped the pole on the patio. "Or come sit with us if you like."

I got up, feeling grateful as the waiter replaced the basket of chapatis, and I tried to give a little laugh that came out as a sniffle. The foreigner was a homeopathic doctor from Romania on his way home from Calcutta and was staying with two young men, friends of friends who lived at the YMCA. They were the perfect respite. When the Romanian asked what I was doing there, I told him about the photography project on Falkland Road. I didn't want to talk about friends. I didn't want to be more than one person.

"Why are you so interested in this topic? What does it have to do with you?" the Romanian asked.

"I've been interested in it since I was a student in Nepal eight years ago," I said, a little unnerved.

"Isn't it dangerous?" one of the Indian men asked.

"Maybe, but I just leave people alone who don't want to talk to me."

The other man swiped at a nearby monkey, who screamed at the pole. I jumped and laughed at my own jitteriness.

"Bugger, right?" the Romanian said.

Will and Maya arrived a few minutes later, n̶
and smiling. When I introduced them all, I saw ₁

men recognize her as a prostitute right away—her casual manner, her clothes, her pidgin English, her Nepaliness. None of which would have given her away in someplace like New York, if she could ever get there. Will, clearly in a sociable mood, pulled over two chairs and ordered food for them, a beer for himself. He talked homeopathy with the Romanian, while I spoke with the other two. From the corner of my eye I watched Maya ward off the monkeys. On the boat the three of us moved away from the others and chose a place up top in the open air this time. I felt quiet, sitting cross-legged, keeping my eyes on the horizon. Maya lay back to sunbathe.

"What's up?" Will asked.

"I guess I found that all a little discomfiting back there, you guys going off while I was asleep."

"We weren't that far away. We just were exploring nearby while you had your nap, and then one thing led to another."

"Okay, but you don't love her. She still wants to be with you. Why confuse her?" He gave me his special gaze. "Quit it. I'm serious."

"All right. Calm down. I just don't think she's confused. She seems to enjoy it. She's remarkably able to live in the moment, especially for someone who's not very spiritually advanced." So he had accepted Mr. Thakur's diagnosis after all.

"I just want to know, are you rescuing her or what?"

"Of course I want to help her, but there's no reason we can't have a little fun at the same time."

Maya sat up. "Why are you upset, *sathi*?"

"Yes, why is she upset?" Will asked. "Everything's fine, isn't it?"

"*Ectum*, fine," she said, pulling me up as the boat docked with a thump. Will split off, going into the Taj Hotel to get some shirts made and said he would see us later. On the way to the guesthouse, Maya held my hand. "*Sathi*, you don't have to worry about me."

"Really?"

"My life is not your problem."

"*Timro, haamro eutay-ho gibon-a*," I sang to her. It was the line from the Nepali folk song that meant, "Your life, our lives are one and the same."

"*Tik*," she laughed. "That's true."

AT THE GUESTHOUSE there was a message from Karsan with his number, finally. I would happily throw myself into an affair with him, I thought, leave Maya and Will to themselves. But when I called he wasn't in, and the older woman who answered didn't speak English. I left a message using Nepali and broken Hindi. I had no idea if she knew what I was saying. Then Will stopped by to say he was going out and to ask if I would check on Maya later. She was watching TV in his room.

"Does she want checking up on? Besides, I might go out myself."

"So just let her know, will you?"

Not long after, she knocked. "I'm bored-*lagyo*," Maya said, sighing wearily.

"You poor thing!" I said, and she laughed. "Do yo~ go out?"

"Maybe. Do you want a massage? You have te

Will, from me. I can see it," she said. She placed her hands on my shoulders and pushed down.

I shrugged. "Okay."

"Good. Take off your dress," she said, closing the windows with their clouded glass. I hesitated.

"There's no need to be shy. We're both the same." I left my underwear on and lay down. Her strong hands were working hands still, despite the fact that she hadn't harvested a field or gathered wood for years. She rubbed my neck and shoulders, which had been hurting since Elephanta. After a while, she said, "Turn over now." I did, holding my dress across my front. She laughed. "Why are you ashamed? We're old friends." She pulled my head gently away from my shoulders, twisting it back and forth, and then I felt her breath on my face and heard her say, "*Sathi?*" I opened my eyes and her tongue fluttered into my mouth. I sat up, bumping teeth and then foreheads with her.

"No, no, I'm sorry. No," I said, quickly pulling on my dress.

"Don't worry, it doesn't matter," she said getting up. She poured herself a glass of water. I moved to open the windows.

"Wait," she said. "Close them for a minute. I won't do anything. I just want to show you something." I did, and she tugged her shirt up to her neck and pulled down her dingy bra, to show me a scattering of a dozen or more small, dark purple circles around the brown nipples.

"What happened?"

"That Nepali guy I told you about did it—"

"Prem, the one you said was your friend?"

"He was mad because I didn't want to be his girlfriend, and

he burned me with his cigarette." She looked down and poked at a few of the scars, watching them whiten and color again. "It doesn't hurt anymore."

"Why is he still your friend?"

"Because . . . because . . ." She smoothed her bra into place and put her shirt on, then crossed her arms and looked at me. "I know what he did was bad, *sathi*, but it's different here. Life is very difficult for many people. He didn't mean it."

I reached out my hand and took hers. "Can I give you money? Can I buy you a plane ticket?"

She considered our hands together. "No, there's nothing you can do."

"Promise?"

"Promise," she said, sighing. "Can we go out now?"

"I think we should have dinner and see a movie." I wanted to wait for Karsan's call, but since I wasn't even sure he would, that seemed like a bad idea, and *Satya*, or "*Truth*," was playing at the Eros and was supposed to be all about a good guy who comes to make a living in Bombay and gets sucked into the underworld.

A few doors down from the theater, I stopped to check my e-mail. I was surprised to see one from Nick among the others from my parents and friends, after two years of silence between us. It was a short note, innocuous enough, saying he'd heard from a friend of mine that I was in India taking pictures, and that he hoped it was going well, and then:

I MISS TALKING TO YOU, ALEX. I DON'T QUITE
STAND WHAT HAPPENED BETWEEN US AT THE

DON'T YOU THINK THAT THERE IS A WAY WE COULD BE
FRIENDS? DON'T YOU THINK ENOUGH TIME HAS PASSED?

"Maya, listen," I said, but when she asked, "What?" I told
her it was nothing. It *was* nothing. Nick and I would never be
friends, and we didn't have to be. I had never considered that
such a luxury before. I logged off without responding.

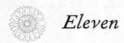 *Eleven*

Part of my slow disengagement plan from Will and Maya was
that I would get back to work. I called his room in the morning
to say I was going to Falkland Road all day.

"Why?" Will asked, as if he'd been counting on me for
something.

"I have to," I said. I didn't want to stand in his way if he
could get her out of here.

Karsan called while I was getting ready and asked if he
could see me today. I said I was busy until late.

"Call me on my mobile then, and I'll meet you for a drink
somewhere," he said.

"Can we play it by ear? Sometimes I can barely stand up at
the end of a day on Falkland Road." The truth was, I felt a
little ashamed at the thought of him.

"Why don't you come over for a late dinner? My mom's going out, and my sister's a good cook. You don't even have to let me know till later. We'll be here. I'm always up till two or so." He wasn't going to take my hesitation personally, and I was relieved.

When I arrived at the girls' house, they were playing cards on the bed, staying out of the strong sun. We all felt *alchi*—lazy. But I still had Nick's e-mail and Karsan's voice knocking around in my head, and a kind of thrumming anxiety about Will and Maya, so I took pictures. It was the one thing I knew how to do. Even if they all came out terribly, at least I had taken them.

I got back to the guesthouse around eight-thirty, earlier than I expected, and Will and Maya were out. I called Karsan, and he said in a low voice, almost a whisper, "You know, my sister's not feeling well. Maybe it's better if we do it another time?"

"Sure," I said, hiding my disappointment. "Just give me a call."

"Tomorrow," he said, and hung up quickly.

I changed my clothes to go get some mediocre pizza at a silly little place called Churchill's around the corner by myself. I needed a break from Indian food anyway; I'd eaten more *dosa*s than I could count. After I'd returned to my room, Will knocked. He looked worried, always an anomaly for him. "Come in. Is everything okay?"

"Do you have some water?" he asked, and scraped back a chair to sit down. He gulped down the glass I handed him and said, "Maya's gone."

"What do you mean?"

"I feel like a jackass, but she gave me no clue. We went off to meet my business partner for lunch at Kemp's Corner, and she seemed fine. Rational, intelligent even. I thought about how maybe she really could have a good life in Kathmandu, find a boyfriend. Then we went to the train station to buy tickets to Goa for next Thursday"—something he hadn't mentioned to me, but that was moot now. "I thought, as long as I'm here, I might as well extend my trip to include some real R and R, with Maya. But at the foreigners' window, the guy insisted Nepalis didn't count as foreign. So we went upstairs to the regular lines, and I left her there while I got us some water. When I came back, she was gone. I asked the woman who had been standing behind her if she knew anything, a proper matronly type, and she said that Maya told her she had to use the ladies' room and would be right back. I waited till Maya's turn passed in line. Then I made a tour of the upstairs hall, scoured downstairs, the platforms—I even had a female police officer go into the bathroom. But nothing. I went all through the bazaar outside. She only had about fifty bucks I'd given her. I was hoping she'd be back here."

"Is her stuff here?"

"Yeah, but she didn't have much—just clothes, a hairbrush, some beads."

"Can I see?" I asked.

Their room was much nicer than mine, spacious, with a small-scale, antique four-poster bed in the middle of a large black-and-white-checked floor—I thought of Alice in Wonderland. They had their own private bath and wooden shutters on the two windows overlooking the park. He laid out her few clothes and creams on the bed, and we figured out she had her sunglasses and Walkman with her. She could have gone back to her brothel, but why? Will had made it clear to her that he would help her. Even if she had to do some smuggling in return, I didn't think that would scare her off. Anywhere else in India fifty dollars would last awhile, but not in this city.

"How did she seem when you last saw her?" I asked.

"She was chatting away with the woman in line behind her—the kind who would normally never talk to someone like her, but Maya had charmed her."

"The one who told you Maya said she'd be back in a few minutes?"

"Yeah, but the longer I waited, the cooler she was with me."

"What was she like?" I wondered if she was a *gharwali*, or a cop for that matter, if she was complicit in any way.

"Catholic, judging by her clothes. You know, a skirt, blouse. Maybe fifty, big sunglasses with graduated lenses." She didn't sound like either a cop or a *gharwali*.

"We have to go back to the train station. Come on," I said, standing up.

Will and I split up when we got there and combed the platforms and waiting areas of the still-crowded train station for more than an hour. The ticket windows were long closed, and we asked people about Maya, showing her picture, but people either didn't know or said they didn't. After looking carefully around the stalls outside lit by candles and little lanterns, we finally took a taxi back to Colaba in silence, sitting at opposite sides of the backseat, watching the streets whiz by.

In the morning, I went to see Manisha & Co. I had updated them on Maya, and while they weren't terribly interested in her before, when I told them another friend of mine, a foreign man who lived in Nepal and used to be her boyfriend, had shown up here in Bombay, they all listened carefully.

"When he met Maya again, he took her to the hotel we're staying at. She was there for a few days, and she seemed happy, but yesterday she disappeared at VT," I said, adding the other details I knew. "We don't know if she left because she was afraid. Maybe she saw a *goondah*, or maybe she didn't want to be with my friend. Maybe she was only pretending to like him. Should I go to the police station?"

Manisha thought I should, to check the women's jail cells. "Don't go yet, though," she said, and leaned out the door. "Raju!" A few moments later their favorite tea boy appeared with a shy smile and long eyelashes. She asked me which house Maya lived in and what the madam looked like, and I told her about the large mole. I was to send two glasses of tea, one for the madam and one for Maya, saying they were from a customer who wanted to know if she would be available later. After ten minutes, Raju reported back that the *gharwali* said Maya was gone for three more days.

Manisha nodded knowingly. "I think she ran away, your friend. If she wanted to return to Nepal, why not go with your *bideshi* friend? Otherwise, why not go back to the brothel?" If she was right, there was no way I would find her. The city was made for disappearing.

I skipped the police station. Who was I kidding that they would help? And when I got back to my room, I found a note wedged into the handle of my door from Will saying, *No Maya, but news. Come see me.*

"Listen to this!" he said, his eyes shining as he let me in. He'd actually spoken to the ticket seller who'd been on duty and remembered the Catholic woman behind Maya in line. "For a hundred rupees he looked up her form. She's Jyoti Pereira, a fifty-two-year-old Indian, who apparently bought a ticket for Mira Sherpa, a twenty-five-year-old Nepali, who could be Maya, don't you think?"

"I don't know."

"They're leaving Saturday morning at eight-fifteen." That was two days away. We made a plan to try to intercept them and I was on my way out when he said, "You know I'm still going to Goa on Monday regardless, by plane now. Do you want to come?"

"Ask me tomorrow," I said. I was surprised, though I shouldn't have been—when had Will let pain outweigh pleasure in his life before?

Back in my room, I flopped down onto my square island of white bed under the ceiling fan and thought about calling Karsan, but it was beginning to feel too much like work keeping his attention, and I fell asleep. When I woke up the next day, the buildings and the quiet street outside my window glistened from an early morning rain. A tan foreign woman in a skimpy sarong and tank top set out her laundry on the rusted balcony railing across the way, while a hotel boy smoked nearby, pretending not to watch her. I stretched like a cat in front of the dresser mirror. The truth was, I wanted to go away. My skin was bad; my stomach had had it. I hadn't exercised in months. My photo project was going fine, but I felt distracted with Maya gone. Soon enough I would be be standing before a class of eighteen-year-olds, and trailing after an older, established photographer, while trying to get my own work done.

Will stopped by in the middle of my breakfast. "So, you want to come?" he asked.

"We'll come back on Friday, and I have my own room, right?" Yes, and I'd have a week after that to finish everything up. I asked him where we were going specifically.

"There's a community of expats I met a few years ago who live in Benaulim. They're very into their hash, but fine if you're not, and they rent cabanas out to support themselves. Lots of fish and fruit to eat. I think it would appeal to the anthropologist side of you. They're like a tribe that got separated from their culture twenty-five years ago."

Then he said he had some business to attend to over the next couple days, but he still wanted to go to the station Saturday morning together to look for Maya. "If she doesn't want to come with us, we can at least give her money so she can make it to Kathmandu safely," he said. "Oh, and there's a party at my friend Dimple's house on Friday night. You should come."

I said I would. It wasn't like I had any other engagements now that I seemed to be off Karsan's list. I spent the next couple of days in the red-light area, staying late and taking pictures—everyone in the immediate area had seen the photos I brought for the girls, and no one even minded about my flash now. Will and I met up to go to Dimple's party over on Nepean Sea Road in a complex of identical pale yellow concrete high-rises. When Dimple opened the door, we entered a room sparkling with people, all Indian except for us, and easily the most uniformly glamorous group I'd ever been a part of: women in silk blouses or glittery tops and blue jeans, faded just so, with long sheets of glossy black hair, the perfect color lipstick, and heavy, simple twenty-two-karat-gold bangles and dangling earrings. The men were dressed in that appealing East-West mix of long Indian shirts over jeans with sandals. Even the few with crooked teeth or bad skin made looking well dressed seem easy. It was the way they carried themselves. They were at the top of a billion-person society, the select few who lived in wealth and beauty. Why shouldn't they feel confident? Even in a new blouse and capris, I felt rumpled and tired. Will, on the other hand, fit right in like the South Asiaophile that he was. Even the way he walked had the local fluidity, whereas I felt all arms and elbows. After meeting Dimple, I went to make myself a gin and tonic before meeting Layla, Prithi, Farrokh, Ramesh, and Biff (yes, Biff), among others. They were mostly in film or fashion or computers, with an architect and a couple of grad students thrown in for good measure.

I was talking to Layla about where to buy gifts to take home when I heard Dimple greet someone with an excited squeal. When I looked over, Karsan walked into the room, and my ears filled with the low, oceanic sound of blood rushing to my head. He was slow, elegant, and unassuming in the jingling atmosphere of the room. and I could feel how people were drawn to him, like fat bumblebees to a can of beer, but I stayed where I was. A woman who was a journalist joined our conversation, and we started talking about the most reliable Indian newspapers when I heard simply, "Alex." I turned around as if I didn't know who it was. Karsan shook my hand and kissed me on the cheek, keeping my hand in his. "How are you?"

"I'm well, thanks, and you?" I asked, the mundane words difficult to get out past the cascade of emotion—part rage, part humiliation, part attraction. I wasn't in love with him, but he and Maya had both disappeared without a good-bye on the same day.

"Good. I'm getting ready to go back to L.A."

"You are? What about your projects here?"

"I can work from there, and I'm afraid if I'm gone too long I'll be forgotten." He lifted his drink with a lopsided, apologetic smile.

"Sounds like a good idea," I said, and raised my glass. I wanted to be a good sport, and there was nothing really to ask of him at this point. I liked him, but I didn't lay claim to him. I guess I only wanted him to like me back.

He turned me gently by the elbow away from the people we were standing with, and said very quietly, "I'm so sorry. I can't explain right now, but it's not personal. My situation at home is more complicated than I let on." I didn't look up, and he lifted my chin with his hand. "I'm really sorry."

"It's fine," I said, and squeezed his hand. "I'm a big girl. Don't worry about it." We turned to rejoin the merriment, and I learned Dimple was a childhood friend of Karsan's. When Karsan heard I knew Will, he said, "You do? I've been hearing about him for years. He's quite an swashbuckler."

"That's one way of describing him," I said.

"What's another?"

"Oh, I don't know. Bounder, rogue, cad. I think I'll have another drink."

He laughed and plucked my empty glass from my hand, asking what I was having. I wanted to follow him, to Velcro myself to him if necessary. I just liked him, liked looking at him, hearing his voice. I found it all very soothing, and it reminded me of what I was now, whereas with Will I felt I was forever trapped at twenty. But I looked out the window instead. When Karsan returned, he asked, "How's your friend from Falkland Road?"

"Missing. The same day you and I were supposed to have dinner. She may be leaving on a train for Delhi tomorrow morning. Will and I are going to try to intercept her before she goes. I have my doubts, though."

The vivacious Dimple appeared and said to Karsan, "Tell me about your latest projects!" as she led him to a squishy peach-colored velvet couch, turning her back to me, and I went out to the balcony and gazed out at the complex of five other tall apartment buildings with their glowing windows and vast parking lot below them. Passing headlights swept through the trees in the distance on Nepean Sea Road.

"You know Karsan?" Will asked.

"A little. Do you?" I kept my face to the breeze.

"No, but Dimple says he's here recovering from a canceled wedding engagement."

"Huh," I said, tapping out a little tune on the hollow metal railing. So that was it.

"Did you know that?"

"I knew something about it," I lied. I was not about to confide in Will about Karsan.

"Apparently it was all set for this October and something happened. Nobody knows what."

"What about you? Are you seeing Dimple?" I craned my neck. She and Karsan were still ensconced on the couch.

"No, she's a lot of fun, and we went out a while ago. We're mostly just friends now," he said. The way he said *mostly* inspired me to hit him on the arm. "Ow——"

"That was for me." I did it again. "And that's for Maya."

"Jealousy doesn't suit you," he said, rubbing his shoulder.

"Jealousy, ha!" I said, turning to go inside. "That was for decency."

As we approached, Dimple looked up at us from a small assembled group and said, "There you two are. Maybe you can set the record straight. How many people does the average

American sleep with before he or she gets married? I say twenty. Prithi says five, and Ramesh says fifty. Karsan is too old-fashioned to say what he thinks."

Will looked at me, and I shrugged and said, "Ten? Fifteen? Twenty? For some people less, and for others maybe a couple hundred or more."

"He would be a total sex maniac!" Dimple cried out. *No, he would just be Will*, I thought. "How many people have you slept with?" she asked me.

"Oh, there've been so many I've lost track," I said, and the group laughed.

"What about you, Will?" she asked.

"One or two in my youth to give myself confidence, but now I'm waiting for my one and only," he said, straight-faced.

"Liar!" Dimple threw a pillow at him, and I choked on a spicy peanut. Someone clapped me on the back.

When I looked up, Karsan was beside me, and a man's voice said, "Say, 'Money!' K-man." A flash went off.

"Ram, don't," Karsan said to the photographer. "That's the last thing I need right now." His words stung, and, afraid I'd cry suddenly, I walked away to find a bathroom to splash water on my face.

"You're too serious, man," Ram said.

"Leave him be," I heard Dimple say. When I returned to the group, I made my way over to her, ready to say good night. As she talked to Karsan, I thought how bubbly, curvy, lovely, light she was, while he was all lines and angles, the way he propped himself on the back of a couch, legs outstretched, his cane beside them. He smiled, nodding, looking down as she babbled on about something.

"Dimple, hi, I—"

"There you are. Alex, right? Will you stay and talk to Karsan? I have to go deal with the maid."

"Sure," I said, abandoning my good-bye.

Karsan motioned at the door with an unlit cigarette in his hand. "You want to come with me?" I gestured at the roomful of smokers. "L.A. habit," he said.

"Why not?" I said, hoping I wouldn't end up in tears. In the dank hallway lit by a single bare bulb, we waited for the elevator, listening to its creaky mechanics. I looked at the winding concrete stairs, wanting to run the six flights, to fly down them.

"Go ahead," Karsan said, as if reading my thoughts.

"No, it's fine." I wasn't letting him out of my sight right now. Outside, we doubled back around the building across an empty lot toward the ocean. Muffled car sounds drifted toward us, and Karsan offered me a drag.

"Only if you don't judge me for the way I can't inhale," I said. I hadn't smoked since college.

"You and our president," he said.

"That's funny. I was just feeling a lot like Monica myself."

"What do you mean?"

"Sort of like 'that woman.' Why were you so upset about the photo?"

"Oh, God, he's a society-pages photographer."

"Standing next to each other doesn't seem too incriminating," I said, as we found a solitary bench by the water.

"I'm sorry," he said. "I didn't mean to be rude."

"*Again*, you mean." The lackluster sea lapped quietly at the rubble and rocks, and the horizon was empty, save for a couple pinpricks of light on faraway boats. "Will you tell me about your fiancée now?"

He looked over, surprised. "I thought I could spare you all this, but I guess that's not fair either." I wrapped my arms around myself. "Madhuri and I went out for three years and were engaged for the last two. She's in residency to become a pediatric cardiologist in L.A., and we were supposed to be married in October, a little over a year after my father died, which we had to wait for."

"What happened?"

"In a word, she got pregnant. It's crazy, with her being a doctor, but she was changing birth control pills. We—she, really—decided an abortion was the right thing, given where she was in her career and that the wedding was six months away. She seemed so certain about it, but we began to fight after that, and we kind of fell apart. In April she moved out. One of the reasons I'm here this summer is to give us some space. But my mother and sister are ticked off at me, especially my mother, who keeps saying my bachelorhood may be the price she has to pay for raising children in America. To most people around us we looked like the perfect couple who threw it all away for no reason. That's why I got mad about the photo, because I knew my family would just start asking questions if they saw you. Their curiosity was already piqued by your calling the house."

"I never would have called if you'd told me. Why didn't you?"

"Because I really didn't think it was their business. That's one of the reasons I'm leaving. I can't bear to hear any more of their opinions on the subject. If anything, I need to talk to her now. But you—any man would be lucky to be with you." He pulled me closer to him, placed his flat palm on mine, turned them over, and held them up to eye level—my hearty Yankee hand resting on his narrow aesthete's.

"And yet this is probably it, I know. It's okay. I feel more hopeful than I did." I wasn't lying either. Even in his rejection, Karsan was one of the nicer parts of the trip, and the fact that he liked me felt redeeming, even if he didn't like me enough to change the course of his life. I looked out at the water and thought of the smugglers out there, taking shifts sleeping in their little skiffs on their way to Saudi Arabia. I wondered if they felt afraid or excited about all they didn't know about what lay ahead of them. I glanced up at the window.

"Do you want to go back in?" he asked.

"God, no. Why would I want to do that?"

"Maybe you're missing your friend Will," he said.

I squinted at him. "Do you really want to go there?"

He shook his head. "Let me try again. So what's the story with your Falkland Road friend?"

I pulled my knees up to my chest and watched the little stripe of froth hitting the rocks and dispersing as I told him everything from the very beginning, since Will first asked me to go find Maya, on the roof of the Hotel Vajra more than eight years before.

When I finished he opened his mouth and closed it again.

"Go ahead. I can take it," I said.

"I think you might be taking too much credit, or blame. It sounds like she would have left home regardless, like she was miserable there."

"But she's miserable here. Would things have gone this badly if I wasn't involved?" I imagined her working from the steps of VT as I spoke.

"You're not God, Alex."

"Just please don't tell me next that this is her karma."

"Okay, easy. I'm just saying that even if she has very few choices, and not very good ones at that, they're her choices."

"And all I'm saying is that I don't think it's unreasonable to want to help a friend who's suffering."

"Unless she doesn't want to be helped. It's a little vain to think it all rests on you . . . and not a little American."

I was pissed off, staring at the black, unvigorous sea—a lifeless body. Our words buzzed like gnats that I wanted to swat away.

"I'm sorry. I know you're upset about it. Is there anything I can do?"

"I keep having this wish, the same one I've always had, that she and I could just talk frankly. Do you have your bike? We could go for a ride."

"Come on, my little *memsahib*," he said, offering his hand. Careening through the near-empty streets, my legs and arms wrapped around his lean body in the lawless city— a tropical, decaying urbanscape, an abandoned futuristic Victoriana—this felt like another version of reckless intimacy, quick and dangerous. They both gave vent to a huge sadness.

When he pulled up to my hotel, the teenage boy at the gate

woke with a start in his plastic chair. I hopped off, and Karsan turned off the engine.

"Well, so, okay," I said. He cupped my face with his hand. I was always amazed by the extra deftness of his movements, as if making up for his bad leg.

"Alex?" he asked, but his eyes said it.

"Sure. Come on in."

I helped him pull his motorcycle into the driveway, and told Mr. Subramanyam, my guardian-slash-nemesis at the front desk, that Karsan was a friend from Los Angeles. Karsan's American accent helped, as did forking over an extra fee (though I knew I was now officially a slut in the management's eyes). Karsan looked at the elevator's faded art deco sign from colonial times that read, *Servants may use the elevator only when accompanied by children.* We took the stairs slowly—his leg was hurting him (a motorcycle accident, he'd finally confessed, when he was twenty)—and he used the bathroom on the way to my room. I poured two glasses of water and tore apart some of the fleshy pods of a custard apple.

When he arrived he took a bite and asked, "Can we just lie next to each other for a while? I haven't really slept in weeks." He spooned himself around me, and I told him to stay the night if he wanted. "I have to be home before morning," he said, and I reached to set my alarm for four. In our clothes, we lay on top of the sheets curled around each other, and he rested his palm on my chest. "Your heart's racing."

"It always does that before I sleep," I lied, and he turned me toward him in the gray dark.

His cheeks were wet, and he asked hoarsely, "Can we make love?"

I kissed his wet face, and sadness moved our limbs the way desire usually does, but more slowly. Afterward, we slept intertwined together under the clock's expectant ticking. When he left in the dishwater light of dawn, it was just a quick kiss and a bye.

A FEW HOURS LATER, Will and I barreled down the empty morning streets in a taxi on our way to the train station. In contrast to the rest of the city, Victoria Terminus was busy inside, its platforms filling up under vaulted ceilings, and flocks of banking pigeons cutting through the sunlight that streamed through high, dirty windows—it reminded me of a secular cathedral. Will and I kept one eye on the departures board while watching the different currents of passengers. Finally, track three was posted for the Delhi train, and with the help of a boyish conductor, we found a car with Mira Sherpa's name on the passenger list but there was no sign of a young Nepali woman inside the train or out. We began to ask people if they'd seen her—she would have stood out by her features—but no one had, and then, ten minutes before the train left, our conductor friend came up to me holding a Nepali girl firmly by her upper arm—she couldn't have been much more than twenty. She wasn't Maya, and she stared at her feet, looking terrified.

"Madam, this is Mira Sherpa," he said.

When he left, I told her I wasn't the police and I apologized, but she kept looking down. "I thought you were a Nepali friend of mine." People watched us from between the window bars of the train as hawkers and food vendors, porters and passengers jostled around us. "I'm looking for my friend. She was here a few days ago and bought a ticket. I thought maybe she used a different name, that she was you. Do you know Maya Gurung?" I held out a photo, and there was the slightest movement of the girl's head as she looked at it. I caught sight of Will and motioned for him to keep away. "Please, I'm afraid she's in danger."

The girl looked up with a kind of silent pleading. "No," she said.

"You don't?"

"No."

"Where are you going, little sister?" I asked.

"To my house," she said, almost inaudibly. The whistle blew, and the girl dashed into the train. I stood on my tiptoes to see if I could catch sight of her again. The train engines had started huffing and rumbling—it was all very Anna Karenina of the tropics—and last-minute passengers bumped past me to get on. Just as the train slowly started pulling away, I glimpsed the girl in the window beside an older Indian woman.

"Did you get any information?" Will asked.

"Nothing," I said, and he started to move quickly through the crowds toward the center of the terminal, dodging people who turned to watch us as we went.

"Come on. Maybe she's here somewhere." Will took the marble stairs up to the ticket counters two at a time, while I skittered behind him. She wasn't there. Of course she wasn't. I had to get to Falkland Road, I decided.

"I'll see you later," I said.

"Let me know if you find anything."

When I hailed a taxi I had every intention of going to FR, but told the driver Sir JJ Hospital in central Bombay, one of the largest public hospitals in the city, where my failed AIDS specialist had his office.

Crossing the hard-packed ground within the gates and still a couple hundred feet off from the main building—badly in need of some white paint—I ran into a hot breeze smelling of Dettol disinfectant and bodily decay. Inside the entrance, the ground floor was almost as busy as the train station, and I found a harried middle-aged man sitting at a rickety metal utility desk with a dirty beige computer and explained that I was looking for a friend who might be in the TB or gynecology units, "Or"—I paused—"maybe in HIV."

At the HIV ward, I knew I should simply ask to see the attending doctor, but no one around seemed official, so I walked through the hallways, looking in the rooms. Almost all the women were young, and many of them were Nepali. I tried to smile at the girls, to *namaste* them as I went. Many were too sick even to see me, let alone respond, and on my way out I found a nurse in a winged hat and told her I was looking for my friend.

"Your friend, madam?" she asked.

"Yes. She's from Nepal." And I told her Maya's full name.

She looked over her charts and found no one by that name. In other units no one found it either.

From there I went to Maya's brothel. I got out of the taxi at a pharmacy directly across from her house, and I stepped inside for a minute before I went across the street. I must have looked dazed, because the guy behind the counter handed me a little wooden stool, which I accepted. I could see the roly-poly *didi* sitting out front on the stoop, attentive to the street in general and nothing in particular. I reached into my bag and got out some photos I knew she'd like.

I was almost in front of her before she saw me.

"Where's your friend?" she asked by way of greeting.

"I don't know. I came to ask you." She looked like a mountain, immovable in her spot, the mole below her left eye just a stopping point before you reached the peak.

"I haven't seen her since she left with that *bideshi* man. Where is he?"

"Here in Bombay."

"She's with him?"

"She left him." The bluntness felt inevitable in this woman's presence, and in many ways, honesty was my most useful tool. "Did your *goondah*s take her?"

"No! Hold on." She heaved herself up and lumbered inside, where I heard her talking to the other girls in a sharp voice about where Maya would have gone. When she came out again, she said nobody knew anything about her disappearance. "Your friend owes me a lot of money."

"Even with the gold bracelet and jewelry she left you?" I said this loudly, so the other girls could hear.

"If you see Maya, tell her that if she doesn't come back, her friends will have to pay her debts," she said. I thought about Maya saying she had no friends in her house and doubted it was true. Maya made friends wherever she went.

"If I see her, I'll tell her," I said. "If you see her, please tell her to call me. I'll give you two thousand rupees—fifty bucks—if she does." I was desperate.

"Okay," she said, perking up. I left her poring over the pictures, looking guardedly pleased.

I tried to tell myself that if Maya wanted to disappear this much, it was her right. Maybe she was better off than I knew, more self-sufficient than I imagined, but I didn't feel good about any of it.

Later that night I was surprised when Karsan called, asking if I wanted to come out to his grandparents' bungalow in the nearby hill town of Lonavala the next day.

"What about your mom and your sister?"

"They'll just have to cope. Besides, you're only a friend, as far as they know."

I caught a nine o'clock train headed toward Pune, and almost three hours later I arrived in a damp, Dickensian train station and made my way into the muddy, ringing bazaar, where a cold drizzle had started. The only phone number I had was for his neighbor's cottage, because they didn't have one at his, and I was calling from a dirty glass booth when I saw the backs of a well-dressed couple walk by—Karsan in a rust-colored Shetland sweater and jeans and a woman in a cream-colored cardigan and long brown skirt. For a moment I thought she must be his ex-fiancée, some cruel joke, but then I realized it had to be his sister.

I stepped from the booth and called after them, wishing I had worn something both nicer and warmer.

"Alex!" he said. "What luck! I wasn't sure we'd find you so easily." We shook hands. "This is my sister, Anupama, and her son, Kamal," he said, referring to an immaculate little boy in her arms who had bright black eyes and wore navy corduroy overalls, a yellow turtleneck, and little green Wellingtons.

"Nice to meet you," she said with a lilting accent. She was maybe five years older, and she had an unreadable smile on her face as she held out her free hand.

"Our driver is down there. We were hoping to find you and then go pick up some vegetables at the market for lunch," Karsan said.

"Sounds great," I said. I hoped my exhaustion didn't show and wished I had been invited to stay the night—it was a long trip out—even though I had my flight to Goa in the morning.

"I want to buy some music for the ride back into town tomorrow," Anupama said as we passed a tented stall filled with cassettes, and we all stopped to bend over the table. Karsan and his sister discussed a few options, settling on one they loved from the seventies. A few stalls down, Kamal cried out at the array of plastic toys, and his mother bought him a hollow cricket bat and ball. The produce market, in a kind of large indoor-outdoor shed, was small, but each stall had a few good-looking vegetables stacked up. Karsan chose a couple of eggplants, some potatoes, and an onion, and then we got into a sedan waiting for us nearby.

The road leading from town was narrow and full of traffic, and I wondered if there was any place that qualified as genuinely bucolic in India to my Iowa-informed sensibility. The driver turned in at a muddy development of white stuccoed houses, minimally landscaped, with low brick walls, scrubby yards, and the occasional sickly tree. The house was part of a cluster, a "colony," owned by diamond merchant families. Karsan called to his mother when we came in, and she appeared from the kitchen area in a black wool turtleneck and a long tan linen skirt, the right kind of clothes for the damp chilliness inside the marble-floored house, compared to my flimsy printed cotton garb.

"Hello," she said, taking in my ragged appearance, and I thought how appropriate it was that the diamond merchant's daughter had a gaze that could cut glass.

"The carrots weren't any good," Karsan said.

"That's a pity. Never mind," she said, taking the vegetables back to the sink.

"Can I get you anything to drink?" Karsan asked me.

"Let's open the wine. It's perfect weather for it," Anupama said. It was delicious red wine, made in India, surprisingly, and it stopped my shivering and helped me get through the conversation, which reminded me of a modern play: witty and decorous and layered with meanings I couldn't quite make out.

"Do you know Madhuri?" his mother asked, and I said no,

but I hoped to meet her, pleased that I could respond unflummoxed. After lunch, Karsan, Anupama, and I left Kamal in his grandmother's care and went for drinks at a little resort that overlooked rolling hills of lush forests through a screen of silver rain and smoky mist. At the center of the otherwise covered patio was a swimming pool open to the sky, where sleek, chubby children frolicked, oblivious to the weather, and a man played Sinatra songs on a shiny white piano.

At six o'clock, Karsan accompanied me to the station while Anupama went to get the newspapers. "There will be lots of questions about you tonight," he said after he finagled a ticket for me on sold-out train by speaking English, a colonial holdover of privilege that he said always amazed him. "I forgot to mention to my family that you were young and pretty." In the face of his mother's and sister's smooth elegance, I couldn't have felt less pretty. He put his hand over mine on the bench between us as we sat in the gloomy dusk under a big, illuminated, dirty yellow clock. I had fifteen minutes if the trains were running on time.

"I'm going to Goa with Will tomorrow," I said, releasing the little nut of information that had been stuck at the back of my throat all day.

"If you were sleeping with him it would be none of my business."

"That's true, but I'm not. I'm just taking a break from Bombay. I'll eat some fresh fish, see some ocean and sky." The crowd on the platform was thickening under the sallow, diffuse light, the train still five minutes off.

"What about your photos?" he asked, the slightest edge to his voice. "Have you done all the work you wanted to? You must be leaving soon after you get back."

"I've actually shot a lot of film. I'm pretty sure there will be some I like, and I'll have a week when I return," I said, and stood to check the tracks. The train's single yellow eye of light approached in the drizzle. "You're going back to her, you know. It's obvious you still love her. I was just a mini escape from all your other concerns. Maybe you were for me too—if that isn't too harsh to say."

He stood and smiled for what felt like the first time in a while. "Can we at least have a beer when you get back?"

"Of course. Thanks for the day in the country," I said, joining the V-shaped crowd funneling onto the train. When I found a seat and looked out the window, Karsan was still there, hands in his pockets, the faintest smile on his lips, and we watched each other until the train pulled away.

I was exhausted by the time I arrived at VT, a little before eleven. Walking through the nighttime crowd I looked up and could have sworn I saw Maya's red-and-black Kipling backpack and her long ponytail swishing behind her, maybe a hundred feet ahead, striding toward the exit. I tried to catch up with her, but I got slowed down by all the people camped out for the night on the floor under the departure boards, and by the time I reached the outside doors she was gone. I kept heading in what seemed like the most likely direction, past the lantern-lit stalls of fruit, snacks, gadgets, and reading material, but I didn't see her anywhere.

After another circuit, I got on a bus back to Colaba and went to sit upstairs in the very front of the bus, where I felt as if I were pitching down the avenue. Halfway home, I looked down at one stop and could have sworn I saw Maya leaving the bus from the lower level—the same ponytail, same backpack, same jeans—not a common outfit here. The bus was already in motion by the time I ran down the narrow spiral stairs at the back end and shouted, "Stop! Please stop!" But the bus didn't until we were almost at Flora Fountain in front of a handful of seafood restaurants just closing up for the night. I found a taxi, but when we reached the corner where Maya had gotten off, the streets were empty, and the stores and restaurants closed. It was as if she had walked into an envelope of night air. Was I losing my mind? Had she ever been there at all?

"Fuck!" I yelled into the thick city night, and burst into tears.

"Madam? Please, madam," the driver said, clearly distressed. "You go to hotel, madam?"

I sniveled out the address, and when I got there dashed upstairs and sobbed some more, from sheer exhaustion as much as anything. It was good that I was going to Goa, where I could lie down on the hot sand and finally rest.

 *Twelve*

Of course, in Benaulim, Will had reserved a cabana with just one bed, after telling me we would have separate rooms. So I went for a walk up the beach and found another place to stay. When I told him over lunch of a scarlet-red tandoori fish and buttery *naan* that I was moving, he smiled as if I'd told him an amusing joke and said, "That's fine."

That night, Will's friends made a fire on the beach and drank Sandpiper beer. Someone with a guitar played songs from *The White Album*. Will's friend Paul pulled a hash pipe from the waistband of his shorts and offered Will the first toke. I watched from the other side of the fire, knowing I'd cough when I tried it, and I did, but the hash quickly dulled the blade of self-consciousness in me as I stared into the orange flames and took a sip of coconut water when it was passed around. I felt less racked with guilt than I had in a while, and when I went with a couple of the other women to go pee outside the ring of firelight, I fell over while squatting and started laughing so hard my eyes teared up.

"That's good. That's great," one of them said. Back at the circle, Will was getting a massage from a girl who reminded me of Audrey Hepburn if she'd been a hippie, much tanner but pixieish and wide-eyed. I got sleepy soon after and lay down to watch the flames. Will woke me up when the fire was just embers, and he and his new girl walked me to my place, making sure I got inside all right. I crawled into bed, sandy and relieved to be alone, and I slept until a damp, salty heat filled the room and the sun made bright outlines around the closed shutters.

I found Will on the beach reading by himself, a gaggle of teenage girl peddlers miraculously leaving him alone.

"Can I join you?"

"Sure," he said, and turned the page.

"How are you?" I asked in Nepali.

"Fine," he said in English, and lay back on his elbows. "So how come you don't want to stay with me?"

"You seemed to be in good company last night."

"She's leaving today. You know, I do feel close to you right now."

I looked at him. "You're kidding, right? I don't feel so close to you, and I blame you for Maya's disappearance." It was nice to be so frank with him, to really not care what he thought anymore. He was no longer the arbiter of how well I was doing here, how much I did or didn't get. He was just Will, with his charm and his foibles. I didn't need to forgive him. There was nothing to forgive.

"I know you do. But the way I see it, we were just reminding her she had other choices, that if she could take a break from brothel living, she might remember other ways to get by. How else do you help someone so hell-bent on wrecking her life?"

"I don't know. By not giving up on her? I also thought that if I could be her friend again, it might help."

"You know, she might have been just using us."

"To get what? New clothes?"

"I'm not sure. Maybe as leverage."

"She didn't do such a great job, did she?" I closed my eyes in the hot sun and listened to the gentle breaking of waves. I could feel Will's stare. It all made me sleepy.

"Henna tattoo, madam. Very lovely for you?" a girl's singsong said, and I opened my eyes to two young girls in blouses and long skirts, one with an armful of sarongs. I pulled a towel around myself and sat up.

"For your girlfriend?" one said to Will.

"She's not my girlfriend," he said. The girls looked at each other, stifling laughter. He turned back to me. "I'm just saying that she might be in better shape and know herself better than we can understand."

"For your sister," the older one said, though she clearly didn't believe it.

"Maybe. I hope so. How much are the tattoos?" I asked, and agreed to a little ornate star on my shoulder.

When they were done and walking away, Will said, "The younger one's pretty, don't you think?"

"For a fourteen-year-old."

"She's probably got a husband and kid."

"I'm not sure that makes pedophilia okay."

"Ah, you've always been tough on me, Larson," he said, running a finger down my arm, and I caught it as if it were a slow-moving fly. *Sé Makas*, One Hundred Flies, Maya had called him.

"Let's go swimming," I said, springing up, and dashed for the water. He passed me and splashed in. The ocean—so warm and flat—was eerie even this far south, especially with no one else in it, and I wondered if there was pollution or sea creatures I should know about, but Will didn't hesitate and I followed.

After swimming, my lunch of spicy fish curry, rice, and salad tasted like the first food I'd eaten in weeks. We shared a Kingfisher.

I was feeding one of the hotel mutts when Will's friend Paul set down a bunch of bananas on the table. He had a few of the others in tow.

"Is that a meal?" Will asked.

"Sure. You don't really need much here," Paul said. In the daylight you could see on their faces that their brains were fried. Their patter was funny, interrupted by song phrases and snatches of drumming on a table, chair, or thigh. Two white girls with sun-scorched dreads ordered beer and peanuts to go with their bananas. Paul told me he'd been a monk in Thailand before coming here. From what I could tell, the gang of them—I think there were eight—all seemed to have slept with one another. At least two had defected from the Bhagwan Shree Rajneesh ashram in Pune.

The next few days melted one into the next as we lived off fruit, fish, and cold—or at least tepid—beer. I washed my clothes in a bucket with the minimal water supply, sunbathed, and went on long walks. Will and I took a boat ride to see the dolphins. At six dollars a person, it was too expensive for the others. They lived on a fisherman's budget, except for the hash and beer.

Will pressed the sex issue with me, lightly, daily, and after the dolphins, I changed my mind. Something about seeing those mammals diving and leaping, with their rubbery, smiling faces, made me think, *What was the big deal?* Why couldn't sex be more like the dolphins swimming around the boat and less like the beginning of a long, impossible riddle?

"Okay, Will, you're on," I said over lunch.

"What do you mean?" he asked.

"Let's go back to your place," I said.

He grinned. "Good girl," he said, getting out money for the check.

I slugged him in the arm. "But don't say things like that."

"How about 'bad girl' then?"

"That's fine."

"YOU SURPRISE ME, ALEX," Will said, after that first afternoon in the sandy sheets.

"I'm glad." It was amazingly uncomplicated, this sex without emotion. I didn't feel like I was betraying anybody. I felt like I was completing some kind of circle. The length of our bodies lay before us in the dappled light, salted, sunned, well fed. The skin on my face and arms was tight with sunburn and hot to the touch, and I shivered under the fan's lazy draft as I watched a gecko in the corner near the ceiling, still as could be.

There were only two more nights after that, but because Will and I ended up finding his friends a little boring in their burnout routine, we'd eat a meal, go have sex, take a walk, go have sex, wake up, have sex. There wasn't a lot else to do. Karsan had called Goa "the Florida of India," and I had to agree about its beachy blandness. Will explained some basic tantra to me, and I in turn felt uninhibited around him, walking naked around the room. It was nice knowing no regrets lay ahead. Still, when I got up and started packing on Friday morning, he seemed surprised.

"You're not going to stay till Monday?" he asked, having extended his own trip.

"I told you I've got stuff to do before I leave next week."

"What 'stuff'?" he said, pulling me onto the bed and pinning me there, his green eyes flashing. "You seemed to be having a good time."

"A great time, and now I'm going back."

"What if I won't let you go?" He held my wrists.

"You will," I said, refusing to wriggle. "It's too much like commitment."

"Okay, then," he said, rolling to the side. "But surely you have time for one more?" His fingertips trailed down my sternum.

"Surely," I said. Sluttiness could be its own reward.

We went for a swim afterward. The beach was mostly empty except for some fishermen bringing in their long wooden boat down the way. Floating in the quiet surf, Will looked innocent under the clear sky, and it was easy to imagine him as the American boy he'd once been, growing up in the suburbs of D.C., part of a world much smaller than and so remote from the one he'd ended up living in. I wondered how much he'd known then, if at ten or twelve or fifteen he saw that he would one day be a man in his early forties, living in a faraway place where he could choose one pretty girl after another like prizes at a county fair, and maybe (if I wasn't mistaken) beginning to tire of that life. That particular boy was rarely visible in the man. Will, like Nick, was largely self-invented, and huge parts of who he once was had been quashed along the way.

ON THE WAY into Bombay from the airport, I shot pictures from the open car window as we passed the outlying slums where shanties were made of flattened cooking-oil tins, plastic sheeting, and cardboard, and people relieved themselves in the muddy ditches at the settlements' edges, their backs to the road. A coffin maker's shop called itself the Last Stop Shop.

Once in town, riding in the flow of carts and bulls, the gaudy trucks, and dust-caked double-deckers, we passed the endless shops, temples, churches, and mosques. I felt a surge of happiness to be back, to be on my own, and to be going home soon. The chatty driver asked what I was doing, if he could be my tour guide, my personal driver.

"No, I've been here for almost two months. I know the city."

"A long time! You are alone? No husband?"

"Alone."

"No friends?"

"Yes, I have friends. Can we take Marine Drive?"

The bay, which usually had at best a squalid grandeur, gave me a place to rest my eyes. The city was what it was. It didn't have any more to give me than I had to give it.

At the guesthouse, Mr. S. was surprisingly courteous and gave me a different room, slightly nicer, a floor above my old one. I went out for a *thali* and shake, and when I came back down my little street, I watched a lithe black cat step haughtily over a pile of garbage on the sidewalk and then past someone leaning against a wall, half hidden by the leafy, early evening shadows. Maya stepped forward.

"*Sathi!*" I yelped, and hugged her. She latched on to my elbow and kept us walking down the street.

"Shh," she said. "I don't want anyone to see me at your hotel. Let's go into the park."

We walked around the block and climbed over the low, locked iron gate.

"Where have you been?" I asked as we chose a bench in the shadows.

"I went to stay with my brother's friend in Bhandup. He's in the army and is married with two children."

"Not Prem?" She had never mentioned a friend of her brother's.

"No, someone else. I saw him in Kathmandu a few years ago and got his address then." I had no idea if she was lying or not.

"But why did you leave so suddenly?" Two noisy birds chattered in the palms high above us.

"I had to go before Will took over my *mon* again. He will never stay with me, and I thought I wouldn't mind, but I do. So I left."

"I understand," I said, remembering Nick's and my final good-bye on a deserted stretch of lower Broadway on a freezing October night. I raged at him for all the ways he had let me down, and afterward I feared that I had amputated my own right arm to save myself. I was only just beginning to see that wasn't true. "What can I do? Your life is so difficult now."

"It's true, and I need your help, Alex."

Finally, I thought. "Tell me."

"I need to stay with you for one night, and after . . ." She paused.

"Yes, what is it?"

"I need some money."

"How much do you need?"

"Twelve thousand rupees." Nearly three hundred bucks. It would clean out most of my cash, but I was on my way home. I could pay my hotel bill with a credit card.

"You don't need more? What about the money you owe the *gharwali*?"

"It's not for that. I'll tell you later," she said, twisting her neck back and forth, cracking it. "Can we go to your room? I don't feel well." She didn't look well either. Her face, puffy in a way I didn't remember, had taken on a yellowish hue, and her eyes were watering. There were goose bumps on her arms.

"Let's go in. You can stay as long as you want."

I negotiated with the concierge while Maya sat on the little couch in the lobby, and I asked for tea and a packet of biscuits to be sent up. I gave her a clean nightgown and a towel for a shower, which she badly needed, and I heard her clearing out her lungs and then possibly retching—TB? Hepatitis? There was always AIDS, of course. I never forgot that. When she came back, she lay down and fell asleep immediately. I stayed up at the table, reading and writing, but mostly watching her and listening to her whimper. I finally lay down at the edge of the bed, hoping she would agree to let me take her to Nepal.

When I woke up at a quarter to ten, Maya was asleep, but I saw her clothes were newly washed and drying on hangers around the room. When she got up around eleven, she looked swollen and wan, and it dawned on me.

"*Sathi*, are you pregnant?" I asked her.

"*Ho, hola*, yes, maybe."

"Is it Will's?"

"No. I don't know whose it is. Mine. It doesn't matter," she said with a little laugh, and yet she'd told me she always used condoms. "The baby's been there since before you arrived. At first I thought I wanted the operation to take it out, and I borrowed money from my *gharwali*, but when you and Will came, I thought maybe it could be different, that maybe I would go to Nepal and Will could help take care of it. I know now that's not possible, so I'll stay here and keep the baby. It'll be fine."

We were sitting on the bed, her propped up against the pillows, and I asked her as gently as I could, "How will it be fine? You're here alone. If you go back to your house on Falkland Road, your baby will grow up in a dangerous place, and probably not go to school." I didn't mean to make her cry, but of course I did, which made me cry, and we hugged.

After a little while she said, "I have so much sorrow, *sathi*. I think maybe I could find some joy with a baby and make it happy, even here."

I blew my nose. "We can figure something out. I can give you some money and send you some more from America. Will can help you too. Everything will be okay, but I don't think you should stay here." I poured us water, and she downed hers, wiped her eyes, and sniffed.

"I'm not going back to Nepal. Everyone will know where the baby came from. My parents will reject me. Here, people will accept us, and the baby and I will have each other. And besides, my brother's friend can adopt the baby. That's why I went to go see them. Then, even if I don't get to see my little girl, he can tell me how she is, and I can send her money and presents."

"It's a girl?"

"I think so." All the more reason to leave. "If I go back to Nepal, I'll just have to beg from people, from Will, from others, and my child will have no future. This way I can send my parents money. Besides, my karma is here."

"I don't agree," I said, and she looked up, perplexed by my tone. "This isn't your karma. This is your choice. You can have a different life."

She said quietly, "In another life maybe things can be different. That's why I need to be kind to people in this life, so that the next time it will be easier. You were my first foreign friend, you know that?" I did know. I also knew I'd been demoted from being the only person who understood her *sukha-dukha* to being her first foreign friend. Maybe I was just a foggy person after all.

I gave her the money and asked her if she would wait to make a decision, think about it a little bit. I still had five more days here. She could stay with me, and I could stay longer if she needed me to. She agreed, and we went out for breakfast and then to walk around Chor Bazaar, where they sold rusty car doors next to live goats alongside mattresses, Victrolas, used kitchen appliances, and old watches. *Chor* means thief, and the joke was if you were robbed you could come here to buy your goods back the next day. We kept walking north all the way up to Mumbadevi, where a limbless beggar writhed on the ground near the temple and sang a frenzied chant. After lunch in a little shop where we were the only women, Maya said suddenly, "I should go see my brother's friend. I told him I'd meet him today, but I'll come to your hotel later, or if I can't get there I'll call you." She kissed me quickly, squeezed my hand, and dashed toward the banged-up double-decker approaching the curb. I couldn't stop her. She wasn't my child, or anyone's anymore, and somehow I had always known our final parting would look like this, mundane as any other with a "see you later" on her lips.

"Wait! *Sathi!*" I called out, but she was already gone, deep in the crowd hustling onto the bus, and I stood helpless on the sidewalk as it pulled away.

Acknowledgments

I was fortunate during the time I wrote this novel to be surrounded by an extremely supportive group of friends and family, but no one person lived with this book more intimately or was more invested in its completion, besides me, than Sean Wilsey. He has both my heart and my enormous gratitude for his enthusiasm, faith, good humor, and many delicious meals along the way.

Katie Baldwin always believed in this book, and her years of unstinting friendship and camaraderie have meant the world to me. Valerie Steiker, too, was integral to the novel's completion, carefully reading drafts and generally being unflagging in her encouragement and wisdom.

Thank you to Alison Smith, Cressida Leyshon, and Paul Greenberg for reading and critiquing drafts and for rooting for the novel all around. Thank you also to David Ebershoff, who not only never wavered in his support, but gave me a place to work for extended periods of time away from the hullabaloo. And to Rob Weiner, who did the same.

On my first trip to Nepal, Carolyn Federman was one of the best fellow travelers I could have hoped for, and I am grateful for her keen eyes, ears, and memory, and her friendship.

In Nepal, for their friendship, hospitality, and many insights, *derei dhanyabad* to Tory Clawson, Susan Hangen, Tika Gurung, Sharmila and Rajendra Suwal, Lila Aryal, Jyoti Adhikari, Bijaya Serchan,

Krishna and Sita Manandhar, John Frederick, Ian Baker, and especially Kamala Gurung.

In India, I am grateful for the kindness and generosity of Suketu Mehta and Sunita Viswanath. Thank you to others who shared their expertise and ideas: Meenakshi Ganguly, Anuradha Mahindra, Meena Menon, Gracie Fernandez, and G.R. Khairnar. Above all, thank you to the many women in the red-light districts who allowed me into their world and told me their stories.

Thank you to my terrific and dedicated agent, Zoe Pagnamenta, and to Lexy Bloom. A more thoughtful or passionate editor, I could not have imagined.

Other people, here and there and everywhere, who played a significant part in this novel's creation, and to whom I owe a true debt of thanks: Sarah Schenck, John Donohue, Sasha Koren, Matt Lane, Gilda Sherwin, Cecily and Bob Mills, Suzanne McNear, Alex McNear, Pat Montandon, David McCormick, Anne Jump, Annie Brewster, Bob Bozic, and Ellery Washington.

I am grateful to the Chinati Foundation, the Lannan Foundation, the Vermont Studio Center, and the New York Times Company Foundation for their support. Thank you, too, to E. L. Doctorow, who has been constant in his encouragement over the years.

And last but not least, my family: Jonathan and Cecily Beal, whose senses of humor and confidence buoyed me; Owen and Mira Wilsey, who arrived late in this process, but who brought with them great joy; and finally, Mom and Dad. You grew me up and let me go, and always welcomed me home. I could not have asked for more. Your love has been the springboard. Thank you.

Sabai-lai, thulo namaste!